2001

1

To Matthew
Hope You Enjoy These
Love Uncle Steve, Aunt
Stephen, Keira + Nicole

D1067534

AN

S. E. Hinton

COLLECTION

The
Outsiders

◆

That Was
Then,
This Is Now

VIKING

THE OUTSIDERS

THE OUTSIDERS

S. E. HINTON

VIKING

VIKING
A Division of Penguin Books USA Inc.,
375 Hudson Street, New York, New York 10014
Penguin Books Ltd, 27 Wrights Lane, London W8 5TZ England
Penguin Books Australia Ltd, Ringwood, Victoria, Australia
Penguin Books Canada Ltd, 10 Alcorn Avenue, Toronto, Ontario, Canada M4V 3B2
Penguin Books (N.Z.) Ltd, 182–190 Wairau Road, Auckland 10, New Zealand

Penguin Books Ltd, Registered Offices: Harmondsworth, Middlesex, England

First published in 1967 by Viking Penguin Inc.
Published simultaneously in Canada
Copyright © S. E. Hinton, 1967
All rights reserved
ISBN 0-670-53257-6
Library of Congress catalog card number: 67-13606

"Nothing Gold Can Stay," on p. 85, is from *Complete Poems of Robert Frost*. Copyright 1923 by Holt, Rinehart and Winston, Inc. Copyright 1951 by Robert Frost. Reprinted by permission of Holt, Rinehart and Winston, Inc.

Printed in the United States of America
Set in Electra

2 4 6 8 10 9 7 5 3 1

For Jimmy

THE OUTSIDERS

Chapter 1

WHEN I STEPPED OUT INTO THE BRIGHT SUNLIGHT FROM the darkness of the movie house, I had only two things on my mind: Paul Newman and a ride home. I was wishing I looked like Paul Newman—he looks tough and I don't—but I guess my own looks aren't so bad. I have light-brown, almost-red hair and greenish-gray eyes. I wish they were more gray, because I hate most guys that have green eyes, but I have to be content with what I have. My hair is longer than a lot of boys wear theirs, squared off in back and long at the front and sides, but I am a greaser and most of my neighborhood rarely bothers to get a haircut. Besides, I look better with long hair.

I had a long walk home and no company, but I usually lone it anyway, for no reason except that I like to watch movies undisturbed so I can get into them and live them with the actors. When I see a movie with someone it's kind of uncomfortable, like having someone read your book over your shoulder. I'm different that way. I mean, my second-oldest brother, Soda, who is sixteen-going-on-seventeen, never cracks a book at all, and my oldest brother, Darrel, who we call Darry, works too long and hard to be interested in a story or drawing a picture, so I'm not like them. And nobody in our gang digs movies and books the way I do. For a while there, I thought I was the only person in the world that did. So I loned it.

Soda tries to understand, at least, which is more than Darry does. But then, Soda is different from anybody; he understands everything, almost. Like he's never hollering at me all the time the way Darry is, or treating me as if I was six instead of fourteen. I love Soda more than I've ever loved anyone, even Mom and Dad. He's always happy-go-lucky and grinning, while Darry's hard and firm and rarely grins at all. But then, Darry's gone through a lot in his twenty years, grown up too fast. Sodapop'll never grow up at all. I don't know which way's the best. I'll find out one of these days.

Anyway, I went on walking home, thinking about the movie, and then suddenly wishing I had some company. Greasers can't walk alone too much or they'll get jumped, or someone will come by and scream "Greaser!" at them, which doesn't make you feel too hot, if you know what I mean. We get jumped by the Socs. I'm not sure how you spell it, but it's the abbreviation for the Socials, the jet set, the West-side rich kids. It's like the term "greaser," which is used to class all us boys on the East Side.

We're poorer than the Socs and the middle class. I reckon we're wilder, too. Not like the Socs, who jump greasers and wreck houses and throw beer blasts for kicks, and get editorials in the paper for being a public disgrace one day and an asset to society the next. Greasers are almost like hoods; we steal things and drive old souped-up cars and hold up gas stations and have a gang fight once in a while. I don't mean I do things like that. Darry would kill me if I got into trouble with the police. Since Mom and Dad were killed in an auto wreck, the three of us get to stay together only as long as we behave. So Soda and I stay out of trouble as much as we can, and we're careful not to get caught when we can't. I only mean that most greasers do things like that, just like we wear our hair long and dress in blue jeans and T-shirts, or leave our shirttails out and wear leather jackets and tennis shoes or boots. I'm not saying that either Socs or greasers are better; that's just the way things are.

I could have waited to go to the movies until Darry or Sodapop got off work. They would have gone with me, or driven me there, or walked along, although Soda just can't sit still long enough to enjoy a movie and they bore Darry to death. Darry thinks his life is enough without inspecting other people's. Or I could have gotten one of the gang to come along, one of the four boys Darry and Soda and I have grown up with and consider family. We're almost as close as brothers; when you grow up in a tight-knit neighborhood like ours you get to know each other real well. If I had thought about it, I could have called Darry and he would have come by on his way home and picked me up, or Two-Bit Mathews—one of our gang—would have come to get me in his car if I had asked him, but sometimes I just don't use my head. It drives my brother Darry nuts when I do stuff like that, 'cause I'm supposed to be smart; I make good grades and have a high IQ and everything, but I don't use my head. Besides, I like walking.

I about decided I didn't like it so much, though, when I spotted that red Corvair trailing me. I was almost two blocks from home then, so I started walking a little faster. I had never been jumped, but I had seen Johnny after four Socs got hold of him, and it wasn't pretty. Johnny was scared of his own shadow after that. Johnny was sixteen then.

I knew it wasn't any use though—the fast walking, I mean—even before the Corvair pulled up beside me and five Socs got out. I got pretty scared—I'm kind of small for fourteen even though I have a good build, and those guys were bigger than me. I automatically hitched my thumbs in my jeans and slouched, wondering if I could get away if I made a break for it. I remembered Johnny— his face all cut up and bruised, and I remembered how he had cried when we found him, half-conscious, in the corner lot. Johnny had it awful rough at home—it took a lot to make him cry.

I was sweating something fierce, although I was cold. I could feel my palms getting clammy and the perspiration running down my back. I get like that when I'm real scared. I glanced around for a pop bottle or a stick or something—Steve Randle, Soda's best buddy, had once held off four guys with a busted pop bottle—but there was nothing. So I stood there like a bump on a log while they surrounded me. I don't use my head. They walked around slowly, silently, smiling.

"Hey, grease," one said in an over-friendly voice. "We're gonna do you a favor, greaser. We're gonna cut all that long greasy hair off."

He had on a madras shirt. I can still see it. Blue madras. One of them laughed, then cussed me out in a low voice. I couldn't think of anything to say. There just isn't a whole lot you can say while waiting to get mugged, so I kept my mouth shut.

"Need a haircut, greaser?" The medium-sized blond pulled a knife out of his back pocket and flipped the blade open.

I finally thought of something to say. "No." I was backing up, away from that knife. Of course I backed right into one of them. They had me down in a second. They had my arms and legs pinned down and one of them was sitting on my chest with his knees on my elbows, and if you don't think that hurts, you're crazy. I could smell English Leather shaving lotion and stale tobacco, and I wondered foolishly if I would suffocate before they did anything. I was scared so bad I was wishing I would. I fought to get loose, and almost did for a second; then they tightened up on me and the one on my chest slugged me a couple of times. So I lay still, swearing at them between gasps. A blade was held against my throat.

"How'd you like that haircut to begin just below the chin?"

It occurred to me then that they could kill me. I went wild. I started screaming for Soda, Darry, anyone. Someone put his hand over my mouth, and I bit it as hard as I could, tasting the blood running through my teeth. I heard a muttered curse and got slugged again, and they were stuffing a handkerchief in my mouth. One of them kept saying, "Shut him up, for Pete's sake, shut him up!"

Then there were shouts and the pounding of feet, and the Socs jumped up and left me lying there, gasping. I lay there and wondered what in the world was happening—people were jumping over me and running by me and I was too dazed to figure it out. Then someone had me under the armpits and was hauling me to my feet. It was Darry.

"Are you all right, Ponyboy?"

He was shaking me and I wished he'd stop. I was dizzy enough anyway. I could tell it was Darry though—partly because of the voice and partly because Darry's always rough with me without meaning to be.

"I'm okay. Quit shaking me, Darry, I'm okay."

He stopped instantly. "I'm sorry."

He wasn't really. Darry isn't ever sorry for anything he does. It seems funny to me that he should look just exactly like my father and act exactly the opposite from him. My father was only forty when he died and he looked twenty-five and a lot of people thought Darry and Dad were brothers instead of father and son. But they only looked alike—my father was never rough with anyone without meaning to be.

Darry is six-feet-two, and broad-shouldered and muscular. He has dark-brown hair that kicks out in front and a slight cowlick in the back—just like Dad's—but Darry's eyes are his own. He's got eyes that are like two pieces of pale blue-green ice. They've got a determined set to them, like the rest of him. He looks older than twenty—tough, cool, and smart. He would be real handsome if his eyes weren't so cold. He doesn't understand anything that is not plain hard fact. But he uses his head.

I sat down again, rubbing my cheek where I'd been slugged the most.

Darry jammed his fists in his pockets. "They didn't hurt you too bad, did they?"

They did. I was smarting and aching and my chest was sore and I was so nervous my hands were shaking and I wanted to start bawling, but you just don't say that to Darry.

"I'm okay."

Sodapop came loping back. By then I had figured that all the noise I had heard was the gang coming to rescue me. He dropped down beside me, examining my head.

"You got cut up a little, huh, Ponyboy?"

I only looked at him blankly. "I did?"

He pulled out a handkerchief, wet the end of it with his tongue, and pressed it gently against the side of my head. "You're bleedin' like a stuck pig."

"I am?"

"Look!" He showed me the handkerchief, reddened as if by magic. "Did they pull a blade on you?"

I remembered the voice: "Need a haircut, greaser?" The blade must have slipped while he was trying to shut me up. "Yeah."

Soda is handsomer than anyone else I know. Not like Darry—Soda's movie-star kind of handsome, the kind that people stop on the street to watch go by. He's not as tall as Darry, and he's a little slimmer, but he has a finely drawn, sensitive face that somehow manages to be reckless and thoughtful at the same time. He's got dark-gold hair that he combs back—long and silky and straight—and in the summer the sun bleaches it to a shining wheat-gold. His eyes are dark brown—lively, dancing, recklessly laughing eyes that can be gentle and sympathetic one moment and blazing with anger the next. He has Dad's eyes, but Soda is one of a kind. He can get drunk in a drag race or dancing without ever getting near alcohol. In our neighborhood it's rare to find a kid who doesn't drink once in a while. But Soda never touches a drop—he doesn't need to. He gets drunk on just plain living. And he understands everybody.

He looked at me more closely. I looked away hurriedly, because, if you want to know the truth, I was starting to bawl. I knew I was as white as I felt and I was shaking like a leaf.

Soda just put his hand on my shoulder. "Easy, Ponyboy. They ain't gonna hurt you no more."

"I know," I said, but the ground began to blur and I felt hot tears running down my cheeks. I brushed them away impatiently. "I'm just a little spooked, that's all." I drew a quivering breath and quit crying. You just don't cry in front of Darry. Not unless you're hurt like Johnny had been that day we found him in the vacant lot. Compared to Johnny I wasn't hurt at all.

Soda rubbed my hair. "You're an okay kid, Pony."

I had to grin at him—Soda can make you grin no matter what. I guess it's because he's always grinning so much himself. "You're crazy, Soda, out of your mind."

Darry looked as if he'd like to knock our heads together. "You're both nuts."

Soda merely cocked one eyebrow, a trick he'd picked up from Two-Bit. "It seems to run in this family."

Darry stared at him for a second, then cracked a grin. Sodapop isn't afraid of him like everyone else and enjoys teasing him. I'd just as soon tease a full-grown grizzly; but for some reason, Darry seems to like being teased by Soda.

Our gang had chased the Socs to their car and heaved rocks at them. They came running toward us now—four lean, hard guys. They were all as tough as nails and looked it. I had grown up with them, and they accepted me, even though I was younger, because I was Darry and Soda's kid brother and I kept my mouth shut good.

Steve Randle was seventeen, tall and lean, with thick greasy hair he kept combed in complicated swirls. He was cocky, smart, and Soda's best buddy since grade school. Steve's specialty was cars. He could lift a hubcap quicker and more quietly than anyone in the neighborhood, but he also knew cars upside-down and backward, and he could drive anything on wheels. He and Soda worked at the same gas station—Steve part time and Soda full time—and their station got more customers than any other in town. Whether that was because Steve was so good with cars or because Soda attracted girls like honey draws flies, I couldn't tell you. I liked Steve only because he was Soda's best friend. He didn't like me—he thought I was a tagalong and a kid; Soda always took me with them when they went places if they weren't taking girls, and that bugged Steve. It wasn't my fault; Soda always asked me, I didn't ask him. Soda doesn't think I'm a kid.

Two-Bit Mathews was the oldest of the gang and the wisecracker of the bunch. He was about six feet tall, stocky

in build, and very proud of his long rusty-colored sideburns.
He had gray eyes and a wide grin, and he couldn't stop making funny remarks to save his life. You couldn't shut up that
guy; he always had to get his two-bits worth in. Hence
his name. Even his teachers forgot his real name was Keith,
and we hardly remembered he had one. Life was one big
joke to Two-Bit. He was famous for shoplifting and his
black-handled switchblade (which he couldn't have acquired without his first talent), and he was always smarting
off to the cops. He really couldn't help it. Everything he
said was so irresistibly funny that he just had to let the
police in on it to brighten up their dull lives. (That's the
way he explained it to me.) He liked fights, blondes, and
for some unfathomable reason, school. He was still a junior
at eighteen and a half and he never learned anything. He
just went for kicks. I liked him real well because he kept
us laughing at ourselves as well as at other things. He reminded me of Will Rogers—maybe it was the grin.

If I had to pick the real character of the gang, it would
be Dallas Winston—Dally. I used to like to draw his
picture when he was in a dangerous mood, for then I could
get his personality down in a few lines. He had an elfish
face, with high cheekbones and a pointed chin, small,
sharp animal teeth, and ears like a lynx. His hair was almost
white it was so blond, and he didn't like haircuts, or hair
oil either, so it fell over his forehead in wisps and kicked
out in the back in tufts and curled behind his ears and
along the nape of his neck. His eyes were blue, blazing ice,
cold with a hatred of the whole world. Dally had spent
three years on the wild side of New York and had been

arrested at the age of ten. He was tougher than the rest of us—tougher, colder, meaner. The shade of difference that separates a greaser from a hood wasn't present in Dally. He was as wild as the boys in the downtown outfits, like Tim Shepard's gang.

In New York, Dally blew off steam in gang fights, but here, organized gangs are rarities—there are just small bunches of friends who stick together, and the warfare is between the social classes. A rumble, when it's called, is usually born of a grudge fight, and the opponents just happen to bring their friends along. Oh, there are a few named gangs around, like the River Kings and the Tiber Street Tigers, but here in the Southwest there's no gang rivalry. So Dally, even though he could get into a good fight sometimes, had no specific thing to hate. No rival gang. Only Socs. And you can't win against them no matter how hard you try, because they've got all the breaks and even whipping them isn't going to change that fact. Maybe that was why Dallas was so bitter.

He had quite a reputation. They have a file on him down at the police station. He had been arrested, he got drunk, he rode in rodeos, lied, cheated, stole, rolled drunks, jumped small kids—he did everything. I didn't like him, but he was smart and you had to respect him.

Johnny Cade was last and least. If you can picture a little dark puppy that has been kicked too many times and is lost in a crowd of strangers, you'll have Johnny. He was the youngest, next to me, smaller than the rest, with a slight build. He had big black eyes in a dark tanned face; his hair was jet-black and heavily greased and combed to the side, but it was so long that it fell in shaggy bangs across his forehead. He had a nervous, suspicious look in his eyes, and that beating he got from the Socs didn't help matters. He was the gang's pet, everyone's kid brother. His father was always beating him up, and his mother ignored him, except when she was hacked off at something, and then you could hear her yelling at him clear down at our house. I think he hated that worse than getting whipped. He would have run away a million times if we hadn't been there. If it hadn't been for the gang, Johnny would never have known what love and affection are.

I wiped my eyes hurriedly. "Didya catch 'em?"

"Nup. They got away this time, the dirty . . ." Two-Bit went on cheerfully, calling the Socs every name he could think of or make up.

"The kid's okay?"

"I'm okay." I tried to think of something to say. I'm usually pretty quiet around people, even the gang. I changed the subject. "I didn't know you were out of the cooler yet, Dally."

"Good behavior. Got off early." Dallas lit a cigarette and handed it to Johnny. Everyone sat down to have a smoke and relax. A smoke always lessens the tension. I had quit trembling and my color was back. The cigarette was calming me down. Two-Bit cocked an eyebrow. "Nice-lookin' bruise you got there, kid."

I touched my cheek gingerly. "Really?"

Two-Bit nodded sagely. "Nice cut, too. Makes you look tough."

Tough and *tuff* are two different words. *Tough* is the same as rough; *tuff* means cool, sharp—like a tuff-looking

Mustang or a tuff record. In our neighborhood both are compliments.

Steve flicked his ashes at me. "What were you doin', walkin' by your lonesome?" Leave it to good old Steve to bring up something like that.

"I was comin' home from the movies. I didn't think . . ."

"You don't ever think," Darry broke in, "not at home or anywhere when it counts. You must think at school, with all those good grades you bring home, and you've always got your nose in a book, but do you ever use your head for common sense? No sirree, bub. And if you did have to go by yourself, you should have carried a blade."

I just stared at the hole in the toe of my tennis shoe. Me and Darry just didn't dig each other. I never could please him. He would have hollered at me for carrying a blade if I *had* carried one. If I brought home B's, he wanted A's, and if I got A's, he wanted to make sure they stayed A's. If I was playing football, I should be in studying, and if I was reading, I should be out playing football. He never hollered at Sodapop—not even when Soda dropped out of school or got tickets for speeding. He just hollered at me.

Soda was glaring at him. "Leave my kid brother alone, you hear? It ain't his fault he likes to go to the movies, and it ain't his fault the Socs like to jump us, and if he had been carrying a blade it would have been a good excuse to cut him to ribbons."

Soda always takes up for me.

Darry said impatiently, "When I want my kid brother to tell me what to do with my other kid brother, I'll ask you—kid brother." But he laid off me. He always does when Sodapop tells him to. Most of the time.

"Next time get one of us to go with you, Ponyboy," Two-Bit said. "Any of us will."

"Speakin' of movies"—Dally yawned, flipping away his cigarette butt—"I'm walkin' over to the Nightly Double tomorrow night. Anybody want to come and hunt some action?"

Steve shook his head. "Me and Soda are pickin' up Evie and Sandy for the game."

He didn't need to look at me the way he did right then. I wasn't going to ask if I could come. I'd never tell Soda, because he really likes Steve a lot, but sometimes I can't stand Steve Randle. I mean it. Sometimes I hate him.

Darry sighed, just like I knew he would. Darry never had time to do anything anymore. "I'm working tomorrow night."

Dally looked at the rest of us. "How about y'all? Two-Bit? Johnnycake, you and Pony wanta come?"

"Me and Johnny'll come," I said. I knew Johnny wouldn't open his mouth unless he was forced to. "Okay, Darry?"

"Yeah, since it ain't a school night." Darry was real good about letting me go places on the weekends. On school nights I could hardly leave the house.

"I was plannin' on getting boozed up tomorrow night," Two-Bit said. "If I don't, I'll walk over and find y'all."

Steve was looking at Dally's hand. His ring, which he had rolled a drunk senior to get, was back on his finger. "You break up with Sylvia again?"

"Yeah, and this time it's for good. That little broad was two-timin' me again while I was in jail."

I thought of Sylvia and Evie and Sandy and Two-Bit's many blondes. They were the only kind of girls that would look at us, I thought. Tough, loud girls who wore too much eye makeup and giggled and swore too much. I liked Soda's girl Sandy just fine, though. Her hair was natural blond and her laugh was soft, like her china-blue eyes. She didn't have a real good home or anything and was our kind—greaser—but she was a real nice girl. Still, lots of times I wondered what other girls were like. The girls who were bright-eyed and had their dresses a decent length and acted as if they'd like to spit on us if given a chance. Some were afraid of us, and remembering Dallas Winston, I didn't blame them. But most looked at us like we were dirt—gave us the same kind of look that the Socs did when they came by in their Mustangs and Corvairs and yelled "Grease!" at us. I wondered about them. The girls, I mean . . . Did they cry when their boys were arrested, like Evie did when Steve got hauled in, or did they run out on them the way Sylvia did Dallas? But maybe their boys didn't get arrested or beaten up or busted up in rodeos.

I was still thinking about it while I was doing my homework that night. I had to read *Great Expectations* for English, and that kid Pip, he reminded me of us—the way he felt marked lousy because he wasn't a gentleman or anything, and the way that girl kept looking down on him. That happened to me once. One time in biology I had to dissect a worm, and the razor wouldn't cut, so I used my switchblade. The minute I flicked it out—I forgot what I was doing or I would never have done it—this girl right beside me kind of gasped, and said, "They are right. You are a hood." That didn't make me feel so hot. There were a lot of Socs in that class—I get put into A classes because I'm supposed to be smart—and most of them thought it was pretty funny. I didn't, though. She was a cute girl. She looked real good in yellow.

We deserve a lot of our trouble, I thought. Dallas deserves everything he gets, and should get worse, if you want the truth. And Two-Bit—he doesn't really want or need half the things he swipes from stores. He just thinks it's fun to swipe everything that isn't nailed down. I can understand why Sodapop and Steve get into drag races and fights so much, though—both of them have too much energy, too much feeling, with no way to blow it off.

"Rub harder, Soda," I heard Darry mumbling. "You're gonna put me to sleep."

I looked through the door. Sodapop was giving Darry a back-rub. Darry is always pulling muscles; he roofs houses and he's always trying to carry two bundles of roofing up the ladder. I knew Soda would put him to sleep, because Soda can put about anyone out when he sets his head to it. He thought Darry worked too hard anyway. I did, too.

Darry didn't deserve to work like an old man when he was only twenty. He had been a real popular guy in school; he was captain of the football team and he had been voted Boy of the Year. But we just didn't have the money for him to go to college, even with the athletic scholarship he won. And now he didn't have time between jobs to even think about college. So he never went anywhere and never did anything anymore, except work out at gyms and go skiing with some old friends of his sometimes.

I rubbed my cheek where it had turned purple. I had

looked in the mirror, and it did make me look tough. But Darry had made me put a Band-aid on the cut.

I remembered how awful Johnny had looked when he got beaten up. I had just as much right to use the streets as the Socs did, and Johnny had never hurt them. Why did the Socs hate us so much? We left them alone. I nearly went to sleep over my homework trying to figure it out.

Sodapop, who had jumped into bed by this time, yelled sleepily for me to turn off the light and get to bed. When I finished the chapter I was on, I did.

Lying beside Soda, staring at the wall, I kept remembering the faces of the Socs as they surrounded me, that blue madras shirt the blond was wearing, and I could still hear a thick voice: "Need a haircut, greaser?" I shivered.

"You cold, Ponyboy?"

"A little," I lied. Soda threw one arm across my neck. He mumbled something drowsily. "Listen, kiddo, when Darry hollers at you . . . he don't mean nothin'. He's just got more worries than somebody his age ought to. Don't take him serious . . . you dig, Pony? Don't let him bug you. He's really proud of you 'cause you're so brainy. It's just because you're the baby—I mean, he loves you a lot. Savvy?"

"Sure," I said, trying for Soda's sake to keep the sarcasm out of my voice.

"Soda?"

"Yeah?"

"How come you dropped out?" I never have gotten over that. I could hardly stand it when he left school.

" 'Cause I'm dumb. The only things I was passing anyway were auto mechanics and gym."

25

"You're not dumb."

"Yeah, I am. Shut up and I'll tell you something. Don't tell Darry, though."

"Okay."

"I think I'm gonna marry Sandy. After she gets out of school and I get a better job and everything. I might wait till you get out of school, though. So I can still help Darry with the bills and stuff."

"Tuff enough. Wait till I get out, though, so you can keep Darry off my back."

"Don't be like that, kid. I told you he don't mean half of what he says. . ."

"You in love with Sandy? What's it like?"

"Hhhmmm." He sighed happily. "It's real nice."

In a moment his breathing was light and regular. I turned my head to look at him and in the moonlight he looked like some Greek god come to earth. I wondered how he could stand being so handsome. Then I sighed. I didn't quite get what he meant about Darry. Darry thought I was just another mouth to feed and somebody to holler at. Darry love me? I thought of those hard, pale eyes. Soda was wrong for once, I thought. Darry doesn't love anyone or anything, except maybe Soda. I didn't hardly think of him as being human. I don't care, I lied to myself, I don't care about him either. Soda's enough, and I'd have him until I got out of school. I don't care about Darry. But I was still lying and I knew it. I lie to myself all the time. But I never believe me.

Chapter 2

DALLY WAS WAITING FOR JOHNNY AND ME UNDER THE STREET
light at the corner of Pickett and Sutton, and since we
got there early, we had time to go over to the drugstore in
the shopping center and goof around. We bought Cokes
and blew the straws at the waitress, and walked around
eyeing things that were lying out in the open until the
manager got wise to us and suggested we leave. He was too
late, though; Dally walked out with two packages of Kools
under his jacket.

Then we went across the street and down Sutton a little
way to The Dingo. There are lots of drive-ins in town—
the Socs go to The Way Out and to Rusty's, and the greasers
go to The Dingo and to Jay's. The Dingo is a pretty rough
hangout; there's always a fight going on there and once a

27

girl got shot. We walked around talking to all the greasers and hoods we knew, leaning in car windows or hopping into the back seats, and getting in on who was running away, and who was in jail, and who was going with who, and who could whip who, and who stole what and when and why. We knew about everybody there. There was a pretty good fight while we were there between a big twenty-three-year-old greaser and a Mexican hitchhiker. We left when the switchblades came out, because the cops would be coming soon and nobody in his right mind wants to be around when the fuzz show.

We crossed Sutton and cut around behind Spencer's Special, the discount house, and chased two junior-high kids across a field for a few minutes; by then it was dark enough to sneak in over the back fence of the Nightly Double drive-in movie. It was the biggest in town, and showed two movies every night, and on weekends four—you could say you were going to the Nightly Double and have time to go all over town.

We all had the money to get in—it only costs a quarter if you're not in a car—but Dally hated to do things the legal way. He liked to show that he didn't care whether there was a law or not. He went around trying to break laws. We went to the rows of seats in front of the concession stand to sit down. Nobody else was there except two girls who were sitting down front. Dally eyed them coolly, then walked down the aisle and sat right behind them. I had a sick feeling that Dally was up to his usual tricks, and I was right. He started talking, loud enough for the two girls to hear. He started out bad and got worse. Dallas could talk awful dirty if he wanted to and I guess he wanted to then. I felt my ears get hot. Two-Bit or Steve or even Soda would have gone right along with him, just to see if they could embarrass the girls, but that kind of kicks just doesn't appeal to me. I sat there, struck dumb, and Johnny left hastily to get a Coke.

I wouldn't have felt so embarrassed if they had been greasey girls—I might even have helped old Dallas. But those two girls weren't our kind. They were tuff-looking girls—dressed sharp and really good-looking. They looked about sixteen or seventeen. One had short dark hair, and the other had long red hair. The redhead was getting mad, or scared. She sat up straight and she was chewing hard on her gum. The other one pretended not to hear Dally. Dally was getting impatient. He put his feet up on the back of the redhead's chair, winked at me, and beat his own record for saying something dirty. She turned around and gave him a cool stare.

"Take your feet off my chair and shut your trap."

Boy, she was good-looking. I'd seen her before; she was a cheerleader at our school. I'd always thought she was stuck-up.

Dally merely looked at her and kept his feet where they were. "Who's gonna make me?"

The other one turned around and watched us. "That's the greaser that jockeys for the Slash J sometimes," she said, as if we couldn't hear her.

I had heard the same tone a million times: "Greaser . . . greaser . . . greaser." Oh, yeah, I had heard that tone before too many times. What are they doing at a drive-in without a car? I thought, and Dallas said, "I know you two. I've seen you around rodeos."

"It's a shame you can't ride bull half as good as you can talk it," the redhead said coolly and turned back around.

That didn't bother Dally in the least. "You two barrel race, huh?"

"You'd better leave us alone," the redhead said in a biting voice, "or I'll call the cops."

"Oh, my, my"—Dally looked bored—"you've got me scared to death. You ought to see my record sometime, baby." He grinned slyly. "Guess what I've been in for?"

"*Please* leave us alone," she said. "Why don't you be nice and leave us alone?"

Dally grinned roguishly. "I'm never nice. Want a Coke?"

She was mad by then. "I wouldn't drink it if I was starving in the desert. Get lost, hood!"

Dally merely shrugged and strolled off.

The girl looked at me. I was half-scared of her. I'm half-scared of all nice girls, especially Socs. "Are you going to start in on us?"

I shook my head, wide-eyed. "No."

Suddenly she smiled. Gosh, she was pretty. "You don't look the type. What's your name?"

I wished she hadn't asked me that. I hate to tell people my name for the first time. "Ponyboy Curtis."

Then I waited for the "You're kidding!" or "That's your real name?" or one of the other remarks I usually get. Ponyboy's my real name and personally I like it.

The redhead just smiled. "That's an original and lovely name."

"My dad was an original person," I said. "I've got a brother named Sodapop, and it says so on his birth certificate."

"My name's Sherri, but I'm called Cherry because of my hair. Cherry Valance."

"I know," I said. "You're a cheerleader. We go to the same school."

"You don't look old enough to be going to high school," the dark-haired girl said.

"I'm not. I got put up a year in grade school."

Cherry was looking at me. "What's a nice, smart kid like you running around with trash like that for?"

I felt myself stiffen. "I'm a grease, same as Dally. He's my buddy."

"I'm sorry, Ponyboy," she said softly. Then she said briskly, "Your brother Sodapop, does he work at a gasoline station? A DX, I think?"

"Yeah."

"Man, your brother is one doll. I might have guessed you were brothers—you look alike."

I grinned with pride—I don't think I look one bit like Soda, but it's not every day I hear Socs telling me they think my brother is a doll.

"Didn't he used to ride in rodeos? Saddle bronc?"

"Yeah. Dad made him quit after he tore a ligament, though. We still hang around rodeos a lot. I've seen you two barrel race. You're good."

"Thanks," Cherry said, and the other girl, who was named Marcia, said, "How come we don't see your brother at school? He's not any older than sixteen or seventeen, is he?"

I winced inside. I've told you I can't stand it that Soda dropped out. "He's a dropout," I said roughly. "Dropout" made me think of some poor dumb-looking hoodlum

31

wandering the streets breaking out street lights—it didn't fit my happy-go-lucky brother at all. It fitted Dally perfectly, but you could hardly say it about Soda.

Johnny came back then and sat down beside me. He looked around for Dally, then managed a shy "Hi" to the girls and tried to watch the movie. He was nervous, though. Johnny was always nervous around strangers. Cherry looked at him, sizing him up as she had me. Then she smiled softly, and I knew she had him sized up right.

Dally came striding back with an armful of Cokes. He handed one to each of the girls and sat down beside Cherry. "This might cool you off."

She gave him an incredulous look; and then she threw her Coke in his face. "That might cool you off, greaser. After you wash your mouth and learn to talk and act decent, I might cool off, too."

Dally wiped the Coke off his face with his sleeve and smiled dangerously. If I had been Cherry I would have beat it out of there. I knew that smile.

"Fiery, huh? Well, that's the way I like 'em." He started to put his arm around her, but Johnny reached over and stopped him.

"Leave her alone, Dally."

"Huh?" Dally was taken off guard. He stared at Johnny in disbelief. Johnny couldn't say "Boo" to a goose. Johnny gulped and got a little pale, but he said, "You heard me. Leave her alone."

Dallas scowled for a second. If it had been me, or Two-Bit, or Soda or Steve, or anyone but Johnny, Dally would have flattened him without a moment's hesitation. You just didn't tell Dally Winston what to do. One time, in a dime store, a guy told him to move over at the candy counter. Dally had turned around and belted him so hard it knocked a tooth loose. A complete stranger, too. But Johnny was the gang's pet, and Dally just couldn't hit him. He was Dally's pet, too. Dally got up and stalked off, his fists jammed in his pockets and a frown on his face. He didn't come back.

Cherry sighed in relief. "Thanks. He had me scared to death."

Johnny managed an admiring grin. "You sure didn't show it. Nobody talks to Dally like that."

She smiled. "From what I saw, you do."

Johnny's ears got red. I was still staring at him. It had taken more than nerve for him to say what he'd said to Dally —Johnny worshiped the ground Dallas walked on, and I had never heard Johnny talk back to anyone, much less his hero.

Marcia grinned at us. She was a little smaller than Cherry. She was cute, but that Cherry Valance was a real looker. "Y'all sit up here with us. You can protect us."

Johnny and I looked at each other. He grinned suddenly, raising his eyebrows so that they disappeared under his bangs. Would we ever have something to tell the boys! his eyes said plainly. We had picked up two girls, and classy ones at that. Not any greasey broads for us, but real Socs. Soda would flip when I told him.

"Okay," I said nonchalantly, "might as well."

I sat between them, and Johnny sat next to Cherry.

"How old are y'all?" Marcia asked.

"Fourteen," I said.

"Sixteen," said Johnny.

"That's funny," Marcia said, "I thought you were both . . ."

"Sixteen," Cherry finished for her.

I was grateful. Johnny looked fourteen and he knew it and it bugged him something awful.

Johnny grinned. "How come y'all ain't scared of us like you were Dally?"

Cherry sighed. "You two are too sweet to scare anyone. First of all, you didn't join in Dallas's dirty talk, and you made him leave us alone. And when we asked you to sit up here with us, you didn't act like it was an invitation to make out for the night. Besides that, I've heard about Dallas Winston, and he looked as hard as nails and twice as tough. And you two don't look mean."

"Sure," I said tiredly, "we're young and innocent."

"No," Cherry said slowly, looking at me carefully, "not innocent. You've seen too much to be innocent. Just not . . . dirty."

"Dally's okay," Johnny said defensively, and I nodded. You take up for your buddies, no matter what they do. When you're a gang, you stick up for the members. If you don't stick up for them, stick together, make like brothers, it isn't a gang any more. It's a pack. A snarling, distrustful, bickering pack like the Socs in their social clubs or the street gangs in New York or the wolves in the timber. "He's tough, but he's a cool old guy."

"He'd leave you alone if he knew you," I said, and that was true. When Steve's cousin from Kansas came down, Dally was decent to her and watched his swearing. We all did around nice girls who were the cousinly type. I don't know how to explain it—we try to be nice to the girls we

34

see once in a while, like cousins or the girls in class; but we still watch a nice girl go by on a street corner and say all kinds of lousy stuff about her. Don't ask me why. I don't know why.

"Well," Marcia said with finality, "I'm glad he doesn't know us."

"I kind of admire him," Cherry said softly, so only I heard, and then we settled down to watch the movie.

Oh, yeah, we found out why they were there without a car. They'd come with their boyfriends, but walked out on them when they found out the boys had brought some booze along. The boys had gotten angry and left.

"I don't care if they did." Cherry sounded annoyed. "It's not my idea of a good time to sit in a drive-in and watch people get drunk."

You could tell by the way she said it that her idea of a good time was probably high-class, and probably expensive. They'd decided to stay and see the movie anyway. It was one of those beach-party movies with no plot and no acting but a lot of girls in bikinis and some swinging songs, so it was all right. We were all four sitting there in silence when suddenly a strong hand came down on Johnny's shoulder and another on mine and a deep voice said, "Okay, greasers, you've had it."

I almost jumped out of my skin. It was like having someone leap out from behind a door and yell "Boo!" at you.

I looked fearfully over my shoulder and there was Two-Bit, grinning like a Chessy cat. "Glory, Two-Bit, scare us to death!" He was good at voice imitations and had sounded for all the world like a snarling Soc. Then I looked at Johnny. His eyes were shut and he was as white as a ghost. His breath was coming in smothered gasps. Two-Bit knew better than to scare Johnny like that. I guess he'd forgotten. He's kind of scatterbrained. Johnny opened his eyes and said weakly, "Hey, Two-Bit."

Two-Bit messed up his hair. "Sorry, kid," he said, "I forgot."

He climbed over the chair and plopped down beside Marcia. "Who's this, your great-aunts?"

"Great-grandmothers, twice removed," Cherry said smoothly.

I couldn't tell if Two-Bit was drunk or not. It's kind of hard to tell with him—he acts boozed up sometimes even when he's sober. He cocked one eyebrow up and the other down, which he always does when something puzzles him, or bothers him, or when he feels like saying something smart. "Shoot, you're ninety-six if you're a day."

"I'm a night," Marcia said brightly.

Two-Bit stared at her admiringly. "Brother, you're a sharp one. Where'd you two ever get to be picked up by a couple of greasey hoods like Pony and Johnny?"

"We really picked them up," Marcia said. "We're really Arabian slave traders and we're thinking about shanghaiing them. They're worth ten camels apiece at least."

"Five," Two-Bit disagreed. "They don't talk Arabian, I don't think. Say somethin' in Arabian, Johnnycake."

"Aw, cut it out!" Johnny broke in. "Dally was bothering them and when he left they wanted us to sit with them to protect them. Against wisecracking greasers like you, probably."

Two-Bit grinned, because Johnny didn't usually get sassy like that. We thought we were doing good if we could get him to talk at all. Incidentally, we don't mind being called greaser by another greaser. It's kind of playful then.

"Hey, where is ol' Dally, anyways?"

"He went hunting some action—booze or dames or a fight. I hope he don't get jailed again. He just got out."

"He'll probably find the fight," Two-Bit stated cheerfully. "That's why I came over. Mr. Timothy Shepard and Co. are looking for whoever so kindly slashed their car's tires, and since Mr. Curly Shepard spotted Dallas doing it . . . well . . . Does Dally have a blade?"

"Not that I know of," I said. "I think he's got a piece of pipe, but he busted his blade this morning."

"Good. Tim'll fight fair if Dally don't pull a blade on him. Dally shouldn't have any trouble."

Cherry and Marcia were staring at us. "You don't believe in playing rough or anything, do you?"

"A fair fight isn't rough," Two-Bit said. "Blades are rough. So are chains and heaters and pool sticks and rumbles. Skin fighting isn't rough. It blows off steam better than anything. There's nothing wrong with throwing a few punches. Socs are rough. They gang up on one or two, or they rumble each other with their social clubs. Us greasers usually stick together, but when we do fight among ourselves, it's a fair fight between two. And Dally deserves whatever he gets, 'cause slashed tires ain't no joke when you've got to work to pay for them. He got spotted, too, and that was his fault. Our one rule, besides Stick together, is Don't get caught. He might get beat up, he might not. Either way there's not going to be any blood feud between our outfit and Shepard's. If we needed them tomorrow they'd show. If Tim beats Dally's head in, and then tomorrow asks us for help in a rumble, we'll show. Dally was getting kicks. He got caught. He pays up. No sweat."

"Yeah, boy," Cherry said sarcastically, "real simple."

"Sure," Marcia said, unconcerned. "If he gets killed or something, you just bury him. No sweat."

"You dig okay, baby." Two-Bit grinned and lit a cigarette. "Anyone want a weed?"

I looked at Two-Bit admiringly. He sure put things into words good. Maybe he was still a junior at eighteen and a half, and maybe his sideburns were too long, and maybe he did get boozed up too much, but he sure understood things.

Cherry and Marcia shook their heads at his offering of cigarettes, but Johnny and I reached for one. Johnny's color was back and his breathing was regular, but his hand was shaking ever so slightly. A cigarette would steady it.

"Ponyboy, will you come with me to get some popcorn?" Cherry asked.

I jumped up. "Sure. Y'all want some?"

"I do," said Marcia. She was finishing the Coke Dally had given her. I realized then that Marcia and Cherry weren't alike. Cherry had said she wouldn't drink Dally's Coke if she was starving, and she meant it. It was the principle of the thing. But Marcia saw no reason to throw away a perfectly good, free Coke.

"Me too," said Two-Bit. He flipped me a fifty-cent piece. "Get Johnny some, too. I'm buyin'," he added as Johnny started to reach into his jeans pocket.

We went to the concession stand and, as usual, there was a line a mile long, so we had to wait. Quite a few kids turned to look at us—you didn't see a kid grease and a Socy cheerleader together often. Cherry didn't seem to notice.

"Your friend—the one with the sideburns—he's okay?"

"He ain't dangerous like Dallas if that's what you mean. He's okay."

She smiled and her eyes showed that her mind was on something else. "Johnny . . . he's been hurt bad sometime, hasn't he?" It was more of a statement than a question. "Hurt and scared."

"It was the Socs," I said nervously, because there were plenty of Socs milling around and some of them were giving me funny looks, as if I shouldn't be with Cherry or something. And I don't like to talk about it either— Johnny getting beat up, I mean. But I started in, talking a little faster than I usually do because I don't like to think about it either.

It was almost four months ago. I had walked down to the DX station to get a bottle of pop and to see Steve and Soda, because they'll always buy me a couple of bottles and let me help work on the cars. I don't like to go on weekends because then there is usually a bunch of girls down there flirting with Soda—all kinds of girls, Socs too. I don't care too much for girls yet. Soda says I'll grow out of it. He did.

It was a warmish spring day with the sun shining bright, but it was getting chilly and dark by the time we started for home. We were walking because we had left Steve's car at the station. At the corner of our block there's a wide, open field where we play football and hang out, and it's often a site for rumbles and fist fights. We were passing it, kicking rocks down the street and finishing our last bottles of Pepsi, when Steve noticed something lying on the ground. He picked it up. It was Johnny's blue-jeans jacket—the only jacket he had.

"Looks like Johnny forgot his jacket," Steve said, slinging it over his shoulder to take it by Johnny's house. Suddenly he stopped and examined it more carefully. There was a stain the color of rust across the collar. He looked at the ground. There were some more stains on the grass. He looked up and across the field with a stricken expression on his face. I think we all heard the low moan and saw the dark motionless hump on the other side of the lot at the same time. Soda reached him first. Johnny was lying face down on the ground. Soda turned him over gently, and I nearly got sick. Someone had beaten him badly.

We were used to seeing Johnny banged up—his father clobbered him around a lot, and although it made us madder than heck, we couldn't do anything about it. But those beatings had been nothing like this. Johnny's face was cut up and bruised and swollen, and there was a wide gash from his temple to his cheekbone. He would carry that scar all his life. His white T-shirt was splattered with blood. I just stood there, trembling with sudden cold. I thought he might be dead; surely nobody could be beaten like that and live. Steve closed his eyes for a second and muffled a groan as he dropped on his knees beside Soda.

Somehow the gang sensed what had happened. Two-Bit was suddenly there beside me, and for once his comical grin was gone and his dancing gray eyes were stormy. Darry had seen us from our porch and ran toward us, suddenly skidding to a halt. Dally was there, too, swearing under his breath, and turning away with a sick expression on his face. I wondered about it vaguely. Dally had seen people killed on the streets of New York's West Side. Why did he look sick now?

"Johnny?" Soda lifted him up and held him against his shoulder. He gave the limp body a slight shake. "Hey, Johnnycake."

Johnny didn't open his eyes, but there came a soft question. "Soda?"

"Yeah, it's me," Sodapop said. "Don't talk. You're gonna be okay."

"There was a whole bunch of them," Johnny went on, swallowing, ignoring Soda's command. "A blue Mustang full . . . I got so scared . . ." He tried to swear, but suddenly started crying, fighting to control himself, then sobbing all the more because he couldn't. I had seen Johnny take a whipping with a two-by-four from his old man and never let out a whimper. That made it worse to see him break now. Soda just held him and pushed Johnny's hair back out of his eyes. "It's okay, Johnnycake, they're gone now. It's okay."

Finally, between sobs, Johnny managed to gasp out his story. He had been hunting our football to practice a few kicks when a blue Mustang had pulled up beside the lot. There were four Socs in it. They had caught him and one of them had a lot of rings on his hand—that's what had cut Johnny up so badly. It wasn't just that they had beaten him half to death—he could take that. They had scared him. They had threatened him with everything under the sun. Johnny was high-strung anyway, a nervous wreck from getting belted every time he turned around and from hearing his parents fight all the time. Living in those conditions might have turned someone else rebellious and bitter; it was killing Johnny. He had never been a coward. He was a good man in a rumble. He stuck up for the gang and kept his mouth shut good around cops. But after the night of the beating, Johnny was jumpier than ever. I didn't think he'd ever get over it. Johnny never walked by himself after that. And Johnny, who was the most law-abiding of us, now carried in his back pocket a six-inch switchblade. He'd use it, too, if he ever got jumped again. They had scared him that much. He would kill the next person who jumped him. Nobody was ever going to beat him like that again. Not over his dead body . . .

I had nearly forgotten that Cherry was listening to me. But when I came back to reality and looked at her, I was startled to find her as white as a sheet.

"All Socs aren't like that," she said. "You have to believe me, Ponyboy. Not all of us are like that."

"Sure," I said.

"That's like saying all you greasers are like Dallas Winston. I'll bet he's jumped a few people."

I digested that. It was true. Dally had jumped people. He had told us stories about muggings in New York that made the hair on the back of my neck stand up. But not all of us were that bad.

Cherry no longer looked sick, only sad. "I'll bet you think the Socs have it made. The rich kids, the West-side Socs. I'll tell you something, Ponyboy, and it may come as a surprise. We have troubles you've never even heard of. You want to know something?" She looked me straight in the eye. "Things are rough all over."

"I believe you," I said. "We'd better get back out there with the popcorn or Two-Bit'll think I ran off with his money."

We went back and watched the movie through again. Marcia and Two-Bit were hitting it off fine. Both had the same scatterbrained sense of humor. But Cherry and Johnny and I just sat there, looking at the movie and not talking. I quit worrying about everything and thought about how nice it was to sit with a girl without having to listen to her swear or to beat her off with a club. I knew Johnny liked it, too. He didn't talk to girls much. Once, while Dallas was in reform school, Sylvia had started hanging on to Johnny and sweet-talking him and Steve got hold of her and told her if she tried any of her tricks with Johnny he'd personally beat the tar out of her. Then he gave Johnny a lecture on girls and how a sneaking little broad like Sylvia would get him into a lot of trouble. As a result, Johnny never spoke to girls much, but whether that was because he was scared of Steve or because he was shy, I couldn't tell.

I got the same lecture from Two-Bit after we'd picked up a couple of girls downtown one day. I thought it was funny, because girls are one subject even Darry thinks I use my head about. And it really had been funny, because Two-Bit was half-crocked when he gave me the lecture, and he told me some stories that about made me want to crawl under the floor or something. But he had been talking about girls like Sylvia and the girls he and Dally and the rest picked up at drive-ins and downtown; he never said anything about Socy girls. So I figured it was all right to be sitting there with them. Even if they did have their own troubles. I really couldn't see what Socs would have to sweat about—good grades, good cars, good girls, madras and Mustangs and Corvairs—Man, I thought, if I had worries like that I'd consider myself lucky.

I know better now.

Chapter 3

AFTER THE MOVIE WAS OVER IT SUDDENLY CAME TO US THAT Cherry and Marcia didn't have a way to get home. Two-Bit gallantly offered to walk them home—the west side of town was only about twenty miles away—but they wanted to call their parents and have them come and get them. Two-Bit finally talked them into letting us drive them home in his car. I think they were still half-scared of us. They were getting over it, though, as we walked to Two-Bit's house to pick up the car. It seemed funny to me that Socs—if these girls were any example—were just like us. They liked the Beatles and thought Elvis Presley was out, and we thought the Beatles were rank and that Elvis was tuff, but that seemed the only difference to me. Of course greasy girls would have acted a lot tougher, but there was a basic sameness. I thought maybe it was money that separated us.

"No," Cherry said slowly when I said this. "It's not just money. Part of it is, but not all. You greasers have a different set of values. You're more emotional. We're sophisticated—cool to the point of not feeling anything. Nothing is for real with us. You know, sometimes I'll catch myself talking to a girl-friend, and realize I don't mean half of what I'm saying. I don't really think a beer blast on the river bottom is super-cool, but I'll rave about one to a girl-friend just to be saying something." She smiled at me. "I never told anyone that. I think you're the first person I've ever really gotten through to."

She was coming through to me all right, probably because I was a greaser, and younger; she didn't have to keep her guard up with me.

"Rat race is a perfect name for it," she said. "We're always going and going and going, and never asking where. Did you ever hear of having more than you wanted? So that you couldn't want anything else and then started looking for something else to want? It seems like we're always searching for something to satisfy us, and never finding it. Maybe if we could lose our cool we could."

That was the truth. Socs were always behind a wall of aloofness, careful not to let their real selves show through. I had seen a social-club rumble once. The Socs even fought coldly and practically and impersonally.

"That's why we're separated," I said. "It's not money, it's feeling—you don't feel anything and we feel too violently."

"And"—she was trying to hide a smile—"that's probably why we take turns getting our names in the paper."

46

Two-Bit and Marcia weren't even listening to us. They were engaged in some wild conversation that made no sense to anyone but themselves.

I have quite a rep for being quiet, almost as quiet as Johnny. Two-Bit always said he wondered why Johnny and I were such good buddies. "You must make such interestin' conversation," he'd say, cocking one eyebrow, "you keepin' your mouth shut and Johnny not sayin' anything." But Johnny and I understood each other without saying anything. Nobody but Soda could really get me talking. Till I met Cherry Valance.

I don't know why I could talk to her; maybe for the same reason she could talk to me. The first thing I knew I was telling her about Mickey Mouse, Soda's horse. I had never told anyone about Soda's horse. It was personal.

Soda had this buckskin horse, only it wasn't his. It belonged to a guy who kept it at the stables where Soda used to work. Mickey Mouse was Soda's horse, though. The first day Soda saw him he said, "There's my horse," and I never doubted it. I was about ten then. Sodapop is horse-crazy. I mean it. He's always hanging around stables and rodeos, hopping on a horse every time he gets a chance. When I was ten I thought that Mickey Mouse and Soda looked alike and were alike. Mickey Mouse was a dark-gold buckskin, sassy and ornery, not much more than a colt. He'd come when Soda called him. He wouldn't come for anyone else. That horse loved Soda. He'd stand there and chew on Soda's sleeve or collar. Gosh, but Sodapop was crazy about that horse. He went down to see him every day. Mickey Mouse was a mean horse. He kicked other horses and was always getting into trouble. "I've got me a ornery pony," Soda'd tell him, rubbing his neck. "How come you're so mean, Mickey Mouse?" Mickey Mouse would just chew on his sleeve and sometimes nip him. But not hard. He may have belonged to another guy, but he was Soda's horse.

"Does Soda still have him?" Cherry asked.

"He got sold," I said. "They came and got him one day and took him off. He was a real valuable horse. Pure quarter."

She didn't say anything else and I was glad. I couldn't tell her that Soda had bawled all night long after they came and got Mickey Mouse. I had cried, too, if you want to know the truth, because Soda never really wanted anything except a horse, and he'd lost his. Soda had been twelve then, going-on-thirteen. He never let on to Mom and Dad how he felt, though, because we never had enough money and usually we had a hard time making ends meet. When you're thirteen in our neighborhood you know the score. I kept saving my money for a year, thinking that someday I could buy Mickey Mouse back for Soda. You're not so smart at ten.

"You read a lot, don't you, Ponyboy?" Cherry asked.

I was startled. "Yeah. Why?"

She kind of shrugged. "I could just tell. I'll bet you watch sunsets, too." She was quiet for a minute after I nodded. "I used to watch them, too, before I got so busy. . ."

I pictured that, or tried to. Maybe Cherry stood still and watched the sun set while she was supposed to be taking the garbage out. Stood there and watched and forgot everything else until her big brother screamed at her to hurry up. I shook my head. It seemed funny to me that the sunset she saw from her patio and the one I saw from the back steps was the same one. Maybe the two different worlds we lived in weren't so different. We saw the same sunset.

Marcia suddenly gasped. "Cherry, look what's coming."

We all looked and saw a blue Mustang coming down the street. Johnny made a small noise in his throat and when I looked at him he was white.

Marcia was shifting nervously. "What are we going to do?"

Cherry bit a fingernail. "Stand here," she said. "There isn't much else we can do."

"Who is it?" Two-Bit asked. "The F.B.I.?"

"No," Cherry said bleakly, "it's Randy and Bob."

"And," Two-Bit added grimly, "a few other of the socially elite checkered-shirt set."

"Your boyfriends?" Johnny's voice was steady, but standing as close to him as I was, I could see he was trembling. I wondered why—Johnny was a nervous wreck, but he never was that jumpy.

Cherry started walking down the street. "Maybe they won't see us. Act normal."

"Who's acting?" Two-Bit grinned. "I'm a natural normal."

"Wish it was the other way around," I muttered, and Two-Bit said, "Don't get mouthy, Ponyboy."

The Mustang passed us slowly and went right on by. Marcia sighed in relief. "That was close."

Cherry turned to me. "Tell me about your oldest brother. You don't talk much about him."

I tried to think of something to say about Darry, and shrugged. "What's to talk about? He's big and handsome and likes to play football."

"I mean, what's he like? I feel like I know Soda from the way you talk about him; tell me about Darry." And when I was silent she urged me on. "Is he wild and reckless like Soda? Dreamy, like you?"

My face got hot as I bit my lip. Darry . . . what was Darry like? "He's . . ." I started to say he was a good ol' guy but I couldn't. I burst out bitterly: "He's not like Sodapop at all and he sure ain't like me. He's hard as a rock and about as human. He's got eyes exactly like frozen ice. He thinks I'm a pain in the neck. He likes Soda— everybody likes Soda—but he can't stand me. I bet he wishes he could stick me in a home somewhere, and he'd do it, too, if Soda'd let him."

Two-Bit and Johnny were staring at me now. "No . . ." Two-Bit said, dumfounded. "No, Ponyboy, that ain't right . . . you got it wrong . . ."

"Gee," Johnny said softly, "I thought you and Darry and Soda got along real well . . ."

"Well, we don't," I snapped, feeling silly. I knew my ears were red by the way they were burning, and I was thankful for the darkness. I felt stupid. Compared to Johnny's home, mine was heaven. At least Darry didn't get drunk and beat me up or run me out of the house, and I had Sodapop to talk things over with. That made me mad, I mean making a fool of myself in front of everyone. "An' you can shut your trap, Johnny Cade, 'cause we all know you ain't wanted at home, either. And you can't blame them."

Johnny's eyes went round and he winced as though I'd belted him. Two-Bit slapped me a good one across the side of the head, and hard.

"Shut your mouth, kid. If you wasn't Soda's kid brother I'd beat the tar out of you. You know better than to talk to Johnny like that." He put his hand on Johnny's shoulder. "He didn't mean it, Johnny."

"I'm sorry," I said miserably. Johnny was my buddy. "I was just mad."

"It's the truth," Johnny said with a bleak grin. "I don't care."

"Shut up talkin' like that," Two-Bit said fiercely, messing up Johnny's hair. "We couldn't get along without you, so you can just shut up!"

"It ain't fair!" I cried passionately. "It ain't fair that we have all the rough breaks!" I didn't know exactly what I meant, but I was thinking about Johnny's father being a drunk and his mother a selfish slob, and Two-Bit's mother being a barmaid to support him and his kid sister after their father ran out on them, and Dally—wild, cunning Dally—turning into a hoodlum because he'd die if he didn't, and Steve—his hatred for his father coming out in his soft, bitter voice and the violence of his temper. Soda-pop . . . a dropout so he could get a job and keep me in school, and Darry, getting old before his time trying to run a family and hang on to two jobs and never having any fun—while the Socs had so much spare time and money that they jumped us and each other for kicks, had beer blasts and river-bottom parties because they didn't know what else to do. Things were rough all over, all right. All over the East Side. It just didn't seem right to me.

"I know," Two Bit said with a good-natured grin, "the chips are always down when it's our turn, but that's the way things are. Like it or lump it."

Cherry and Marcia didn't say anything. I guess they didn't know what to say. We had forgotten they were there. Then the blue Mustang was coming down the street again, more slowly.

"Well," Cherry said resignedly, "they've spotted us."

The Mustang came to a halt beside us, and the two boys in the front seat got out. They were Socs all right. One had on a white shirt and a madras ski jacket, and the other a light-yellow shirt and a wine-colored sweater. I looked at their clothes and realized for the first time that evening that all I had was a pair of jeans and Soda's old navy sweat shirt with the sleeves cut short. I swallowed. Two-Bit started to tuck in his shirttail, but stopped himself in time; he just flipped up the collar of his black leather jacket and lit a cigarette. The Socs didn't even seem to see us.

"Cherry, Marcia, listen to us . . ." the handsome black-haired Soc with the dark sweater began.

Johnny was breathing heavily and I noticed he was staring at the Soc's hand. He was wearing three heavy rings. I looked quickly at Johnny, an idea dawning on me. I remembered that it was a blue Mustang that had pulled up beside the vacant lot and that Johnny's face had been cut up by someone wearing rings . . .

The Soc's voice broke into my thoughts: ". . . just because we got a little drunk last time . . ."

Cherry looked mad. "A little? You call reeling and passing out in the streets 'a little'? Bob, I told you, I'm never going out with you while you're drinking, and I mean it.

Too many things could happen while you're drunk. It's me or the booze."

The other Soc, a tall guy with a semi-Beatle haircut, turned to Marcia. "Baby, you know we don't get drunk very often . . ." When she only gave him a cold stare he got angry. "And even if you are mad at us, that's no reason to go walking the streets with these bums."

Two-Bit took a long drag on his cigarette, Johnny slouched and hooked his thumbs in his pockets, and I stiffened. We can look meaner than anything when we want to—looking tough comes in handy. Two-Bit put his elbow on Johnny's shoulder. "Who you callin' bums?"

"Listen, greasers, we got four more of us in the back seat . . ."

"Then pity the back seat," Two-Bit said to the sky.

"If you're looking for a fight . . ."

Two-Bit cocked an eyebrow, but it only made him look more cool. "You mean if I'm looking for a good jumping, you outnumber us, so you'll give it to us? Well . . ." He snatched up an empty bottle, busted off the end, and gave it to me, then reached in his back pocket and flipped out his switchblade. "Try it, pal."

"No!" Cherry cried. "Stop it!" She looked at Bob. "We'll ride home with you. Just wait a minute."

"Why?" Two-Bit demanded. "We ain't scared of them."

Cherry shuddered. "I can't stand fights . . . I can't stand them . . ."

I pulled her to one side. "I couldn't use this," I said, dropping the pop bottle. "I couldn't ever cut anyone. . . ." I had to tell her that, because I'd seen her eyes when Two-Bit flicked out his switch.

"I know," she said quietly, "but we'd better go with them. Ponyboy . . . I mean . . . if I see you in the hall at school or someplace and don't say hi, well, it's not personal or anything, but . . ."

"I know," I said.

"We couldn't let our parents see us with you all. You're a nice boy and everything . . ."

"It's okay," I said, wishing I was dead and buried somewhere. Or at least that I had on a decent shirt. "We aren't in the same class. Just don't forget that some of us watch the sunset too."

She looked at me quickly. "I could fall in love with Dallas Winston," she said. "I hope I never see him again, or I will."

She left me standing there with my mouth dropped open, and the blue Mustang vroomed off.

We walked on home, mostly in silence. I wanted to ask Johnny if those were the same Socs that had beaten him up, but I didn't mention it. Johnny never talked about it and we never said anything.

"Well, those were two good-lookin' girls if I ever saw any." Two-Bit yawned as we sat down on the curb at the vacant lot. He took a piece of paper out of his pocket and tore it up.

"What was that?"

"Marcia's number. Probably a phony one, too. I must have been outa my mind to ask for it. I think I'm a little soused."

So he had been drinking. Two-Bit was smart. He knew the score. "Y'all goin' home?" he asked.

"Not right now," I said. I wanted to have another

smoke and to watch the stars. I had to be in by twelve, but I thought I had plenty of time.

"I don't know why I handed you that busted bottle," Two-Bit said, getting to his feet. "You'd never use it."

"Maybe I would' have," I said. "Where you headed?"

"Gonna go play a little snooker and hunt up a poker game. Maybe get rip-roarin' drunk. I dunno. See y'all tomorrow."

Johnny and I stretched out on our backs and looked at the stars. I was freezing—it was a cold night and all I had was that sweat shirt, but I could watch stars in sub-zero weather. I saw Johnny's cigarette glowing in the dark and wondered vaguely what it was like inside a burning ember . . .

"It was because we're greasers," Johnny said, and I knew he was talking about Cherry. "We could have hurt her reputation."

"I reckon," I said, wondering if I ought to tell Johnny what she had said about Dallas.

"Man, that was a tuff car. Mustangs are tuff."

"Big-time Socs, all right," I said, a nervous bitterness growing inside me. It wasn't fair for the Socs to have every-thing. We were as good as they were; it wasn't our fault we were greasers. I couldn't just take it or leave it, like Two-Bit, or ignore it and love life anyway, like Sodapop, or harden myself beyond caring, like Dally, or actually en-joy it, like Tim Shepard. I felt the tension growing inside of me and I knew something had to happen or I would ex-plode.

"I can't take much more." Johnny spoke my own feel-ings. "I'll kill myself or something."

"Don't," I said, sitting up in alarm. "You can't kill yourself, Johnny."

"Well, I won't. But I gotta do something. It seems like there's gotta be someplace without greasers or Socs, with just people. Plain ordinary people."

"Out of the big towns," I said, lying back down. "In the country . . ."

In the country . . . I loved the country. I wanted to be out of towns and away from excitement. I only wanted to lie on my back under a tree and read a book or draw a picture, and not worry about being jumped or carrying a blade or ending up married to some scatterbrained broad with no sense. The country would be like that, I thought dreamily. I would have a yeller cur dog, like I used to, and Sodapop could get Mickey Mouse back and ride in all the rodeos he wanted to, and Darry would lose that cold, hard look and be like he used to be, eight months ago, before Mom and Dad were killed. Since I was dreaming I brought Mom and Dad back to life . . . Mom could bake some more chocolate cakes and Dad would drive the pickup out early to feed the cattle. He would slap Darry on the back and tell him he was getting to be a man, a regular chip off the block, and they would be as close as they used to be. Maybe Johnny could come and live with us, and the gang could come out on weekends, and maybe Dallas would see that there was some good in the world after all, and Mom would talk to him and make him grin in spite of himself. "You've got quite a mom," Dally used to say. "She knows the score." She could talk to Dallas and kept him from getting into a lot of trouble. My mother was golden and beautiful . . .

"Ponyboy"—Johnny was shaking me—"Hey, Pony, wake up."

I sat up, shivering. The stars had moved. "Glory, what time is it?"

"I don't know. I went to sleep, too, listening to you rattle on and on. You'd better get home. I think I'll stay all night out here." Johnny's parents didn't care if he came home or not.

"Okay." I yawned. Gosh, but it was cold. "If you get cold or something come on over to our house."

"Okay."

I ran home, trembling at the thought of facing Darry. The porch light was on. Maybe they were asleep and I could sneak in, I thought. I peeked in the window. Soda-pop was stretched out on the sofa, sound asleep, but Darry was in the armchair under the lamp, reading the newspaper. I gulped, and opened the door softly. Darry looked up from his paper. He was on his feet in a second. I stood there, chewing on my fingernail.

"Where the heck have you been? Do you know what time it is?" He was madder than I'd seen him in a long time. I shook my head wordlessly.

"Well, it's two in the morning, kiddo. Another hour and I would have had the police out after you. Where were you, Ponyboy?"—his voice was rising—"Where in the almighty universe were you?"

It sounded dumb, even to me, when I stammered, "I . . . I went to sleep in the lot . . ."

"You what?" He was shouting, and Sodapop sat up and rubbed his eyes.

"Hey, Ponyboy," he said sleepily, "where ya been?"

"I didn't mean to." I pleaded with Darry. "I was talking to Johnny and we both dropped off . . ."

"I reckon it never occurred to you that your brothers might be worrying their heads off and afraid to call the police because something like that could get you two thrown in a boys' home so quick it'd make your head spin. And you were asleep in the lot? Ponyboy, what on earth is the matter with you? Can't you use your head? You haven't even got a coat on."

I felt hot tears of anger and frustration rising. "I said I didn't mean to . . ."

"I didn't mean to!" Darry shouted, and I almost shook. "I didn't think! I forgot! That's all I hear out of you! Can't you think of anything?"

"Darry . . ." Sodapop began, but Darry turned on him. "You keep your trap shut! I'm sick and tired of hearin' you stick up for him."

He should never yell at Soda. Nobody should ever holler at my brother. I exploded. "You don't yell at him!" I shouted. Darry wheeled around and slapped me so hard that it knocked me against the door.

Suddenly it was deathly quiet. We had all frozen. Nobody in my family had ever hit me. Nobody. Soda was wide-eyed. Darry looked at the palm of his hand where it had turned red and then looked back at me. His eyes were huge. "Ponyboy . . ."

I turned and ran out the door and down the street as fast as I could. Darry screamed, "Pony, I didn't mean to!" but I was at the lot by then and pretended I couldn't hear. I was running away. It was plain to me that Darry didn't want me around. And I wouldn't stay if he did. He wasn't ever going to hit me again.

"Johnny?" I called, and started when he rolled over and jumped up almost under my feet. "Come on, Johnny, we're running away."

Johnny asked no questions. We ran for several blocks until we were out of breath. Then we walked. I was crying by then. I finally just sat down on the curb and cried, burying my face in my arms. Johnny sat down beside me, one hand on my shoulder. "Easy, Ponyboy," he said softly, "we'll be okay."

I finally calmed down and wiped my eyes on my bare arm. My breath was coming in quivering sobs. "Gotta cigarette?"

He handed me one and struck a match.

"Johnny, I'm scared."

"Well, don't be. You're scarin' me. What happened? I never seen you bawl like that."

"I don't very often. It was Darry. He hit me. I don't know what happened, but I couldn't take him hollering at me and hitting me too. I don't know . . . sometimes we get along okay, then all of a sudden he blows up on me or else is naggin' at me all the time. He didn't use to be like that . . . we used to get along okay . . . before Mom and Dad died. Now he just can't stand me."

"I think I like it better when the old man's hittin' me." Johnny sighed. "At least then I know he knows who I am. I walk in that house, and nobody says anything. I walk out, and nobody says anything. I stay away all night, and nobody notices. At least you got Soda. I ain't got nobody."

59

"Shoot," I said, startled out of my misery, "you got the whole gang. Dally didn't slug you tonight 'cause you're the pet. I mean, golly, Johnny, you got the whole gang."

"It ain't the same as having your own folks care about you," Johnny said simply. "It just ain't the same."

I was beginning to relax and wonder if running away was such a great idea. I was sleepy and freezing to death and I wanted to be home in bed, safe and warm under the covers with Soda's arm across me. I decided I would go home and just not speak to Darry. It was my house as much as Darry's, and if he wanted to pretend I wasn't alive, that was just fine with me. He couldn't stop me from living in my own house.

"Let's walk to the park and back. Then maybe I'll be cooled off enough to go home."

"Okay," Johnny said easily. "Okay."

Things gotta get better, I figured. They couldn't get worse. I was wrong.

Chapter 4

THE PARK WAS ABOUT TWO BLOCKS SQUARE, WITH A FOUN-
tain in the middle and a small swimming pool for the little
kids. The pool was empty now in the fall, but the fountain
was going merrily. Tall elm trees made the park shadowy
and dark, and it would have been a good hangout, but we
preferred our vacant lot, and the Shepard outfit liked the
alleys down by the tracks, so the park was left to lovers and
little kids.

Nobody was around at two-thirty in the morning, and it
was a good place to relax and cool off. I couldn't have
gotten much cooler without turning into a popsicle. Johnny
snapped up his jeans jacket and flipped up the collar.

"Ain't you about to freeze to death, Pony?"

"You ain't a'woofin'," I said, rubbing my bare arms between drags on my cigarette. I started to say something about the film of ice developing on the outer edges of the fountain when a sudden blast from a car horn made us both jump. The blue Mustang was circling the park slowly.

Johnny swore under his breath, and I muttered, "What do they want? This is our territory. What are Socs doing this far east?"

Johnny shook his head. "I don't know. But I bet they're looking for us. We picked up their girls."

"Oh, glory," I said with a groan, "this is all I need to top off a perfect night." I took one last drag on my weed and ground the stub under my heel. "Want to run for it?"

"It's too late now," Johnny said. "Here they come."

Five Socs were coming straight at us, and from the way they were staggering I figured they were reeling pickled. That scared me. A cool deadly bluff could sometimes shake them off, but not if they outnumbered you five to two and were drunk. Johnny's hand went to his back pocket and I remembered his switchblade. I wished for that broken bottle. I'd sure show them I could use it if I had to. Johnny was scared to death. I mean it. He was as white as a ghost and his eyes were wild-looking, like the eyes of an animal in a trap. We backed against the fountain and the Socs surrounded us. They smelled so heavily of whiskey and English Leather that I almost choked. I wished desperately that Darry and Soda would come along hunting for me. The four of us could handle them easily. But no one was around, and I knew Johnny and I were going to have to fight it out alone. Johnny had a blank, tough look on his face—you'd have had to know him to see the panic in his eyes. I stared at the Socs coolly. Maybe they could scare us to death, but we'd never let them have the satisfaction of knowing it.

It was Randy and Bob and three other Socs, and they recognized us. I knew Johnny recognized them; he was watching the moonlight glint off Bob's rings with huge eyes.

"Hey, whatta ya know?" Bob said a little unsteadily, "here's the little greasers that picked up our girls. Hey, greasers."

"You're outa your territory," Johnny warned in a low voice. "You'd better watch it."

Randy swore at us and they stepped in closer. Bob was eyeing Johnny. "Nup, pal, yer the ones who'd better watch it. Next time you want a broad, pick up yer own kind—dirt."

I was getting mad. I was hating them enough to lose my head.

"You know what a greaser is?" Bob asked. "White trash with long hair."

I felt the blood draining from my face. I've been cussed out and sworn at, but nothing ever hit me like that did. Johnnycake made a kind of gasp and his eyes were smoldering.

"You know what a Soc is?" I said, my voice shaking with rage. "White trash with Mustangs and madras." And then, because I couldn't think of anything bad enough to call them, I spit at them.

Bob shook his head, smiling slowly. "You could use a bath, greaser. And a good working over. And we've got all night to do it. Give the kid a bath, David."

63

I ducked and tried to run for it, but the Soc caught my arm and twisted it behind my back, and shoved my face into the fountain. I fought, but the hand at the back of my neck was strong and I had to hold my breath. I'm dying, I thought, and wondered what was happening to Johnny. I couldn't hold my breath any longer. I fought again desperately but only sucked in water. I'm drowning, I thought, they've gone too far . . . A red haze filled my mind and I slowly relaxed.

The next thing I knew I was lying on the pavement beside the fountain, coughing water and gasping. I lay there weakly, breathing in air and spitting out water. The wind blasted through my soaked sweat shirt and dripping hair. My teeth chattered unceasingly and I couldn't stop them. I finally pushed myself up and leaned back against the fountain, the water running down my face. Then I saw Johnny.

He was sitting next to me, one elbow on his knee, and staring straight ahead. He was a strange greenish-white, and his eyes were huger than I'd ever seen them.

"I killed him," he said slowly. "I killed that boy."

Bob, the handsome Soc, was lying there in the moonlight, doubled up and still. A dark pool was growing from him, spreading slowly over the blue-white cement. I looked at Johnny's hand. He was clutching his switchblade, and it was dark to the hilt. My stomach gave a violent jump and my blood turned icy.

"Johnny," I managed to say, fighting the dizziness, "I think I'm gonna be sick."

"Go ahead," he said in the same steady voice. "I won't look at you."

I turned my head and was quietly sick for a minute. Then I leaned back and closed my eyes so I wouldn't see Bob lying there.

This can't be happening. This can't be happening. This can't be . . .

"You really killed him, huh, Johnny?"

"Yeah." His voice quavered slightly. "I had to. They were drowning you, Pony. They might have killed you. And they had a blade. . . they were gonna beat me up. . . ."

"Like . . ."—I swallowed—"like they did before?"

Johnny was quiet for a minute. "Yeah," he said, "like they did before."

Johnny told me what had happened: "They ran when I stabbed him. They all ran . . ."

A panic was rising in me as I listened to Johnny's quiet voice go on and on. "Johnny!" I nearly screamed. "What are we gonna do? They put you in the electric chair for killing people!" I was shaking. I want a cigarette. I want a cigarette. I want a cigarette. We had smoked our last pack. "I'm scared, Johnny. What are we gonna do?"

Johnny jumped up and dragged me up by my sweat shirt. He shook me. "Calm down, Ponyboy. Get ahold of yourself."

I hadn't realized I was screaming. I shook loose. "Okay," I said, "I'm okay now."

Johnny looked around, slapping his pockets nervously. "We gotta get outa here. Get somewhere. Run away. The police'll be here soon." I was trembling, and it wasn't all from cold. But Johnny, except for the fact that his hands were twitching, looked as cool as Darry ever had. "We'll need money. And maybe a gun. And a plan."

Money. Maybe a gun? A plan. Where in the world would we get these things?

"Dally," Johnny said with finality. "Dally'll get us outa here."

I heaved a sigh. Why hadn't I thought of that? But I never thought of anything. Dallas Winston could do anything.

"Where can we find him?"

"I think at Buck Merril's place. There's a party over there tonight. Dally said somethin' about it this afternoon."

Buck Merril was Dally's rodeo partner. He was the one who'd got Dally the job as a jockey for the Slash J. Buck raised a few quarter horses, and made most of his money on fixed races and a little bootlegging. I was under strict orders from both Darry and Soda not to get caught within ten miles of his place, which was dandy with me. I didn't like Buck Merril. He was a tall lanky cowboy with blond hair and buckteeth. Or he used to be bucktoothed before he had the front two knocked out in a fight. He was out of it. He dug Hank Williams—how gross can you get?

Buck answered the door when we knocked, and a roar of cheap music came with him. The clinking of glasses, loud, rough laughter and female giggles, and Hank Williams. It scraped on my raw nerves like sandpaper. A can of beer in one hand, Buck glared down at us. "Whatta ya want?"

"Dally!" Johnny gulped, looking back over his shoulder. "We gotta see Dally."

"He's busy," Buck snapped, and someone in his living room yelled "A-ha!" and then "Yee-ha," and the sound of it almost made my nerves snap.

"Tell him it's Pony and Johnny," I commanded. I knew Buck, and the only way you could get anything from him was to bully him. I guess that's why Dallas could handle him so easily, although Buck was in his mid-twenties and Dally was seventeen. "He'll come."

Buck glared at me for a second, then stumbled off. He was pretty well crocked, which made me apprehensive. If Dally was drunk and in a dangerous mood. . . .

He appeared in a few minutes, clad only in a pair of low-cut blue jeans, scratching the hair on his chest. He was sober enough, and that surprised me. Maybe he hadn't been there long.

"Okay, kids, whatta ya need me for?"

As Johnny told him the story, I studied Dally, trying to figure out what there was about this tough-looking hood that a girl like Cherry Valance could love. Towheaded and shifty-eyed, Dally was anything but handsome. Yet in his hard face there was character, pride, and a savage defiance of the world. He could never love Cherry Valance back. It would be a miracle if Dally loved anything. The fight for self-preservation had hardened him beyond caring.

He didn't bat an eye when Johnny told him what had happened, only grinned and said "Good for you" when Johnny told how he had knifed the Soc. Finally Johnny finished. "We figured you could get us out if anyone could. I'm sorry we got you away from the party."

"Oh, shoot, kid"—Dally glanced contemptuously over his shoulder—"I was in the bedroom."

He suddenly stared at me. "Glory, but your ears can get red, Ponyboy."

I was remembering what usually went on in the bedrooms at Buck's parties. Then Dally grinned in amused realization. "It wasn't anything like that, kid. I was asleep, or tryin' to be, with all this racket. Hank Williams"—he rolled his eyes and added a few adjectives after 'Hank Williams.' "Me and Shepard had a run-in and I cracked some ribs. I just needed a place to lay over." He rubbed his side ruefully. "Ol' Tim sure can pack a punch. He won't be able to see outa one eye for a week." He looked us over and sighed. "Well, wait a sec and I'll see what I can do about this mess." Then he took a good look at me. "Ponyboy, are you wet?"

"Y-y-yes-s," I stammered through chattering teeth.

"Glory hallelujah!" He opened the screen door and pulled me in, motioning for Johnny to follow. "You'll die of pneumonia 'fore the cops ever get you."

He half-dragged me into an empty bedroom, swearing at me all the way. "Get that sweat shirt off." He threw a towel at me. "Dry off and wait here. At least Johnny's got his jeans jacket. You ought to know better than to run away in just a sweat shirt, and a wet one at that. Don't you ever use your head?" He sounded so much like Darry that I stared at him. He didn't notice, and left us sitting on the bed.

Johnny lay back on it. "Wish I had me a weed."

My knees were shaking as I finished drying off, sitting there in my jeans.

Dally appeared after a minute. He carefully shut the door. "Here"—he handed us a gun and a roll of bills— "the gun's loaded. For Pete's sake, Johnny, don't point the thing at me. Here's fifty bucks. That's all I could get out of Merril tonight. He's blowin' his loot from that last race."

You might have thought it was Dally who fixed those races for Buck, being a jockey and all, but it wasn't. The last guy to suggest it lost three teeth. It's the truth. Dally rode the ponies honestly and did his best to win. It was the only thing Dally did honestly.

"Pony, do Darry and Sodapop know about this?"

I shook my head. Dally sighed. "Boy howdy, I ain't itchin' to be the one to tell Darry and get my head busted."

"Then don't tell him," I said. I hated to worry Sodapop, and would have liked to let him know I had gotten this far okay, but I didn't care if Darry worried himself gray-headed. I was too tired to tell myself I was being mean and unreasonable. I convinced myself it wouldn't be fair to make Dally tell him. Darry would beat him to death for giving us the money and the gun and getting us out of town.

"Here!" Dally handed me a shirt about sixty-million sizes too big. "It's Buck's—you an' him ain't exactly the same size, but it's dry." He handed me his worn brown leather jacket with the yellow sheep's-wool lining. "It'll get cold where you're going, but you can't risk being loaded down with blankets."

I started buttoning up the shirt. It about swallowed me. "Hop the three-fifteen freight to Windrixville," Dally instructed. "There's an old abandoned church on top of Jay Mountain. There's a pump in back so don't worry about water. Buy a week's supply of food as soon as you get there —this morning, before the story gets out, and then don't

69

so much as stick your noses out the door. I'll be up there as soon as I think it's clear. Man, I thought New York was the only place I could get mixed up in a murder rap."

At the word "murder," Johnny made a small noise in his throat and shuddered.

Dally walked us back to the door, turning off the porch light before we stepped out. "Git goin'!" He messed up Johnny's hair. "Take care, kid," he said softly.

"Sure, Dally, thanks." And we ran into the darkness.

We crouched in the weeds beside the railroad tracks, listening to the whistle grow louder. The train slowed to a screaming halt. "Now," whispered Johnny. We ran and pulled ourselves into an open boxcar. We pressed against the side, trying to hold our breath while we listened to the railroad workers walk up and down outside. One poked his head inside, and we froze. But he didn't see us, and the boxcar rattled as the train started up.

"The first stop'll be Windrixville," Johnny said, laying the gun down gingerly. He shook his head. "I don't see why he gave me this. I couldn't shoot anybody."

Then for the first time, really, I realized what we were in for. Johnny had killed someone. Quiet, soft-spoken little Johnny, who wouldn't hurt a living thing on purpose, had taken a human life. We were really running away, with the police after us for murder and a loaded gun by our side. I wished we'd asked Dally for a pack of cigarettes. . . .

I stretched out and used Johnny's legs for a pillow. Curling up, I was thankful for Dally's jacket. It was too big, but it was warm. Not even the rattling of the train could keep me awake, and I went to sleep in a hoodlum's jacket, with a gun lying next to my hand.

I was hardly awake when Johnny and I leaped off the train into a meadow. Not until I landed in the dew and got a wet shock did I realize what I was doing. Johnny must have woke me up and told me to jump, but I didn't remember it. We lay in the tall weeds and damp grass, breathing heavily. The dawn was coming. It was lightening the sky in the east and a ray of gold touched the hills. The clouds were pink and meadow larks were singing. This is the country, I thought, half asleep. My dream's come true and I'm in the country.

"Blast it, Ponyboy"—Johnny was rubbing his legs— "you must have put my legs to sleep. I can't even stand up. I barely got off that train."

"I'm sorry. Why didn't you wake me up?"

"That's okay. I didn't want to wake you up until I had to."

"Now how do we find Jay Mountain?" I asked Johnny. I was still groggy with sleep and wanted to sleep forever right there in the dew and the dawn.

"Go ask someone. The story won't be in the paper yet. Make like a farm boy taking a walk or something."

"I don't look like a farm boy," I said. I suddenly thought of my long hair, combed back, and the slouching stride I used from habit. I looked at Johnny. He didn't look like any farm boy to me. He still reminded me of a lost puppy who had been kicked too often, but for the first time I saw him as a stranger might see him. He looked hard and tough, because of his black T-shirt and his blue jeans and jacket, and because his hair was heavily greased and so long. I saw how his hair curled behind his ears and I thought: We both need a haircut and some decent clothes. I looked down at my worn, faded blue jeans, my too-big shirt, and Dally's worn-out jacket. They'll know we're hoods the minute they see us, I thought.

"I'll have to stay here," Johnny said, rubbing his legs. "You go down the road and ask the first person you see where Jay Mountain is." He winced at the pain in his legs. "Then come back. And for Pete's sake, run a comb through your hair and quit slouching down like a thug."

So Johnny had noticed it too. I pulled a comb from my back pocket and combed my hair carefully. "I guess I look okay now, huh, Johnny?"

He was studying me. "You know, you look an awful lot like Sodapop, the way you've got your hair and everything. I mean, except your eyes are green."

"They ain't green, they're gray," I said, reddening. "And I look about as much like Soda as you do." I got to my feet. "He's good-looking."

"Shoot," Johnny said with a grin, "you are, too."

I climbed over the barbed-wire fence without saying anything else. I could hear Johnny laughing at me, but I didn't care. I went strolling down the red dirt road, hoping my natural color would come back before I met anyone. I wonder what Darry and Sodapop are doing now, I thought, yawning. Soda had the whole bed to himself for once. I bet Darry's sorry he ever hit me. He'll really get worried when he finds out Johnny and I killed that Soc. Then, for a moment, I pictured Sodapop's face when he heard about it. I wish I was home, I thought absently, I wish I was home and still in bed. Maybe I am. Maybe I'm just dreaming . . .

It was only last night that Dally and I had sat down behind those girls at the Nightly Double. Glory, I thought with a bewildering feeling of being rushed, things are happening too quick. Too fast. I figured I couldn't get into any worse trouble than murder. Johnny and I would be hiding for the rest of our lives. Nobody but Dally would know where we were, and he couldn't tell anyone because he'd get jailed again for giving us that gun. If Johnny got caught, they'd give him the electric chair, and if they caught me, I'd be sent to a reformatory. I'd heard about reformatories from Curly Shepard and I didn't want to go to one at all. So we'd have to be hermits for the rest of our lives, and never see anyone but Dally. Maybe I'd never see Darry or Sodapop again. Or even Two-Bit or Steve. I was in the country, but I knew I wasn't going to like it as much as I'd thought I would. There are things worse than being a greaser.

I met a sunburned farmer driving a tractor down the road. I waved at him and he stopped.

"Could you tell me where Jay Mountain is?" I asked as politely as I could.

He pointed on down the road. "Follow this road to that big hill over there. That's it. Taking a walk?"

"Yessir." I managed to look sheepish. "We're playing army and I'm supposed to report to headquarters there."

I can lie so easily that it spooks me sometimes—Soda says it comes from reading so much. But then, Two-Bit lies all the time too, and he never opens a book.

73

"Boys will be boys," the farmer said with a grin, and I thought dully that he sounded as corn-poney as Hank Williams. He went on and I walked back to where Johnny was waiting.

We climbed up the road to the church, although it was a lot farther away than it looked. The road got steeper with every step. I was feeling kind of drunk—I always do when I get too sleepy—and my legs got heavier and heavier. I guess Johnny was sleepier than I was—he had stayed awake on the train to make sure we got off at the right place. It took us about forty-five minutes to get there. We climbed in a back window. It was a small church, real old and spooky and spiderwebby. It gave me the creeps.

I'd been in church before. I used to go all the time, even after Mom and Dad were gone. Then one Sunday I talked Soda into coming with Johnny and me. He didn't want to come unless Steve did, and Two-Bit decided he might as well come too. Dally was sleeping off a hangover, and Darry was working. When Johnny and I went, we sat in the back, trying to get something out of the sermon and avoiding the people, because we weren't dressed so sharp most of the time. Nobody seemed to mind, and Johnny and I really liked to go. But that day . . . well, Soda can't sit still long enough to enjoy a movie, much less a sermon. It wasn't long before he and Steve and Two-Bit were throwing paper wads at each other and clowning around, and finally Steve dropped a hymn book with a bang—accidentally, of course. Everyone in the place turned around to look at us, and Johnny and I nearly crawled under the pews. And then Two-Bit *waved* at them.

I hadn't been to church since.

But this church gave me a kind of creepy feeling. What do you call it? Premonition? I flopped down on the floor—and immediately decided not to do any more flopping. That floor was stone, and hard. Johnny stretched out beside me, resting his head on his arm. I started to say something to him, but I went to sleep before I could get the words out of my mouth. But Johnny didn't notice. He was asleep, too.

Chapter 5

I WOKE UP LATE IN THE AFTERNOON. FOR A SECOND I DIDN'T know where I was. You know how it is, when you wake up in a strange place and wonder where in the world you are, until memory comes rushing over you like a wave. I half convinced myself that I had dreamed everything that had happened the night before. I'm really home in bed, I thought. It's late and both Darry and Sodapop are up. Darry's cooking breakfast, and in a minute he and Soda will come in and drag me out of bed and wrestle me down and tickle me until I think I'll die if they don't stop. It's me and Soda's turn to do the dishes after we eat, and then we'll all go outside and play football. Johnny and Two-Bit and I will get Darry on our side, since Johnny and I are so small and Darry's the best player. It'll go like the usual

76

weekend morning. I tried telling myself that while I lay on the cold rock floor, wrapped up in Dally's jacket and listening to the wind rushing through the trees' dry leaves outside.

Finally I quit pretending and pushed myself up. I was stiff and sore from sleeping on that hard floor, but I had never slept so soundly. I was still groggy. I pushed off Johnny's jeans jacket, which had somehow got thrown across me, and blinked, scratching my head. It was awful quiet, with just the sound of rushing wind in the trees. Suddenly I realized that Johnny wasn't there.

"Johnny?" I called loudly, and that old wooden church echoed me, onny onny . . . I looked around wildly, almost panic-stricken, but then caught sight of some crooked lettering written in the dust of the floor. *Went to get supplies. Be back soon. J.C.*

I sighed, and went to the pump to get a drink. The water from it was like liquid ice and it tasted funny, but it was water. I splashed some on my face and that woke me up pretty quick. I wiped my face off on Johnny's jacket and sat down on the back steps. The hill the church was on dropped off suddenly about twenty feet from the back door, and you could see for miles and miles. It was like sitting on the top of the world.

When you haven't got anything to do, you remember things in spite of yourself. I could remember every detail of the whole night, but it had the unreal quality of a dream. It seemed much longer than twenty-four hours since Johnny and I had met Dally at the corner of Pickett and Sutton. Maybe it was. Maybe Johnny had been gone a whole week and I had just slept. Maybe he had already been worked over by the fuzz and was waiting to get the electric chair since he wouldn't tell where I was. Maybe Dally had been killed in a car wreck or something and no one would ever know where I was, and I'd just die up here, alone, and turn into a skeleton. My over-active imagination was running away with me again. Sweat ran down my face and back, and I was trembling. My head swam, and I leaned back and closed my eyes. I guess it was partly delayed shock. Finally my stomach calmed down and I relaxed a little, hoping that Johnny would remember cigarettes. I was scared, sitting there by myself.

I heard someone coming up through the dead leaves toward the back of the church, and I ducked inside the door. Then I heard a whistle, long and low, ending in a sudden high note. I knew that whistle well enough. It was used by us and the Shepard gang for "Who's there?" I returned it carefully, then darted out the door so fast that I fell off the steps and sprawled flat under Johnny's nose.

I propped myself on my elbows and grinned up at him. "Hey, Johnny. Fancy meetin' you here."

He looked down at me over a big package. "I swear, Ponyboy, you're gettin' to act more like Two-Bit every day."

I tried unsuccessfully to cock an eyebrow. "Who's acting?" I rolled over and sprang up, happy that someone was there. "What'd you get?"

"Come on inside. Dally told us to stay inside."

We went in. Johnny dusted off a table with his jacket and started taking things out of the sack and lining them up neatly. "A week's supply of baloney, two loaves of bread, a box of matches . . ." Johnny went on.

I got tired of watching him do it all, so I started digging into the sack myself. "Wheee!" I sat down on a dusty chair and stared. "A paperback copy of *Gone with the Wind*! How'd you know I always wanted one?"

Johnny reddened. "I remembered you sayin' something about it once. And me and you went to see that movie, 'member? I thought you could maybe read it out loud and help kill time or something."

"Gee, thanks." I put the book down reluctantly. I wanted to start it right then. "Peroxide? A deck of cards . . ." Suddenly I realized something. "Johnny, you ain't thinking of . . ."

Johnny sat down and pulled out his knife. "We're gonna cut our hair, and you're gonna bleach yours." He looked at the ground carefully. "They'll have our descriptions in the paper. We can't fit 'em."

"Oh, no!" My hand flew to my hair. "No, Johnny, not my hair!"

It was my pride. It was long and silky, just like Soda's, only a little redder. Our hair was tuff—we didn't have to use much grease on it. Our hair labeled us greasers, too—it was our trademark. The one thing we were proud of. Maybe we couldn't have Corvairs or madras shirts, but we could have hair.

"We'd have to anyway if we got caught. You know the first thing the judge does is make you get a haircut."

"I don't see why," I said sourly. "Dally could just as easily mug somebody with short hair."

"I don't know either—it's just a way of trying to break us. They can't really do anything to guys like Curly Shepard or Tim; they've had about everything done to

79

them. And they can't take anything away from them because they don't have anything in the first place. So they cut their hair."

I looked at Johnny imploringly. Johnny sighed. "I'm gonna cut mine too, and wash the grease out, but I can't bleach it. I'm too dark-skinned to look okay blond. Oh, come on, Ponyboy," he pleaded. "It'll grow back."

"Okay," I said, wide-eyed. "Get it over with."

Johnny flipped out the razor-edge of his switch, took hold of my hair, and started sawing on it. I shuddered. "Not too short," I begged. "Johnny, please . . ."

Finally it was over with. My hair looked funny, scattered over the floor in tufts. "It's lighter than I thought it was," I said, examining it. "Can I see what I look like now?"

"No," Johnny said slowly, staring at me. "We gotta bleach it first."

After I'd sat in the sun for fifteen minutes to dry the bleach, Johnny let me look in the old cracked mirror we'd found in a closet. I did a double take. My hair was even lighter than Sodapop's. I'd never combed it to the side like that. It just didn't look like me. It made me look younger, and scareder, too. Boy howdy, I thought, this really makes me look tuff. I look like a blasted pansy. I was miserable.

Johnny handed me the knife. He looked scared, too. "Cut the front and thin out the rest. I'll comb it back after I wash it."

"Johnny," I said tiredly, "you can't wash your hair in that freezing water in this weather. You'll get a cold."

He only shrugged. "Go ahead and cut it."

I did the best I could. He went ahead and washed it

anyway, using the bar of soap he'd bought. I was glad I had had to run away with him instead of with Two-Bit or Steve or Dally. That would be one thing they'd never think of—soap. I gave him Dally's jacket to wrap up in, and he sat shivering in the sunlight on the back steps, leaning against the door, combing his hair back. It was the first time I could see that he had eyebrows. He didn't look like Johnny. His forehead was whiter where his bangs had been; it would have been funny if we hadn't been so scared. He was still shivering with cold. "I guess," he said weakly, "I guess we're disguised."

I leaned back next to him sullenly. "I guess so."

"Oh, shoot," Johnny said with fake cheerfulness, "it's just hair."

"Shoot nothing," I snapped. "It took me a long time to get that hair just the way I wanted it. And besides, this just ain't us. It's like being in a Halloween costume we can't get out of."

"Well, we got to get used to it," Johnny said with finality. "We're in big trouble and it's our looks or us."

I started eating a candy bar. "I'm still tired," I said. To my surprise, the ground blurred and I felt tears running down my cheeks. I brushed them off hurriedly. Johnny looked as miserable as I felt.

"I'm sorry I cut your hair off, Ponyboy."

"Oh, it ain't that," I said between bites of chocolate. "I mean, not all of it. I'm just a little spooky. I really don't know what's the matter. I'm just mixed up."

"I know," Johnny said through chattering teeth as we went inside. "Things have been happening so fast . . ." I put my arm across his shoulders to warm him up.

"Two-Bit shoulda been in that little one-horse store. Man, we're in the middle of nowhere; the nearest house is two miles away. Things were layin' out wide open, just waitin' for somebody slick like Two-Bit to come and pick 'em up. He coulda walked out with half the store." He leaned back beside me, and I could feel him trembling. "Good ol' Two-Bit," he said in a quavering voice. He must have been as homesick as I was.

"Remember how he was wisecrackin' last night?" I said. "Last night . . . just last night we were walkin' Cherry and Marcia over to Two-Bit's. Just last night we were layin' in the lot, lookin' up at the stars and dreaming . . ."

"Stop it!" Johnny gasped from between clenched teeth. "Shut up about last night! I killed a kid last night. He couldn't of been over seventeen or eighteen, and I killed him. How'd you like to live with that?" He was crying. I held him like Soda had held him the day we found him lying in the lot.

"I didn't mean to," he finally blurted out, "but they were drownin' you, and I was so scared . . ." He was quiet for a minute. "There sure is a lot of blood in people."

He got up suddenly and began pacing back and forth, slapping his pockets.

"Whata we gonna do?" I was crying by then. It was getting dark and I was cold and lonesome. I closed my eyes and leaned my head back, but the tears came anyway.

"This is my fault," Johnny said in a miserable voice. He had stopped crying when I started. "For bringin' a little thirteen-year-old kid along. You ought to go home. You can't get into any trouble. You didn't kill him."

"No!" I screamed at him. "I'm fourteen! I've been

fourteen for a month! And I'm in it as much as you are. I'll stop crying in a minute . . . I can't help it."

He slumped down beside me. "I didn't mean it like that, Ponyboy. Don't cry, Pony, we'll be okay. Don't cry . . ." I leaned against him and bawled until I went to sleep.

I woke up late that night. Johnny was resting against the wall and I was asleep on his shoulder. "Johnny?" I yawned. "You awake?" I was warm and sleepy.

"Yeah," he said quietly.

"We ain't gonna cry no more, are we?"

"Nope. We're all cried out now. We're gettin' used to the idea. We're gonna be okay now."

"That's what I thought," I said drowsily. Then for the first time since Dally and I had sat down behind those girls at the Nightly Double, I relaxed. We could take whatever was coming now.

The next four or five days were the longest days I've ever spent in my life. We killed time by reading *Gone with the Wind* and playing poker. Johnny sure did like that book, although he didn't know anything about the Civil War and even less about plantations, and I had to explain a lot of it to him. It amazed me how Johnny could get more meaning out of some of the stuff in there than I could—I was supposed to be the deep one. Johnny had failed a year in school and never made good grades—he couldn't grasp anything that was shoved at him too fast, and I guess his teachers thought he was just plain dumb. But he wasn't. He was just a little slow to get things, and he liked to explore things once he did get them. He was especially stuck on the Southern gentlemen—impressed with their manners and charm.

"I bet they were cool ol' guys," he said, his eyes glowing, after I had read the part about them riding into sure death because they were gallant. "They remind me of Dally."

"Dally?" I said, startled. "Shoot, he ain't got any more manners than I do. And you saw how he treated those girls the other night. Soda's more like them Southern boys."

"Yeah . . . in the manners bit, and the charm, too, I guess," Johnny said slowly, "but one night I saw Dally gettin' picked up by the fuzz, and he kept real cool and calm the whole time. They was gettin' him for breakin' out the windows in the school building, and it was Two-Bit who did that. And Dally knew it. But he just took the sentence without battin' an eye or even denyin' it. That's gallant."

That was the first time I realized the extent of Johnny's hero-worship for Dally Winston. Of all of us, Dally was the one I liked least. He didn't have Soda's understanding or dash, or Two-Bit's humor, or even Darry's superman qualities. But I realized that these three appealed to me because they were like the heroes in the novels I read. Dally was real. I liked my books and clouds and sunsets. Dally was so real he scared me.

Johnny and I never went to the front of the church. You could see the front from the road, and sometimes farm kids rode their horses by on their way to the store. So we stayed in the very back, usually sitting on the steps and looking across the valley. We could see for miles; see the ribbon of highway and the small dots that were houses and cars. We couldn't watch the sunset, since the back faced east, but I loved to look at the colors of the fields and the soft shadings of the horizon.

One morning I woke up earlier than usual. Johnny and I slept huddled together for warmth—Dally had been right when he said it would get cold where we were going. Being careful not to wake Johnny up, I went to sit on the steps and smoke a cigarette. The dawn was coming then. All the lower valley was covered with mist, and sometimes little pieces of it broke off and floated away in small clouds. The sky was lighter in the east, and the horizon was a thin golden line. The clouds changed from gray to pink, and the mist was touched with gold. There was a silent moment when everything held its breath, and then the sun rose. It was beautiful.

"Golly"—Johnny's voice beside me made me jump—"that sure was pretty."

"Yeah." I sighed, wishing I had some paint to do a picture with while the sight was still fresh in my mind.

"The mist was what was pretty," Johnny said. "All gold and silver."

"Uhmmmm," I said, trying to blow a smoke ring.

"Too bad it couldn't stay like that all the time."

"Nothing gold can stay." I was remembering a poem I'd read once.

"What?"

> "Nature's first green is gold,
> Her hardest hue to hold.
> Her early leaf's a flower;
> But only so an hour.
> Then leaf subsides to leaf.
> So Eden sank to grief,

So dawn goes down to day.
Nothing gold can stay."

Johnny was staring at me. "Where'd you learn that? That was what I meant."

"Robert Frost wrote it. He meant more to it than I'm gettin', though." I was trying to find the meaning the poet had in mind, but it eluded me. "I always remembered it because I never quite got what he meant by it."

"You know," Johnny said slowly, "I never noticed colors and clouds and stuff until you kept reminding me about them. It seems like they were never there before." He thought for a minute. "Your family sure is funny."

"And what happens to be so funny about it?" I asked stiffly.

Johnny looked at me quickly. "I didn't mean nothing. I meant, well, Soda kinda looks like your mother did, but he acts just exactly like your father. And Darry is the spittin' image of your father, but he ain't wild and laughing all the time like he was. He acts like your mother. And you don't act like either one."

"I know," I said. "Well," I said, thinking this over, "you ain't like any of the gang. I mean, I couldn't tell Two-Bit or Steve or even Darry about the sunrise and clouds and stuff. I couldn't even remember that poem around them. I mean, they just don't dig. Just you and Sodapop. And maybe Cherry Valance."

Johnny shrugged. "Yeah," he said with a sigh. "I guess we're different."

"Shoot," I said, blowing a perfect smoke ring, "maybe *they* are."

By the fifth day I was so tired of baloney I nearly got sick every time I looked at it. We had eaten all our candy bars in the first two days. I was dying for a Pepsi. I'm what you might call a Pepsi addict. I drink them like a fiend, and going for five days without one was about to kill me. Johnny promised to get some if we ran out of supplies and had to get some more, but that didn't help me right then. I was smoking a lot more there than I usually did—I guess because it was something to do—although Johnny warned me that I would get sick smoking so much. We were careful with our cigarettes—if that old church ever caught fire there'd be no stopping it.

On the fifth day I had read up to Sherman's siege of Atlanta in *Gone with the Wind*, owed Johnny a hundred and fifty bucks from poker games, smoked two packs of Camels, and as Johnny had predicted, got sick. I hadn't eaten anything all day; and smoking on an empty stomach doesn't make you feel real great. I curled up in a corner to sleep off the smoke. I was just about asleep when I heard, as if from a great distance, a low long whistle that went off in a sudden high note. I was too sleepy to pay any attention, although Johnny didn't have any reason to be whistling like that. He was sitting on the back steps trying to read *Gone with the Wind*. I had almost decided that I had dreamed the outside world and there was nothing real but baloney sandwiches and the Civil War and the old church and the mist in the valley. It seemed to me that I had always lived in the church, or maybe lived during the Civil War and had somehow got transplanted. That shows you what a wild imagination I have.

87

A toe nudged me in the ribs. "Glory," said a rough but familiar voice, "he looks different with his hair like that."

I rolled over and sat up, rubbing the sleep out of my eyes and yawning. Suddenly I blinked.

"Hey, Dally!"

"Hey, Ponyboy!" He grinned down at me. "Or should I say Sleeping Beauty?"

I never thought I'd live to see the day when I would be so glad to see Dally Winston, but right then he meant one thing: contact with the outside world. And it suddenly became real and vital.

"How's Sodapop? Are the fuzz after us? Is Darry all right? Do the boys know where we are? What . . ."

"Hold on, kid," Dally broke in. "I can't answer everything at once. You two want to go get something to eat first? I skipped breakfast and I'm about starved."

"You're starved?" Johnny was so indignant he nearly squeaked. I remembered the baloney.

"Is it safe to go out?" I asked eagerly.

"Yep." Dally searched his shirt pocket for a cigarette, and finding none, said, "Gotta cancer stick, Johnnycake?"

Johnny tossed him a whole package.

"The fuzz won't be lookin' for you around here," Dally said, lighting up. "They think you've lit out for Texas. I've got Buck's T-bird parked down the road a little way. Goshamighty, boys, ain't you been eatin' anything?"

Johnny looked startled. "Yeah. Whatever gave you the idea we ain't?"

Dally shook his head. "You're both pale and you've lost weight. After this, get out in the sun more. You look like you've been through the mill."

I started to say "Look who's talking" but decided it would be safer not to. Dally needed a shave—a stubble of colorless beard covered his jaw—and he looked like he was the one who'd been sleeping in his clothes for a week instead of us; I knew he hadn't seen a barber in months. But it was safer not to get mouthy with Dally Winston.

"Hey, Ponyboy"—he fumbled with a piece of paper in his back pocket—"I gotta letter for you."

"A letter? Who from?"

"The President, of course, stupid. It's from Soda."

"Sodapop?" I said, bewildered. "But how did he know . . . ?"

"He came over to Buck's a couple of days ago for something and found that sweat shirt. I told him I didn't know where you were, but he didn't believe me. He gave me this letter and half his pay check to give you. Kid, you ought to see Darry. He's takin' this mighty hard . . ."

I wasn't listening. I leaned back against the side of the church and read:

Ponyboy,

Well I guess you got into some trouble, huh? Darry and me nearly went nuts when you ran out like that. Darry is awful sorry he hit you. You know he didn't mean it. And then you and Johnny turned up mising and what with that dead kid in the park and Dally getting hauled into the station, well it scared us something awful. The police came by to question us and we told them as much as we could. I can't believe little old Johnny could kill somebody. I know Dally knows where you are, but you know him. He keeps his trap shut and won't tell me nothing. Darry *hasn't got the slightest notion where you're at and it is nearly killing him. I wish you'd come back and turn your selves in but I guess you can't since Johnny might get hurt. You sure are famous. You got a paragraph in the newspaper even. Take care and say hi to Johnny for us.*

Sodapop Curtis

He could improve his spelling, I thought after reading it through three or four times. "How come you got hauled in?" I asked Dally.

"Shoot, kid"—he grinned wolfishly—"them boys at the station know me by now. I get hauled in for everything that happens in our turf. While I was there I kinda let it slip that y'all were headin' for Texas. So that's where they're lookin'."

He took a drag on his cigarette and cussed it good-naturedly for not being a Kool. Johnny listened in admiration. "You sure can cuss good, Dally."

"Sure can," Dally agreed wholeheartedly, proud of his vocabulary. "But don't you kids get to pickin' up my bad habits."

He gave me a hard rub on the head. "Kid, I swear it don't look like you with your hair all cut off. It used to look tuff. You and Soda had the coolest-lookin' hair in town."

"I know," I said sourly. "I look lousy, but don't rub it in."

"Do y'all want somethin' to eat or not?"

Johnny and I leaped up. "You'd better believe it."

"Gee," Johnny said wistfully, "it sure will be good to get into a car again."

"Well," Dally drawled, "I'll give you a ride for your money."

Dally always did like to drive fast, as if he didn't care whether he got where he was going or not, and we came down the red dirt road off Jay Mountain doing eighty-five. I like fast driving and Johnny was crazy about drag races, but we both got a little green around the gills when Dally took a corner on two wheels with the brakes screaming. Maybe it was because we hadn't been in a car for so long.

We stopped at a Dairy Queen and the first thing I got was a Pepsi. Johnny and I gorged on barbecue sandwiches and banana splits.

"Glory," Dallas said, amazed, watching us gulp the stuff down. "You don't need to make like every mouthful's your last. I got plenty of money. Take it easy, I don't want you gettin' sick on me. And I thought I was hungry!"

Johnny merely ate faster. I didn't slow down until I got a headache.

"I didn't tell y'all something," Dally said, finishing his third hamburger. "The Socs and us are having all-out warfare all over the city. That kid you killed had plenty of friends and all over the town it's Soc against grease. We can't walk alone at all. I started carryin' a heater . . ."

"Dally!" I said, frightened. "You kill people with heaters!"

"Ya kill 'em with switchblades, too, don't ya, kid?" Dally said in a hard voice. Johnny gulped. "Don't worry," Dally went on, "it ain't loaded. I ain't aimin' to get picked up for murder. But it sure does help a bluff. Tim Shepard's gang and our outfit are havin' it out with the Socs tomorrow night at the vacant lot. We got hold of the president of one of their social clubs and had a war council. Yeah"— Dally sighed, and I knew he was remembering New York— "just like the good old days. If they win, things go on as usual. If we do, they stay outa our territory but good. Two-Bit got jumped a few days ago. Darry and me came along in time, but he wasn't havin' too much trouble. Two-Bit's a good fighter. Hey, I didn't tell you we got us a spy."

"A spy?" Johnny looked up from his banana split. "Who?"

"That good-lookin' broad I tried to pick up that night you killed the Soc. The redhead, Cherry what's-her-name."

Chapter 6

J<small>OHNNY</small> <small>GAGGED AND</small> I <small>ALMOST DROPPED MY HOT-FUDGE</small> sundae. "Cherry?" we both said at the same time. "The Soc?"

"Yeah," Dally said. "She came over to the vacant lot the night Two-Bit was jumped. Shepard and some of his outfit and us were hanging around there when she drives up in her little ol' Sting Ray. That took a lot of nerve. Some of us was for jumping her then and there, her bein' the dead kid's girl and all, but Two-Bit stopped us. Man, next time I want a broad I'll pick up my own kind."

"Yeah," Johnny said slowly, and I wondered if, like me, he was remembering another voice, also tough and just deepened into manhood, saying: "Next time you want a broad, pick up your own kind . . ." It gave me the creeps.

Dally was going on: "She said she felt that the whole mess was her fault, which it is, and that she'd keep up with what was comin' off with the Socs in the rumble and would testify that the Socs were drunk and looking for a fight and that you fought back in self-defense." He gave a grim laugh. "That little gal sure does hate me. I offered to take her over to The Dingo for a Coke and she said 'No, thank you' and told me where I could go in very polite terms."

She was afraid of loving you, I thought. So Cherry Valance, the cheerleader, Bob's girl, the Soc, was trying to help us. No, it wasn't Cherry the Soc who was helping us, it was Cherry the dreamer who watched sunsets and couldn't stand fights. It was hard to believe a Soc would help us, even a Soc that dug sunsets. Dally didn't notice. He had forgotten about it already.

"Man, this place is out of it. What do they do for kicks around here, play checkers?" Dally surveyed the scene without interest. "I ain't never been in the country before. Have you two?"

Johnny shook his head but I said, "Dad used to take us all huntin'. I've been in the country before. How'd you know about the church?"

"I got a cousin that lives around here somewheres. Tipped me off that it'd make a tuff hide-out in case of something. Hey, Ponyboy, I heard you was the best shot in the family."

"Yeah," I said. "Darry always got the most ducks, though. Him and Dad. Soda and I goofed around too much, scared most of our game away." I couldn't tell Dally that I hated to shoot things. He'd think I was soft.

94

"That was a good idea, I mean cuttin' your hair and bleachin' it. They printed your descriptions in the paper but you sure wouldn't fit 'em now."

Johnny had been quietly finishing his fifth barbecue sandwich, but now he announced: "We're goin' back and turn ourselves in."

It was Dally's turn to gag. Then he swore awhile. Then he turned to Johnny and demanded: "What?"

"I said we're goin' back and turn ourselves in," Johnny repeated in a quiet voice. I was surprised but not shocked. I had thought about turning ourselves in lots of times, but apparently the whole idea was a jolt to Dallas.

"I got a good chance of bein' let off easy," Johnny said desperately, and I didn't know if it was Dally he was try-ing to convince or himself. "I ain't got no record with the fuzz and it was self-defense. Ponyboy and Cherry can testify to that. And I don't aim to stay in that church all my life."

That was quite a speech for Johnny. His big black eyes grew bigger than ever at the thought of going to the police station, for Johnny had a deathly fear of cops, but he went on: "We won't tell that you helped us, Dally, and we'll give you back the gun and what's left of the money and say we hitchhiked back so you won't get into trouble. Okay?"

Dally was chewing the corner of his ID card, which gave his age as twenty-one so he could buy liquor. "You sure you want to go back? Us greasers get it worse than anyone else."

Johnny nodded. "I'm sure. It ain't fair for Ponyboy to have to stay up in that church with Darry and Soda worryin' about him all the time. I don't guess . . ."—he swallowed and tried not to look eager—"I don't guess my parents are worried about me or anything?"

"The boys are worried," Dally said in a matter-of-fact voice. "Two-Bit was for going to Texas to hunt for you."

"My parents," Johnny repeated doggedly, "did they ask about me?"

"No," snapped Dally, "they didn't. Blast it, Johnny, what do they matter? Shoot, my old man don't give a hang whether I'm in jail or dead in a car wreck or drunk in the gutter. That don't bother me none."

Johnny didn't say anything. But he stared at the dashboard with such hurt bewilderment that I could have bawled.

Dally cussed under his breath and nearly tore out the transmission of the T-bird as we roared out of the Dairy Queen. I felt sorry for Dally. He meant it when he said he didn't care about his parents. But he and the rest of the gang knew Johnny cared and did everything they could to make it up to him. I don't know what it was about Johnny—maybe that lost-puppy look and those big scared eyes were what made everyone his big brother. But they couldn't, no matter how hard they tried, take the place of his parents. I thought about it for a minute—Darry and Sodapop were my brothers and I loved both of them, even if Darry did scare me; but not even Soda could take Mom and Dad's place. And they were my real brothers, not just sort of adopted ones. No wonder Johnny was hurt because his parents didn't want him. Dally could take it— Dally was of the breed that could take anything, because he was hard and tough, and when he wasn't, he could turn hard and tough. Johnny was a good fighter and could play it cool, but he was sensitive and that isn't a good way to be when you're a greaser.

"Blast it, Johnny," Dally growled as we flew along the red road, "why didn't you think of turning yourself in five days ago? It would have saved a lot of trouble."

"I was scared," Johnny said with conviction. "I still am." He ran his finger down one of his short black sideburns. "I guess we ruined our hair for nothing, Ponyboy."

"I guess so." I was glad we were going back. I was sick of that church. I didn't care if I was bald.

Dally was scowling, and from long and painful experience I knew better than to talk to him when his eyes were blazing like that. I'd likely as not get clobbered over the head. That had happened before, just as it had happened to all the gang at one time or another. We rarely fought among ourselves—Darry was the unofficial leader, since he kept his head best, Soda and Steve had been best friends since grade school and never fought, and Two-Bit was just too lazy to argue with anyone. Johnny kept his mouth shut too much to get into arguments, and nobody ever fought with Johnny. I kept my mouth shut, too. But Dally was a different matter. If something beefed him, he didn't keep quiet about it, and if you rubbed him the wrong way —look out. Not even Darry wanted to tangle with him. He was dangerous.

Johnny just sat there and stared at his feet. He hated for any one of us to be mad at him. He looked awful sad. Dally glanced at him out of the corner of his eye. I looked out the window.

"Johnny," Dally said in a pleading, high voice, using a tone I had never heard from him before, "Johnny, I

97

ain't mad at you. I just don't want you to get hurt. You
don't know what a few months in jail can do to you. Oh,
blast it, Johnny"—he pushed his white-blond hair back out
of his eyes—"you get hardened in jail. I don't want that to
happen to you. Like it happened to me . . ."

I kept staring out the window at the rapidly passing
scenery, but I felt my eyes getting round. Dally never
talked like that. Never. Dally didn't give a Yankee dime
about anyone but himself, and he was cold and hard and
mean. He never talked about his past or being in jail that
way—if he talked about it at all, it was to brag. And I
suddenly thought of Dally . . . in jail at the age of ten . . .
Dally growing up in the streets . . .

"Would you rather have me living in hide-outs for the
rest of my life, always on the run?" Johnny asked seriously.

If Dally had said yes, Johnny would have gone back to
the church without hesitation. He figured Dally knew more
than he did, and Dally's word was law. But he never heard
Dally's answer, for we had reached the top of Jay Mountain
and Dally suddenly slammed on the brakes and stared.
"Oh, glory!" he whispered. The church was on fire!

"Let's go see what the deal is," I said, hopping out.

"What for?" Dally sounded irritated. "Get back in here
before I beat your head in."

I knew Dally would have to park the car and catch me
before he could carry out his threat, and Johnny was already out and following me, so I figured I was safe. We
could hear him cussing us out, but he wasn't mad enough to
come after us. There was a crowd at the front of the
church, mostly little kids, and I wondered how they'd

gotten there so quickly. I tapped the nearest grownup. "What's going on?"

"Well, we don't know for sure," the man said with a good-natured grin. "We were having a school picnic up here and the first thing we knew, the place is burning up. Thank goodness this is a wet season and the old thing is worthless anyway." Then, to the kids, he shouted, "Stand back, children. The firemen will be coming soon."

"I bet we started it," I said to Johnny. "We must have dropped a lighted cigarette or something."

About that time a lady came running up. "Jerry, some of the kids are missing."

"They're probably around here somewhere. You can't tell with all this excitement where they might be."

"No." She shook her head. "They've been missing for at least a half an hour. I thought they were climbing the hill . . ."

Then we all froze. Faintly, just faintly, you could hear someone yelling. And it sounded like it was coming from inside the church.

The woman went white. "I told them not to play in the church . . . I told them . . ." She looked like she was going to start screaming, so Jerry shook her.

"I'll get them, don't worry!" I started at a dead run for the church, and the man caught my arm. "I'll get them. You kids stay out!"

I jerked loose and ran on. All I could think was: We started it. We started it. We started it!

I wasn't about to go through that flaming door, so I slammed a big rock through a window and pulled myself in. It was a wonder I didn't cut myself to death, now that I think about it.

"Hey, Ponyboy."

I looked around, startled. I hadn't realized Johnny had been right behind me all the way. I took a deep breath, and started coughing. The smoke filled my eyes and they started watering. "Is that guy coming?"

Johnny shook his head. "The window stopped him."

"Too scared?"

"Naw . . ." Johnny gave me a grin. "Too fat."

I couldn't laugh because I was scared I'd drown in the smoke. The roar and crackling was getting louder, and Johnny shouted the next question.

"Where's the kids?"

"In the back, I guess," I hollered, and we started stumbling through the church. I should be scared, I thought with an odd detached feeling, but I'm not. The cinders and embers began falling on us, stinging and smarting like ants. Suddenly, in the red glow and the haze, I remembered wondering what it was like in a burning ember, and I thought: Now I know, it's a red hell. Why aren't I scared?

We pushed open the door to the back room and found four or five little kids, about eight years old or younger, huddled in a corner. One was screaming his head off, and Johnny yelled, "Shut up! We're goin' to get you out!" The kid looked surprised and quit hollering. I blinked myself—Johnny wasn't behaving at all like his old self. He looked over his shoulder and saw that the door was blocked by flames, then pushed open the window and tossed out the nearest kid. I caught one quick look at his face; it was red-marked from falling embers and sweat-streaked, but he grinned at me. He wasn't scared either. That was the only time I can think of when I saw him without that defeated, suspicious look in his eyes. He looked like he was having the time of his life.

I picked up a kid, and he promptly bit me, but I leaned out the window and dropped him as gently as I could, being in a hurry like that. A crowd was there by that time. Dally was standing there, and when he saw me he screamed, "For Pete's sake, get outa there! That roof's gonna cave in any minute. Forget those blasted kids!"

I didn't pay any attention, although pieces of the old roof were crashing down too close for comfort. I snatched up another kid, hoping he didn't bite, and dropped him without waiting to see if he landed okay or not. I was coughing so hard I could hardly stand up, and I wished I had time to take off Dally's jacket. It was hot. We dropped the last of the kids out as the front of the church started to crumble. Johnny shoved me toward the window. "Get out!"

I leaped out the window and heard timber crashing and the flames roaring right behind me. I staggered, almost falling, coughing and sobbing for breath. Then I heard Johnny scream, and as I turned to go back for him, Dally swore at me and clubbed me across the back as hard as he could, and I went down into a peaceful darkness.

When I came to, I was being bounced around, and I ached and smarted, and wondered dimly where I was. I tried to think, but there was a high-pitched screaming going on, and I couldn't tell whether it was inside my head or out. Then I realized it was a siren. The fuzz, I thought dully. The cops have come for us. I tried to swallow a groan and wished wildly for Soda. Someone with a cold wet rag was gently sponging off my face, and a voice said, "I think he's coming around."

I opened my eyes. It was dark. I'm moving, I thought. Are they taking me to jail?

"Where . . . ?" I said hoarsely, not able to get anything else out of my mouth. My throat was sore. I blinked at the stranger sitting beside me. But he wasn't a stranger . . . I'd seen him before . . .

"Take it easy, kid. You're in an ambulance."

"Where's Johnny?" I cried, frightened at being in this car with strangers. "And Dallas?"

"They're in the other ambulance, right behind us. Just calm down. You're going to be okay. You just passed out."

"I didn't either," I said in the bored, tough voice we reserved for strangers and cops. "Dallas hit me. How come?"

"Because your back was in flames, that's why."

I was surprised. "It was? Golly, I didn't feel it. It don't hurt."

"We put it out before you got burned. That jacket saved you from a bad burning, maybe saved your life. You just keeled over from smoke inhalation and a little shock— of course, that slap on the back didn't help much."

I remembered who he was then—Jerry somebody-or-other who was too heavy to get in the window. He must be a school teacher, I thought. "Are you taking us to the police station?" I was still a little mixed up as to what was coming off.

"The police station?" It was his turn to be surprised.

"What would we want to take you to the police station for? We're taking all three of you to the hospital."

I let his first remark slide by. "Are Johnny and Dally all right?"

"Which one's which?"

"Johnny has black hair. Dally's the mean-looking one."

He studied his wedding ring. Maybe he's thinking about his wife, I thought. I wished he'd say something.

"We think the towheaded kid is going to be all right. He burned one arm pretty badly, though, trying to drag the other kid out the window. Johnny, well, I don't know about him. A piece of timber caught him across the back— he might have a broken back, and he was burned pretty severely. He passed out before he got out the window. They're giving him plasma now." He must have seen the look on my face because he hurriedly changed the subject. "I swear, you three are the bravest kids I've seen in a long time. First you and the black-haired kid climbing in that window, and then the tough-looking kid going back in to save him. Mrs. O'Briant and I think you were sent straight from heaven. Or are you just professional heroes or something?"

Sent from heaven? Had he gotten a good look at Dallas? "No, we're greasers," I said. I was too worried and scared to appreciate the fact that he was trying to be funny.

"You're what?"

"Greasers. You know, like hoods, JD's. Johnny is wanted for murder, and Dallas has a record with the fuzz a mile long."

"Are you kidding me?" Jerry stared at me as if he thought I was still in shock or something.

"I am not. Take me to town and you'll find out pretty quick."

"We're taking you to a hospital there anyway. The address card in your billfold said that was where you lived. Your name's really Ponyboy?"

"Yeah. Even on my birth certificate. And don't bug me about it. Are . . ."—I felt weak—"are the little kids okay?"

"Just fine. A little frightened maybe. There were some short explosions right after you all got out. Sounded just exactly like gunfire."

Gunfire. There went our gun. And *Gone with the Wind*. Were we sent from heaven? I started to laugh weakly. I guess that guy knew how close to hysterics I really was, for he talked to me in a low soothing voice all the way to the hospital.

I was sitting in the waiting room, waiting to hear how Dally and Johnny were. I had been checked over, and except for a few burns and a big bruise across my back, I was all right. I had watched them bring Dally and Johnny in on stretchers. Dally's eyes were closed, but when I spoke he had tried to grin and had told me that if I ever did a stupid thing like that again he'd beat the tar out of me. He was still swearing at me when they took him on in. Johnny was unconscious. I had been afraid to look at him, but I was relieved to see that his face wasn't burned. He just looked very pale and still and sort of sick. I would have cried at the sight of him so still except I couldn't in front of people.

Jerry Wood had stayed with me all the time. He kept thanking me for getting the kids out. He didn't seem to mind our being hoods. I told him the whole story—starting when Dallas and Johnny and I had met at the corner of Pickett and Sutton. I left out the part about the gun and our hitching a ride in the freight car. He was real nice about it and said that being heroes would help get us out of trouble, especially since it was self-defense and all.

I was sitting there, smoking a cigarette, when Jerry came back in from making a phone call. He stared at me for a second. "You shouldn't be smoking."

I was startled. "How come?" I looked at my cigarette. It looked okay to me. I looked around for a "No Smoking" sign and couldn't find one. "How come?"

"Why, uh," Jerry stammered, "uh, you're too young."

"I am?" I had never thought about it. Everyone in our neighborhood, even the girls, smoked. Except for Darry, who was too proud of his athletic health to risk a cigarette, we had all started smoking at an early age. Johnny had been smoking since he was nine; Steve started at eleven. So no one thought it unusual when I started. I was the weed-fiend in my family—Soda smokes only to steady his nerves or when he wants to look tough.

Jerry simply sighed, then grinned. "There are some people here to see you. Claim to be your brothers or something."

I leaped up and ran for the door, but it was already open and Soda had me in a bear hug and was swinging me around. I was so glad to see him I could have bawled. Finally he set me down and looked at me. He pushed my hair back. "Oh, Ponyboy, your hair . . . your tuff, tuff hair . . ."

Then I saw Darry. He was leaning in the doorway, wearing his olive jeans and black T-shirt. He was still tall, broad-shouldered Darry; but his fists were jammed in his pockets and his eyes were pleading. I simply looked at him. He swallowed and said in a husky voice, "Ponyboy . . ."

I let go of Soda and stood there for a minute. Darry didn't like me . . . he had driven me away that night . . . he had hit me . . . Darry hollered at me all the time . . . he didn't give a hang about me. . . . Suddenly I realized, horrified, that Darry was crying. He didn't make a sound, but tears were running down his cheeks. I hadn't seen him cry in years, not even when Mom and Dad had been killed. (I remembered the funeral. I had sobbed in spite of myself; Soda had broken down and bawled like a baby; but Darry had only stood there, his fists in his pockets and that look on his face, the same helpless, pleading look that he was wearing now.)

In that second what Soda and Dally and Two-Bit had been trying to tell me came through. Darry did care about me, maybe as much as he cared about Soda, and because he cared he was trying too hard to make something of me. When he yelled "Pony, where have you been all this time?" he meant "Pony, you've scared me to death. Please be careful, because I couldn't stand it if anything happened to you."

Darry looked down and turned away silently. Suddenly I broke out of my daze.

"Darry!" I screamed, and the next thing I knew I had him around the waist and was squeezing the daylights out of him.

"Darry," I said, "I'm sorry . . ."

He was stroking my hair and I could hear the sobs racking him as he fought to keep back the tears. "Oh, Pony, I thought we'd lost you . . . like we did Mom and Dad . . ."

That was his silent fear then—of losing another person he loved. I remembered how close he and Dad had been, and I wondered how I could ever have thought him hard and unfeeling. I listened to his heart pounding through his T-shirt and knew everything was going to be okay now. I had taken the long way around, but I was finally home. To stay.

Chapter 7

Now there were three of us sitting in the waiting room waiting to hear how Dally and Johnny were. Then the reporters and the police came. They asked too many questions too fast, and got me mixed up. If you want to know the truth, I wasn't feeling real good in the first place. Kind of sick, really. And I'm scared of policemen anyway. The reporters fired one question right after another at me and got me so confused I didn't know what was coming off. Darry finally told them I wasn't in any shape to be yelled at so much and they slowed down a little. Darry's kinda big.

Sodapop kept them in stitches. He'd grab one guy's press hat and another's camera and walk around interviewing the nurses and mimicking TV reporters. He tried to lift a policeman's gun and grinned so crazily when he was caught that the policeman had to grin too. Soda can make anyone grin. I managed to get hold of some hair grease and comb my hair back so that it looked a little better before they got any pictures. I'd die if I got my picture in the paper with my hair looking so lousy. Darry and Sodapop were in the pictures too; Jerry Wood told me that if Soda-pop and Darry hadn't been so good-looking, they wouldn't have taken so many. That was public appeal, he said.

Soda was really getting a kick out of all this. I guess he would have enjoyed it more if it hadn't been so serious, but he couldn't resist anything that caused that much excitement. I swear, sometimes he reminds me of a colt. A long-legged palomino colt that has to get his nose into everything. The reporters stared at him admiringly; I told you he looks like a movie star, and he kind of radiates.

Finally, even Sodapop got tired of the reporters—he gets bored with the same old thing after a time—and stretching out on the long bench, he put his head in Darry's lap and went to sleep. I guess both of them were tired—it was late at night and I knew they hadn't had much sleep during the week. Even while I was answering questions I remembered that it had been only a few hours since I was sleeping off a smoke in the corner of the church. Already it was an unreal dream and yet, at the time I couldn't have imagined any other world. Finally, the reporters started to leave, along with the police. One of them turned and asked, "What would you do right now if you could do anything you wanted?"

I looked at him tiredly. "Take a bath."

They thought that was pretty funny, but I meant it. I

felt lousy. The hospital got real quiet after they left. The only noise was the nurse's soft footsteps and Soda's light breathing. Darry looked down at him and grinned half-heartedly. "He didn't get much sleep this week," he said softly. "He hardly slept at all."

"Hhhmmmm," Soda said drowsily, "you didn't either."

The nurses wouldn't tell us anything about Johnny and Dally, so Darry got hold of the doctor. The doctor told us that he would talk only to the family, but Darry finally got it through the guy's head that we were about as much family as Dally and Johnny had.

Dally would be okay after two or three days in the hospital, he said. One arm was badly burned and would be scarred for the rest of his life, but he would have full use of it in a couple of weeks. Dally'll be okay, I thought. Dallas is always okay. He could take anything. It was Johnny I was worried about.

He was in critical condition. His back had been broken when that piece of timber fell on him. He was in severe shock and suffering from third-degree burns. They were doing everything they could to ease the pain, although since his back was broken he couldn't even feel the burns below his waist. He kept calling for Dallas and Ponyboy. If he lived . . . *If?* Please, no, I thought. Please not "if." The blood was draining from my face and Darry put an arm across my shoulder and squeezed hard. . . . Even if he lived he'd be crippled for the rest of his life. "You wanted it straight and you got it straight," the doctor said. "Now go home and get some rest."

I was trembling. A pain was growing in my throat and I wanted to cry, but greasers don't cry in front of strangers.

Some of us never cry at all. Like Dally and Two-Bit and Tim Shepard—they forgot how at an early age. Johnny crippled for life? I'm dreaming, I thought in panic, I'm dreaming. I'll wake up at home or in the church and everything'll be like it used to be. But I didn't believe myself. Even if Johnny did live he'd be crippled and never play football or help us out in a rumble again. He'd have to stay in that house he hated, where he wasn't wanted, and things could never be like they used to be. I didn't trust myself to speak. If I said one word, the hard knot in my throat would swell and I'd be crying in spite of myself.

I took a deep breath and kept my mouth shut. Soda was awake by then, and although he looked stony-faced, as if he hadn't heard a word the doctor had said, his eyes were bleak and stunned. Serious reality has a hard time coming through to Soda, but when it does, it hits him hard. He looked like I felt when I had seen that black-haired Soc lying doubled up and still in the moonlight.

Darry was rubbing the back of my head softly. "We'd better go home. We can't do anything here."

In our Ford I was suddenly overcome by sleepiness. I leaned back and closed my eyes and we were home before I knew it. Soda was shaking me gently. "Hey, Ponyboy, wake up. You still got to get to the house."

"Hmmmmm," I said sleepily, and lay down in the seat. I couldn't have gotten up to save my life. I could hear Soda and Darry, but as if from a great distance.

"Oh, come on, Ponyboy," Soda pleaded, shaking me a little harder, "we're sleepy, too."

I guess Darry was tired of fooling around, because he picked me up and carried me in.

"He's getting mighty big to be carried," Soda said. I wanted to tell him to shut up and let me sleep but I only yawned.

"He's sure lost a lot of weight," Darry said.

I thought sleepily that I should at least pull off my shoes, but I didn't. I went to sleep the minute Darry tossed me on the bed. I'd forgotten how soft a bed really was.

I was the first one up the next morning. Soda must have pulled my shoes and shirt off for me; I was still wearing my jeans. He must have been too sleepy to undress himself, though; he lay stretched out beside me fully clothed. I wiggled out from under his arm and pulled the blanket up over him, then went to take a shower. Asleep, he looked a lot younger than going-on-seventeen, but I had noticed that Johnny looked younger when he was asleep, too, so I figured everyone did. Maybe people are younger when they are asleep.

After my shower, I put on some clean clothes and spent five minutes or so hunting for a hint of beard on my face and mourning over my hair. That bum haircut made my ears stick out.

Darry was still asleep when I went into the kitchen to fix breakfast. The first one up has to fix breakfast and the other two do the dishes. That's the rule around our house, and usually it's Darry who fixes breakfast and me and Soda who are left with the dishes. I hunted through the icebox and found some eggs. We all like our eggs done differently. I like them hard, Darry likes them in a bacon-and-tomato sandwich, and Sodapop eats his with grape jelly. All three of us like chocolate cake for breakfast. Mom had never allowed it with ham and eggs, but Darry let Soda and me talk him into it. We really didn't have to twist his arm; Darry loves chocolate cake as much as we do. Sodapop always makes sure there's some in the icebox every night and if there isn't he cooks one up real quick. I like Darry's cakes better; Sodapop always puts too much sugar in the icing. I don't see how he stands jelly and eggs and chocolate cake all at once, but he seems to like it. Darry drinks black coffee, and Sodapop and I drink chocolate milk. We could have coffee if we wanted it, but we like chocolate milk. All three of us are crazy about chocolate stuff. Soda says if they ever make a chocolate cigarette I'll have it made.

"Anybody home?" a familiar voice called through the front screen, and Two-Bit and Steve came in. We always just stick our heads into each other's houses and holler "Hey" and walk in. Our front door is always unlocked in case one of the boys is hacked off at his parents and needs a place to lay over and cool off. We never could tell who we'd find stretched out on the sofa in the morning. It was usually Steve, whose father told him about once a week to get out and never come back. It kind of bugs Steve, even if his old man does give him five or six bucks the next day to make up for it. Or it might be Dally, who lived anywhere he could. Once we even found Tim Shepard, leader of the Shepard gang and far from his own turf, reading the morning paper in the armchair. He merely looked up, said "Hi," and strolled out without staying for breakfast. Two-Bit's mother warned us about burglars, but Darry, flexing his muscles so that they bulged like oversized baseballs, drawled that he wasn't afraid of any burglars, and that we didn't really have anything worth taking. He'd risk a robbery, he said, if it meant keeping one of the boys from blowing up and robbing a gas station or something. So the door was never locked.

"In here!" I yelled, forgetting that Darry and Sodapop were still asleep. "Don't slam the door."

They slammed the door, of course, and Two-Bit came running into the kitchen. He caught me by the upper arms and swung me around, ignoring the fact that I had two uncooked eggs in my hand.

"Hey, Ponyboy," he cried gleefully, "long time no see."

You would have thought it had been five years instead of five days since I'd seen him last, but I didn't mind. I like ol' Two-Bit; he's a good buddy to have. He spun me into Steve, who gave me a playful slap on my bruised back and shoved me across the room. One of the eggs went flying. It landed on the clock and I tightened my grip on the other one, so that it crushed and ran all over my hand.

"Now look what you did," I griped. "There went our breakfast. Can't you two wait till I set the eggs down before you go shovin' me all over the country?" I really was a little mad, because I had just realized how long it had been since I'd eaten anything. The last thing I'd eaten was a hot-fudge sundae at the Dairy Queen in Windrixville, and I was hungry.

Two-Bit was walking in a slow circle around me, and I sighed because I knew what was coming.

"Man, dig baldy here!" He was staring at my head as he circled me. "I wouldn't have believed it. I thought all the wild Indians in Oklahoma had been tamed. What little squaw's got that tuff-lookin' mop of yours, Ponyboy?"

"Aw, lay off," I said. I wasn't feeling too good in the first place, kind of like I was coming down with something. Two-Bit winked at Steve, and Steve said, "Why, he had to get a haircut to get his picture in the paper. They'd never believe a little greasey-lookin' mug could be a hero. How do you like bein' a hero, big shot?"

"How do I like *what*?"

"Being a hero. You know"—he shoved the morning paper at me impatiently—"like a big shot, even."

I stared at the newspaper. On the front page of the second section was the headline: JUVENILE DELINQUENTS TURN HEROES.

"What I like is the 'turn' bit," Two-Bit said, cleaning the egg up off the floor. "Y'all were heroes from the beginning. You just didn't 'turn' all of a sudden."

I hardly heard him. I was reading the paper. That whole page was covered with stories about us—the fight, the murder, the church burning, the Socs being drunk, everything. My picture was there, with Darry and Sodapop. The article told how Johnny and I had risked our lives saving those little kids, and there was a comment from one of the parents, who said that they would all have burned to death if it hadn't been for us. It told the whole story of our fight with the Socs—only they didn't say "Socs," because most grownups don't know about the battles that go on between us. They had interviewed Cherry Valance, and she said Bob had been drunk and that the boys had been looking for a fight when they took her home. Bob had told her he'd fix us for picking up his girl. His buddy Randy Adderson, who had helped jump us, also said it was their fault and that we'd only fought back in self-defense. But they were charging Johnny with manslaughter. Then I discovered that I was supposed to appear at juvenile court for running away, and Johnny was too, if he recovered. (Not *if*, I thought again. Why do they keep saying *if?*) For once, there weren't any charges against Dally, and I knew he'd be mad because the paper made him out a hero for saving Johnny and didn't say much about his police record, which he was kind of proud of. He'd kill those reporters if he got hold of them. There was another column about just Darry and Soda and me: how Darry worked on two jobs at once and made good at both of them, and about his outstanding record at school; it mentioned Sodapop dropping out of school so we could stay together, and that I made the honor roll at school all the time and might be a future track star. (Oh, yeah, I forgot—I'm on the A-squad track team, the youngest one. I'm a good runner.) Then it said we shouldn't be separated after we had worked so hard to stay together.

The meaning of that last line finally hit me. "You mean . . ."—I swallowed hard—"that they're thinking about putting me and Soda in a boys' home or something?"

Steve was carefully combing back his hair in complicated swirls. "Somethin' like that."

I sat down in a daze. We couldn't get hauled off now. Not after me and Darry had finally got through to each other, and now that the big rumble was coming up and we would settle this Soc-greaser thing once and for all. Not now, when Johnny needed us and Dally was still in the hospital and wouldn't be out for the rumble.

"No," I said out loud, and Two-Bit, who was scraping the egg off the clock, turned to stare at me.

"No what?"

"No, they ain't goin' to put us in a boys' home."

"Don't worry about it," Steve said, cocksure that he and Sodapop could handle anything that came up. "They don't do things like that to heroes. Where're Soda and Superman?"

That was as far as he got, because Darry, shaved and dressed, came in behind Steve and lifted him up off the floor, then dropped him. We all call Darry "Superman" or "Muscles" at one time or another; but one time Steve made the mistake of referring to him as "all brawn and no brain," and Darry almost shattered Steve's jaw. Steve didn't call him that again, but Darry never forgave him; Darry has never really gotten over not going to college. That was the only time I've ever seen Soda mad at Steve, although Soda attaches no importance to education. School bored him. No action.

Soda came running in. "Where's that blue shirt I washed yesterday?" He took a swig of chocolate milk out of the container.

"Hate to tell you, buddy," Steve said, still flat on the floor, "but you have to wear clothes to work. There's a law or something."

"Oh, yeah," Soda said. "Where're those wheat jeans, too?"

"I ironed. They're in my closet," Darry said. "Hurry up, you're gonna be late."

Soda ran back, muttering, "I'm hurryin', I'm hurryin'."

Steve followed him and in a second there was the general racket of a pillow fight. I absent-mindedly watched Darry as he searched the icebox for chocolate cake

"Darry," I said suddenly, "did you know about the juvenile court?"

Without turning to look at me he said evenly, "Yeah, the cops told me last night."

I knew then that he realized we might get separated. I didn't want to worry him any more, but I said, "I had one of those dreams last night. The one I can't ever remember."

Darry spun around to face me, genuine fear on his face. "What?"

I had a nightmare the night of Mom and Dad's funeral. I'd had nightmares and wild dreams every once in a while when I was little, but nothing like this one. I woke up screaming bloody murder. And I never could remember what it was that had scared me. It scared Sodapop and Darry almost as bad as it scared me; for night after night, for weeks on end, I would dream this dream and wake up in a cold sweat or screaming. And I never could remember exactly what happened in it. Soda began sleeping with me, and it stopped recurring so often, but it happened often enough for Darry to take me to a doctor. The doctor said I had too much imagination. He had a simple cure, too: Study harder, read more, draw more, and play football more. After a hard game of football and four or five hours of reading, I was too exhausted, mentally and physically, to dream anything. But Darry never got over it, and every once in a while he would ask me if I ever dreamed any more.

"Was it very bad?" Two-Bit questioned. He knew the whole story, and having never dreamed about anything but blondes, he was interested.

"No," I lied. I had awakened in a cold sweat and shivering, but Soda was dead to the world. I had just wiggled closer to him and stayed awake for a couple of hours, trembling under his arm. That dream always scared the heck out of me.

Darry started to say something, but before he could begin, Sodapop and Steve came in.

"You know what?" Sodapop said to no one in particular. "When we stomp the Socies good, me and Stevie here are gonna throw a big party and everybody can get stoned. Then we'll go chase the Socs clear to Mexico."

"Where you gonna get the dough, little man?" Darry had found the cake and was handing out pieces.

"I'll think of somethin'," Sodapop assured him between bites.

"You going to take Sandy to the party?" I asked, just to be saying something. Instant silence. I looked around. "What's the deal?"

Sodapop was staring at his feet, but his ears were reddening. "No. She went to live with her grandmother in Florida."

"How come?"

"Look," Steve said, surprisingly angry, "does he have to draw you a picture? It was either that or get married, and her parents almost hit the roof at the idea of her marryin' a sixteen-year-old kid."

"Seventeen," Soda said softly. "I'll be seventeen in a couple of weeks."

"Oh," I said, embarrassed. Soda was no innocent; I had been in on bull sessions and his bragging was as loud as anyone's. But never about Sandy. Not ever about Sandy. I

119

remembered how her blue eyes had glowed when she looked at him, and I was sorry for her.

There was a heavy silence. Then Darry said, "We'd better get on to work, Pepsi-Cola." Darry rarely called Soda by Dad's pet nickname for him, but he did so then because he knew how miserable Sodapop was about Sandy.

"I hate to leave you here by yourself, Ponyboy," Darry said slowly. "Maybe I ought to take the day off."

"I've stayed by my lonesome before. You can't afford a day off."

"Yeah, but you just got back and I really ought to stay . . ."

"I'll baby-sit him," Two-Bit said, ducking as I took a swing at him. "I haven't got anything better to do."

"Why don't you get a job?" Steve said. "Ever consider working for a living?"

"Work?" Two-Bit was aghast. "And ruin my rep? I wouldn't be baby-sittin' the kid here if I knew of some good day-nursery open on Saturdays."

I pulled his chair over backward and jumped on him, but he had me down in a second. I was kind of short on wind. I've got to cut out smoking or I won't make track next year.

"Holler uncle."

"Nope," I said, struggling, but I didn't have my usual strength.

Darry was pulling on his jacket. "You two do up the dishes. You can go to the movies if you want to before you go see Dally and Johnny." He paused for a second, watching Two-Bit squash the heck out of me. "Two-Bit, lay off. He ain't lookin' so good. Ponyboy, you take a couple of aspirins and go easy. You smoke more than a pack today and I'll skin you. Understood?"

"Yeah," I said, getting to my feet. "You carry more than one bundle of roofing at a time today and me and Soda'll skin you. Understood?"

He grinned one of his rare grins. "Yeah. See y'all this afternoon."

"Bye," I said. I heard our Ford's vvrrrroooooom and thought: Soda's driving. And they left.

". . . anyway, I was walking around downtown and started to take this short cut through an alley"—Two-Bit was telling me about one of his many exploits while we did the dishes. I mean, while I did the dishes. He was sitting on the cabinet, sharpening that black-handled switchblade he was so proud of—". . . and I ran into three guys. I says 'Howdy' and they just look at each other. Then one says 'We would jump you but since you're as slick as us we figger you don't have nothin' worth takin'.' I says 'Buddy, that's the truth' and went right on. Moral: What's the safest thing to be when one is met by a gang of social outcasts in an alley?"

"A judo expert?" I suggested.

"No, another social outcast!" Two-Bit yelped, and nearly fell off the cabinet from laughing so hard. I had to grin, too. He saw things straight and made them into something funny.

"We're gonna clean up the house," I said. "The reporters or police or somebody might come by, and anyway, it's time for those guys from the state to come by and check up on us."

"This house ain't messy. You oughtta see my house."

"I have. And if you had the sense of a billy goat you'd try to help around your place instead of bumming around."

"Shoot, kid, if I ever did that my mom would die of shock."

I liked Two-Bit's mother. She had the same good humor and easygoing ways that he did. She wasn't lazy like him, but she let him get away with murder. I don't know, though—it's just about impossible to get mad at him.

When we had finished, I pulled on Dally's brown leather jacket—the back was burned black—and we started for Tenth Street.

"I would drive us," Two-Bit said as we walked up the street trying to thumb a ride, "but the brakes are out on my car. Almost killed me and Kathy the other night." He flipped the collar of his black leather jacket up to serve as a windbreak while he lit a cigarette. "You oughtta see Kathy's brother. Now there's a hood. He's so greasy he glides when he walks. He goes to the barber for an oil change, not a haircut."

I would have laughed, but I had a terrific headache. We stopped at the Tasty Freeze to buy Cokes and rest up, and the blue Mustang that had been trailing us for eight blocks pulled in. I almost decided to run, and Two-Bit must have guessed this, for he shook his head ever so slightly and tossed me a cigarette. As I lit up, the Socs who had jumped Johnny and me at the park hopped out of the Mustang. I recognized Randy Adderson, Marcia's boyfriend, and the tall guy that had almost drowned me. I hated them. It was their fault Bob was dead; their fault Johnny was dying; their fault Soda and I might get put in a boys' home. I hated them as bitterly and as contemptuously as Dally Winston hated.

Two-Bit put an elbow on my shoulder and leaned against me, dragging on his cigarette. "You know the rules. No jazz before the rumble," he said to the Socs.

"We know," Randy said. He looked at me. "Come here. I want to talk to you."

I glanced at Two-Bit. He shrugged. I followed Randy over to his car, out of earshot of the rest. We sat there in his car for a second, silent. Golly, that was the tuffest car I've ever been in.

"I read about you in the paper," Randy said finally. "How come?"

"I don't know. Maybe I felt like playing hero."

"I wouldn't have. I would have let those kids burn to death."

"You might not have. You might have done the same thing."

Randy pulled out a cigarette and pressed in the car lighter. "I don't know. I don't know anything anymore. I would never have believed a greaser could pull something like that."

" 'Greaser' didn't have anything to do with it. My buddy over there wouldn't have done it. Maybe you would have done the same thing, maybe a friend of yours wouldn't have. It's the individual."

"I'm not going to show at the rumble tonight," Randy said slowly.

I took a good look at him. He was seventeen or so, but he was already old. Like Dallas was old. Cherry had said her friends were too cool to feel anything, and yet she could remember watching sunsets. Randy was supposed to be too cool to feel anything, and yet there was pain in his eyes.

"I'm sick of all this. Sick and tired. Bob was a good guy. He was the best buddy a guy ever had. I mean, he was a good fighter and tuff and everything, but he was a real person too. You dig?"

I nodded.

"He's dead—his mother has had a nervous breakdown. They spoiled him rotten. I mean, most parents would be proud of a kid like that—good-lookin' and smart and everything, but they gave in to him all the time. He kept trying to make someone say 'No' and they never did. They never did. That was what he wanted. For somebody to tell him 'No.' To have somebody lay down the law, set the limits, give him something solid to stand on. That's what we all want, really. One time . . ."—Randy tried to grin, but I could tell he was close to tears—"one time he came home drunker than anything. He thought sure they were gonna raise the roof. You know what they did? They thought it was something *they'd* done. They thought it was their fault—that they'd failed him and driven him to it or something. They took all the blame and didn't do anything to him. If his old man had just belted him—just once, he might still be alive. I don't know why I'm telling you this. I couldn't tell anyone else. My friends—they'd think I was off my rocker or turning soft. Maybe I am. I just know that I'm sick of this whole mess. That kid—your buddy, the one that got burned—he might die?"

"Yeah," I said, trying not to think about Johnny.

"And tonight . . . people get hurt in rumbles, maybe killed. I'm sick of it because it doesn't do any good. You can't win, you know that, don't you?" And when I remained silent he went on: "You can't win, even if you whip us. You'll still be where you were before—at the bottom. And we'll still be the lucky ones with all the breaks. So it doesn't do any good, the fighting and the killing. It doesn't prove a thing. We'll forget it if you win, or if you don't. Greasers will still be greasers and Socs will still be Socs. Sometimes I think it's the ones in the middle that are really the lucky stiffs . . ." He took a deep breath. "So I'd fight if I thought it'd do any good. I think I'm going to leave town. Take my little old Mustang and all the dough I can carry and get out."

"Running away won't help."

"Oh, hell, I know it," Randy half-sobbed, "but what can I do? I'm marked chicken if I punk out at the rumble, and I'd hate myself if I didn't. I don't know what to do."

"I'd help you if I could," I said. I remembered Cherry's voice: *Things are rough all over.* I knew then what she meant.

He looked at me. "No, you wouldn't. I'm a Soc. You get a little money and the whole world hates you."

"No," I said, "you hate the whole world."

He just looked at me—from the way he looked he could have been ten years older than he was. I got out of the car. "You would have saved those kids if you had been there," I said. "You'd have saved them the same as we did."

"Thanks, grease," he said, trying to grin. Then he stopped. "I didn't mean that. I meant, thanks, kid."

"My name's Ponyboy," I said. "Nice talkin' to you, Randy."

I walked over to Two-Bit, and Randy honked for his friends to come and get into the car.

"What'd he want?" Two-Bit asked. "What'd Mr. Super-Soc have to say?"

"He ain't a Soc," I said, "he's just a guy. He just wanted to talk."

"You want to see a movie before we go see Johnny and Dallas?"

"Nope," I said, lighting up another weed. I still had a headache, but I felt better. Socs were just guys after all. Things were rough all over, but it was better that way. That way you could tell the other guy was human too.

Chapter 8

THE NURSES WOULDN'T LET US SEE JOHNNY. HE WAS IN critical condition. No visitors. But Two-Bit wouldn't take no for an answer. That was his buddy in there and he aimed to see him. We both begged and pleaded, but we were getting nowhere until the doctor found out what was going on.

"Let them go in," he said to the nurse. "He's been asking for them. It can't hurt now."

Two-Bit didn't notice the expression in his voice. It's true, I thought numbly, he is dying. We went in, practically on tiptoe, because the quietness of the hospital scared us. Johnny was lying still, with his eyes closed, but when Two-Bit said, "Hey, Johnnykid," he opened them and looked at us, trying to grin. "Hey, y'all."

The nurse, who was pulling the shades open, smiled and said, "So he can talk after all."

Two-Bit looked around. "They treatin' you okay, kid?"

"Don't . . ."—Johnny gasped—"don't let me put enough grease on my hair."

"Don't talk," Two-Bit said, pulling up a chair, "just listen. We'll bring you some hair grease next time. We're havin' the big rumble tonight."

Johnny's huge black eyes widened a little, but he didn't say anything.

"It's too bad you and Dally can't be in it. It's the first big rumble we've had—not countin' the time we whipped Shepard's outfit."

"He came by," Johnny said.

"Tim Shepard?"

Johnny nodded. "Came to see Dally."

Tim and Dallas had always been buddies.

"Did you know you got your name in the paper for being a hero?"

Johnny almost grinned as he nodded. "Tuff enough," he managed, and by the way his eyes were glowing, I figured Southern gentlemen had nothing on Johnny Cade.

I could see that even a few words were tiring him out; he was as pale as the pillow and looked awful. Two-Bit pretended not to notice.

"You want anything besides hair grease, kid?"

Johnny barely nodded. "The book"—he looked at me—"can you get another one?"

Two-Bit looked at me too. I hadn't told him about *Gone with the Wind*.

"He wants a copy of *Gone with the Wind* so I can read

it to him," I explained. "You want to run down to the drugstore and get one?"

"Okay," Two-Bit said cheerfully. "Don't y'all run off."

I sat down in Two-Bit's chair and tried to think of something to say. "Dally's gonna be okay," I said finally. "And Darry and me, we're okay now."

I knew Johnny understood what I meant. We had always been close buddies, and those lonely days in the church strengthened our friendship. He tried to smile again, and then suddenly went white and closed his eyes tight.

"Johnny!" I said, alarmed. "Are you okay?"

He nodded, keeping his eyes closed. "Yeah, it just hurts sometimes. It usually don't . . . I can't feel anything below the middle of my back . . ."

He lay breathing heavily for a moment. "I'm pretty bad off, ain't I, Pony?"

"You'll be okay," I said with fake cheerfulness. "You gotta be. We couldn't get along without you."

The truth of that last statement hit me. We couldn't get along without him. We needed Johnny as much as he needed the gang. And for the same reason.

"I won't be able to walk again," Johnny started, then faltered. "Not even on crutches. Busted my back."

"You'll be okay," I repeated firmly. Don't start crying, I commanded myself, don't start crying, you'll scare Johnny.

"You want to know something, Ponyboy? I'm scared stiff. I used to talk about killing myself . . ." He drew a quivering breath. "I don't want to die now. It ain't long enough. Sixteen years ain't long enough. I wouldn't mind it so much if there wasn't so much stuff I ain't done yet and so many things I ain't seen. It's not fair. You know what? That time we were in Windrixville was the only time I've been away from our neighborhood."

"You ain't gonna die," I said, trying to hold my voice down. "And don't get juiced up, because the doc won't let us see you no more if you do."

Sixteen years on the streets and you can learn a lot. But all the wrong things, not the things you want to learn. Sixteen years on the streets and you see a lot. But all the wrong sights, not the sights you want to see.

Johnny closed his eyes and rested quietly for a minute. Years of living on the East Side teaches you how to shut off your emotions. If you didn't, you would explode. You learn to cool it.

A nurse appeared in the doorway. "Johnny," she said quietly, "your mother's here to see you."

Johnny opened his eyes. At first they were wide with surprise, then they darkened. "I don't want to see her," he said firmly.

"She's your mother."

"I said I don't want to see her." His voice was rising. "She's probably come to tell me about all the trouble I'm causing her and about how glad her and the old man'll be when I'm dead. Well, tell her to leave me alone. For once"—his voice broke—"for once just to leave me alone." He was struggling to sit up, but he suddenly gasped, went whiter than the pillowcase, and passed out cold.

The nurse hurried me out the door. "I was afraid of something like this if he saw anyone."

I ran into Two-Bit, who was coming in.

"You can't see him now," the nurse said, so Two-Bit handed her the book. "Make sure he can see it when he comes around." She took it and closed the door behind her. Two-Bit stood and looked at the door a long time. "I wish it was any one of us except Johnny," he said, and his voice was serious for once. "We could get along without anyone but Johnny."

Turning abruptly, he said, "Let's go see Dallas."

As we walked out into the hall, we saw Johnny's mother. I knew her. She was a little woman, with straight black hair and big black eyes like Johnny's. But that was as far as the resemblance went. Johnnycake's eyes were fearful and sensitive; hers were cheap and hard. As we passed her she was saying, "But I have a right to see him. He's my son. After all the trouble his father and I've gone to to raise him, this is our reward! He'd rather see those no-count hoodlums than his own folks . . ." She saw us and gave us such a look of hatred that I almost backed up. "It was your fault. Always running around in the middle of the night getting jailed and heaven knows what else . . ." I thought she was going to cuss us out. I really did.

Two-Bit's eyes got narrow and I was afraid he was going to start something. I don't like to hear women get sworn at, even if they deserve it. "No wonder he hates your guts," Two-Bit snapped. He was going to tell her off real good, but I shoved him along. I felt sick. No wonder Johnny didn't want to see her. No wonder he stayed overnight at Two-Bit's or at our house, and slept in the vacant lot in good weather. I remembered my mother . . . beautiful and golden, like Soda, and wise and firm, like Darry.

"Oh, lordy!" There was a catch in Two-Bit's voice and he was closer to tears than I'd ever seen him. "He has to live with that."

We hurried to the elevator to get to the next floor. I hoped the nurse would have enough sense not to let Johnny's mother see him. It would kill him.

Dally was arguing with one of the nurses when we came in. He grinned at us. "Man, am I glad to see you! These ——— hospital people won't let me smoke, and I want out!"

We sat down, grinning at each other. Dally was his usual mean, ornery self. He was okay.

"Shepard came by to see me a while ago."

"That's what Johnny said. What'd he want?"

"Said he saw my picture in the paper and couldn't believe it didn't have 'Wanted Dead or Alive' under it. He mostly came to rub it in about the rumble. Man, I hate not bein' in that."

Only last week Tim Shepard had cracked three of Dally's ribs. But Dally and Tim Shepard had always been buddies; no matter how they fought, they were two of a kind, and they knew it.

Dally was grinning at me. "Kid, you scared the devil outa me the other day. I thought I'd killed you."

"Me?" I said, puzzled. "Why?"

"When you jumped out of the church. I meant to hit you just hard enough to knock you down and put out the fire, but when you dropped like a ton of lead I thought I'd aimed too high and broke your neck." He thought for a minute. "I'm glad I didn't, though."

"I'll bet," I said with a grin. I'd never liked Dally— but then, for the first time, I felt like he was my buddy. And all because he was glad he hadn't killed me.

Dally looked out the window. "Uh . . ."—he sounded very casual—"how's the kid?"

"We just left him," Two-Bit said, and I could tell that he was debating whether to tell Dally the truth or not. "I don't know about stuff like this . . . but . . . well, he seemed pretty bad to me. He passed out cold before we left him."

Dally's jaw line went white as he swore between clenched teeth.

"Two-Bit, you still got that fancy black-handled switch?"

"Yeah."

"Give it here."

Two-Bit reached into his back pocket for his prize possession. It was a jet-handled switchblade, ten inches long, that would flash open at a mere breath. It was the reward of two hours of walking aimlessly around a hardware store to divert suspicion. He kept it razor sharp. As far as I knew, he had never pulled it on anyone; he used his plain pocket-knife when he needed a blade. But it was his showpiece, his pride and joy—every time he ran into a new hood he pulled it out and showed off with it. Dally knew how much that knife meant to Two-Bit, and if he needed a blade bad enough to ask for it, well, he needed a blade. That was all there was to it. Two-Bit handed it over to Dally without a moment's hesitation.

"We gotta win that fight tonight," Dally said. His voice was hard. "We gotta get even with the Socs. For Johnny."

He put the switch under his pillow and lay back, staring at the ceiling. We left. We knew better than to talk to Dally when his eyes were blazing and he was in a mood like that.

133

We decided to catch a bus home. I just didn't feel much like walking or trying to hitch a ride. Two-Bit left me sitting on the bench at the bus stop while he went to a gas station to buy some cigarettes. I was kind of sick to my stomach and sort of groggy. I was nearly asleep when I felt someone's hand on my forehead. I almost jumped out of my skin. Two-Bit was looking down at me worriedly. "You feel okay? You're awful hot."

"I'm all right," I said, and when he looked at me as if he didn't believe me, I got a little panicky. "Don't tell Darry, okay? Come on, Two-Bit, be a buddy. I'll be well by to-night. I'll take a bunch of aspirins."

"All right," Two-Bit said reluctantly. "But Darry'll kill me if you're really sick and go ahead and fight anyway."

"I'm okay," I said, getting a little angry. "And if you keep your mouth shut, Darry won't know a thing."

"You know somethin'?" Two-Bit said as we were riding home on the bus. "You'd think you could get away with murder, living with your big brother and all, but Darry's stricter with you than your folks were, ain't he?"

"Yeah," I said, "but they'd raised two boys before me. Darry hasn't."

"You know, the only thing that keeps Darry from bein' a Soc is us."

"I know," I said. I had known it for a long time. In spite of not having much money, the only reason Darry couldn't be a Soc was us. The gang. Me and Soda. Darry was too smart to be a greaser. I don't know how I knew, I just did. And I was kind of sorry.

I was silent most of the way home. I was thinking about

the rumble. I had a sick feeling in my stomach and it
wasn't from being ill. It was the same kind of helplessness
I'd felt that night Darry yelled at me for going to sleep in
the lot. I had the same deathly fear that something was
going to happen that none of us could stop. As we got
off the bus I finally said it. "Tonight—I don't like it one
bit."

Two-Bit pretended not to understand. "I never knew you
to play chicken in a rumble before. Not even when you
was a little kid."

I knew he was trying to make me mad, but I took the
bait anyway. "I ain't chicken, Two-Bit Mathews, and you
know it," I said angrily. "Ain't I a Curtis, same as Soda and
Darry?"

Two-Bit couldn't deny this, so I went on: "I mean, I
got an awful feeling something's gonna happen."

"Somethin' *is* gonna happen. We're gonna stomp the
Socs' guts, that's what."

Two-Bit knew what I meant, but doggedly pretended
not to. He seemed to feel that if you said something was
all right, it immediately was, no matter what. He's been that
way all his life, and I don't expect he'll change. Sodapop
would have understood, and we would have tried to figure
it out together, but Two-Bit just ain't Soda. Not by a long
shot.

Cherry Valance was sitting in her Corvette by the vacant
lot when we came by. Her long hair was pinned up, and in
daylight she was even better looking. That Sting Ray was
one tuff car. A bright red one. It was cool.

"Hi, Ponyboy," she said. "Hi, Two-Bit."

Two-Bit stopped. Apparently Cherry had shown up there before during the week Johnny and I had spent in Windrixville.

"What's up with the big-times?"

She tightened the strings on her ski jacket. "They play your way. No weapons, fair deal. Your rules."

"You sure?"

She nodded. "Randy told me. He knows for sure."

Two-Bit turned and started home. "Thanks, Cherry."

"Ponyboy, stay a minute," Cherry said. I stopped and went back to her car. "Randy's not going to show up at the rumble."

"Yeah," I said, "I know."

"He's not scared. He's just sick of fighting. Bob . . ." She swallowed, then went on quietly. "Bob was his best buddy. Since grade school."

I thought of Soda and Steve. What if one of them saw the other killed? Would that make them stop fighting? No, I thought, maybe it would make Soda stop, but not Steve. He'd go on hating and fighting. Maybe that was what Bob would have done if it had been Randy instead of him.

"How's Johnny?"

"Not so good," I said. "Will you go up to see him?"

She shook her head. "No. I couldn't."

"Why not?" I demanded. It was the least she could do. It was her boyfriend who had caused it all . . . and then I stopped. Her boyfriend . . .

"I couldn't," she said in a quiet, desperate voice. "He killed Bob. Oh, maybe Bob asked for it. I know he did.

But I couldn't ever look at the person who killed him. You only knew his bad side. He could be sweet sometimes, and friendly. But when he got drunk . . . it was that part of him that beat up Johnny. I knew it was Bob when you told me the story. He was so proud of his rings. Why do people sell liquor to boys? Why? I know there's a law against it, but kids get it anyway. I can't go see Johnny. I know I'm too young to be in love and all that, but Bob was something special. He wasn't just any boy. He had something that made people follow him, something that marked him different, maybe a little better, than the crowd. Do you know what I mean?"

I did. Cherry saw the same things in Dallas. That was why she was afraid to see him, afraid of loving him. I knew what she meant all right. But she also meant she wouldn't go see Johnny because he had killed Bob. "That's okay," I said sharply. It wasn't Johnny's fault Bob was a booze-hound and Cherry went for boys who were bound for trouble. "I wouldn't want you to see him. You're a traitor to your own kind and not loyal to us. Do you think your spying for us makes up for the fact that you're sitting there in a Corvette while my brother drops out of school to get a job? Don't you ever feel sorry for us. Don't you ever try to give us handouts and then feel high and mighty about it."

I started to turn and walk off, but something in Cherry's face made me stop. I was ashamed—I can't stand to see girls cry. She wasn't crying, but she was close to it.

"I wasn't trying to give you charity, Ponyboy. I only wanted to help. I liked you from the start . . . the way you talked. You're a nice kid, Ponyboy. Do you realize how scarce nice kids are nowadays? Wouldn't you try to help me if you could?"

I would. I'd help her and Randy both, if I could. "Hey," I said suddenly, "can you see the sunset real good from the West Side?"

She blinked, startled, then smiled. "Real good."

"You can see it good from the East Side, too," I said quietly.

"Thanks, Ponyboy." She smiled through her tears. "You dig okay."

She had green eyes. I went on, walking home slowly.

Chapter 9

IT WAS ALMOST SIX-THIRTY WHEN I GOT HOME. THE RUMBLE
was set for seven, so I was late for supper, as usual. I always come in late. I forget what time it is. Darry had
cooked dinner: baked chicken and potatoes and corn—
two chickens because all three of us eat like horses. Especially Darry. But although I love baked chicken, I could
hardly swallow any. I swallowed five aspirins, though, when
Darry and Soda weren't looking. I do that all the time because I can't sleep very well at night. Darry thinks I take
just one, but I usually take four. I figured five would keep
me going through the rumble and maybe get rid of my
headache.

Then I hurried to take a shower and change clothes. Me
and Soda and Darry always got spruced up before a rumble.

And besides, we wanted to show those Socs we weren't trash, that we were just as good as they were.

"Soda," I called from the bathroom, "when did you start shaving?"

"When I was fifteen," he yelled back.

"When did Darry?"

"When he was thirteen. Why? You figgerin' on growing a beard for the rumble?"

"You're funny. We ought to send you in to the *Reader's Digest.* I hear they pay a lot for funny things."

Soda laughed and went right on playing poker with Steve in the living room. Darry had on a tight black T-shirt that showed every muscle on his chest and even the flat hard muscles of his stomach. I'd hate to be the Soc who takes a crack at him, I thought as I pulled on a clean T-shirt and a fresh pair of jeans. I wished my T-shirt was tighter—I have a pretty good build for my size, but I'd lost a lot of weight in Windrixville and it just didn't fit right. It was a chilly night and T-shirts aren't the warmest clothes in the world, but nobody ever gets cold in a rumble, and besides, jackets interfere with your swinging ability.

Soda and Steve and I had put on more hair oil than was necessary, but we wanted to show that we were greasers. Tonight we could be proud of it. Greasers may not have much, but they have a rep. That and long hair. (What kind of world is it where all I have to be proud of is a reputation for being a hood, and greasy hair? I don't want to be a hood, but even if I don't steal things and mug people and get boozed up, I'm marked lousy. Why should I be proud of it? Why should I even pretend to be proud of it?)

Darry never went in for long hair. His was short and clean all the time.

I sat in the armchair in the living room, waiting for the rest of the outfit to show up. But of course, tonight the only one coming would be Two-Bit; Johnny and Dallas wouldn't show. Soda and Steve were playing cards and arguing as usual. Soda was keeping up a steady stream of wisecracks and clowning, and Steve had turned up the radio so loud that it almost broke my eardrums. Of course everybody listens to it loud like that, but it wasn't just the best thing for a headache.

"You like fights, don't you, Soda?" I asked suddenly.

"Yeah, sure." He shrugged. "I like fights."

"How come?"

"I don't know." He looked at me, puzzled. "It's action. It's a contest. Like a drag race or a dance or something."

"Shoot," said Steve, "I want to beat those Socs' heads in. When I get in a fight I want to stomp the other guy good. I like it, too."

"How come you like fights, Darry?" I asked, looking up at him as he stood behind me, leaning in the kitchen doorway. He gave me one of those looks that hide what he's thinking, but Soda piped up: "He likes to show off his muscles."

"I'm gonna show 'em off on you, little buddy, if you get any mouthier."

I digested what Soda had said. It was the truth. Darry liked anything that took strength, like weight-lifting or playing football or roofing houses, even if he was proud of being smart too. Darry never said anything about it, but I knew he liked fights. I felt out of things. I'll fight anyone anytime, but I don't like to.

"I don't know if you ought to be in this rumble, Pony," Darry said slowly.

Oh, no, I thought in mortal fear, I've got to be in it. Right then the most important thing in my life was helping us whip the Socs. Don't let him make me stay home now. I've got to be in it.

"How come? I've always come through before, ain't I?"

"Yeah," Darry said with a proud grin. "You fight real good for a kid your size. But you were in shape before. You've lost weight and you don't look so great, kid. You're tensed up too much."

"Shoot," said Soda, trying to get the ace out of his shoe without Steve's seeing him, "we all get tensed up before a rumble. Let him fight tonight. Skin never hurt anyone— no weapons, no danger."

"I'll be okay," I pleaded. "I'll get hold of a little one, okay?"

"Well, Johnny won't be there this time . . ."—Johnny and I sometimes ganged up on one big guy—"but then, Curly Shepard won't be there either, or Dally, and we'll need every man we can get."

"What happened to Shepard?" I asked, remembering Tim Shepard's kid brother. Curly, who was a tough, cool, hard-as-nails Tim in miniature, and I had once played chicken by holding our cigarette ends against each other's fingers. We had stood there, clenching our teeth and grimacing, with sweat pouring down our faces and the smell of burning flesh making us sick, each refusing to holler, until Tim happened to stroll by. When he saw that we were really burning holes in each other he cracked our heads together, swearing to kill us both if we ever pulled a stunt like that again. I still have the scar on my forefinger. Curly was an average downtown hood, tough and not real bright, but I liked him. He could take anything.

"He's in the cooler," Steve said, kicking the ace out of Soda's shoe. "In the reformatory."

Again? I thought, and said, "Let me fight, Darry. If it was blades or chains or something it'd be different. Nobody ever gets really hurt in a skin rumble."

"Well"—Darry gave in—"I guess you can. But be careful, and if you get in a jam, holler and I'll get you out."

"I'll be okay," I said wearily. "How come you never worry about Sodapop as much? I don't see you lecturin' him."

"Man"—Darry grinned and put his arm across Soda's shoulders—"this is one kid brother I don't have to worry about."

Soda punched him in the ribs affectionately.

"This kiddo can use his head."

Sodapop looked down at me with mock superiority, but Darry went on: "You can see he uses it for one thing—to grow hair on." He ducked Soda's swing and took off for the door.

Two-Bit stuck his head in the door just as Darry went flying out of it. Leaping as he went off the steps, Darry turned a somersault in mid-air, hit the ground, and bounced up before Soda could catch him.

"Welup," Two-Bit said cheerfully, cocking an eyebrow, "I see we are in prime condition for a rumble. Is everybody happy?"

"Yeah!" screamed Soda as he too did a flying somersault off the steps. He flipped up to walk on his hands and then did a no-hands cartwheel across the yard to beat Darry's performance. The excitement was catching. Screeching like an Indian, Steve went running across the lawn in flying leaps, stopped suddenly, and flipped backward. We could all do acrobatics because Darry had taken a course at the Y and then spent a whole summer teaching us everything he'd learned on the grounds that it might come in handy in a fight. It did, but it also got Two-Bit and Soda jailed once. They were doing mid-air flips down a downtown sidewalk, walking on their hands, and otherwise disturbing the public and the police. Leave it to those two to pull something like that.

With a happy whoop I did a no-hands cartwheel off the porch steps, hit the ground, and rolled to my feet. Two-Bit followed me in a similar manner.

"I am a greaser," Sodapop chanted. "I am a JD and a hood. I blacken the name of our fair city. I beat up people. I rob gas stations. I am a menace to society. Man, do I have fun!"

"Greaser . . . greaser . . . greaser . . ." Steve singsonged. "O victim of environment, underprivileged, rotten, no-count hood!"

"Juvenile delinquent, you're no good!" Darry shouted.

"Get thee hence, white trash," Two-Bit said in a snobbish voice. "I am a Soc. I am the privileged and the well-dressed. I throw beer blasts, drive fancy cars, break windows at fancy parties."

"And what do you do for fun?" I inquired in a serious, awed voice.

"I jump greasers!" Two-Bit screamed, and did a cart-wheel.

We settled down as we walked to the lot. Two-Bit was the only one wearing a jacket; he had a couple of cans of beer stuffed in it. He always gets high before a rumble. Before anything else, too, come to think of it. I shook my head. I'd hate to see the day when I had to get my nerve from a can. I'd tried drinking once before. The stuff tasted awful, I got sick, had a headache, and when Darry found out, he grounded me for two weeks. But that was the last time I'd ever drink. I'd seen too much of what drinking did for you at Johnny's house.

"Hey, Two-Bit," I said, deciding to complete my survey, "how come you like to fight?"

He looked at me as if I was off my nut. "Shoot, everybody fights."

If everybody jumped in the Arkansas River, ol' Two-Bit would be right on their heels. I had it then. Soda fought for fun, Steve for hatred, Darry for pride, and Two-Bit for conformity. Why do I fight? I thought, and couldn't think of any real good reason. There isn't any real good reason for fighting except self-defense.

"Listen, Soda, you and Ponyboy," Darry said as we strode down the street, "if the fuzz show, you two beat it out of there. The rest of us can only get jailed. You two can get sent to a boys' home."

"Nobody in this neighborhood's going to call the fuzz," Steve said grimly. "They know what'd happen if they did."

"All the same, you two blow at the first sign of trouble. You hear me?"

"You sure don't need an amplifier," Soda said, and stuck

out his tongue at the back of Darry's head. I stifled a giggle. If you want to see something funny, it's a tough hood sticking his tongue out at his big brother.

Tim Shepard and company were already waiting when we arrived at the vacant lot, along with a gang from Brumly, one of the suburbs. Tim was a lean, catlike eighteen-year-old who looked like the model JD you see in movies and magazines. He had the right curly black hair, smoldering dark eyes, and a long scar from temple to chin where a tramp had belted him with a broken pop bottle. He had a tough, hard look to him, and his nose had been broken twice. Like Dally's, his smile was grim and bitter. He was one of those who enjoy being a hood. The rest of his bunch were the same way. The boys from Brumly, too. Young hoods—who would grow up to be old hoods. I'd never thought about it before, but they'd just get worse as they got older, not better. I looked at Darry. He wasn't going to be any hood when he got old. He was going to get somewhere. Living the way we do would only make him more determined to get somewhere. That's why he's better than the rest of us, I thought. He's going somewhere. And I was going to be like him. I wasn't going to live in a lousy neighborhood all my life.

Tim had the tense, hungry look of an alley cat—that's what he's always reminded me of, an alley cat—and he was constantly restless. His boys ranged from fifteen to nineteen, hard-looking characters who were used to the strict discipline Tim gave out. That was the difference between his gang and ours—they had a leader and were organized; we were just buddies who stuck together—each man was his own leader. Maybe that was why we could whip them.

Tim and the leader of the Brumly outfit moved forward to shake hands with each of us—proving that our gangs were on the same side in this fight, although most of the guys in those two outfits weren't exactly what I'd like to call my friends. When Tim got to me he studied me, maybe remembering how his kid brother and I had played chicken. "You and the quiet black-headed kid were the ones who killed that Soc?"

"Yeah," I said, pretending to be proud of it; then I thought of Cherry and Randy and got a sick feeling in my stomach.

"Good goin', kid. Curly always said you were a good kid. Curly's in the reformatory for the next six months." Tim grinned ruefully, probably thinking of his roughneck, hard-headed brother. "He got caught breakin' into a liquor store, the little . . ." He went on to call Curly every unprintable name under the sun—in Tim's way of thinking, terms of affection.

I surveyed the scene with pride. I was the youngest one there. Even Curly, if he had been there, had turned fifteen, so he was older than me. I could tell Darry realized this too, and although he was proud, I also knew he was worried. Shoot, I thought, I'll fight so good this time he won't ever worry about me again. I'll show him that someone besides Sodapop can use his head.

One of the Brumly guys waved me over. We mostly stuck with our own outfits, so I was a little leery of going over to him, but I shrugged. He asked to borrow a weed, then lit up. "That big guy with y'all, you know him pretty well?"

"I ought to, he's my brother," I said. I couldn't honestly say "Yes." I knew Darry as well as he knew me, and that isn't saying a whole lot.

"No kiddin'? I got a feelin' he's gonna be asked to start the fireworks around here. He a pretty good bopper?"

He meant rumbler. Those Brumly boys have weird vocabularies. I doubt if half of them can read a newspaper or spell much more than their names, and it comes out in their speech. I mean, you take a guy that calls a rumble "bop-action," and you can tell he isn't real educated.

"Yep," I said. "But why him?"

He shrugged. "Why anybody else?"

I looked our outfits over. Most greasers don't have real tuff builds or anything. They're mostly lean and kind of panther-looking in a slouchy way. This is partly because they don't eat much and partly because they're slouchy. Darry looked like he could whip anyone there. I think most of the guys were nervous because of the 'no weapons' rule. I didn't know about the Brumly boys, but I knew Shepard's gang were used to fighting with anything they could get their hands on—bicycle chains, blades, pop bottles, pieces of pipe, pool sticks, or sometimes even heaters. I mean guns. I have a kind of lousy vocabulary, too, even if I am educated. Our gang never went in for weapons. We're just not that rough. The only weapons we ever used were knives, and shoot, we carried them mostly just for looks. Like Two-Bit with his black-handled switch. None of us had ever really hurt anybody, or wanted to. Just Johnny. And he hadn't wanted to.

"Hey, Curtis!" Tim yelled. I jumped.

"Which one?" I heard Soda yell back.

"The big one. Come on over here."

The guy from Brumly looked at me. "What did I tell ya?"

I watched Darry going toward Tim and the leader of the Brumly boys. He shouldn't be here, I thought suddenly. I shouldn't be here and Steve shouldn't be here and Soda shouldn't be here and Two-Bit shouldn't be here. We're greasers, but not hoods, and we don't belong with this bunch of future convicts. We could end up like them, I thought. We could. And the thought didn't help my headache.

I went back to stand with Soda and Steve and Two-Bit then, because the Socs were arriving. Right on time. They came in four carloads, and filed out silently. I counted twenty-two of them. There were twenty of us, so I figured the odds were as even as we could get them. Darry always likes to take on two at a time anyway. They looked like they were all cut from the same piece of cloth: clean-shaven with semi-Beatle haircuts, wearing striped or checkered shirts with light-red or tan-colored jackets or madras ski jackets. They could just as easily have been going to the movies as to a rumble. That's why people don't ever think to blame the Socs and are always ready to jump on us. We look hoody and they look decent. It could be just the other way around—half of the hoods I know are pretty decent guys underneath all that grease, and from what I've heard, a lot of Socs are just cold-blooded mean—but people usually go by looks.

They lined up silently, facing us, and we lined up facing

them. I looked for Randy but didn't see him. I hoped he wasn't there. A guy with a madras shirt stepped up. "Let's get the rules straight—nothing but our fists, and the first to run lose. Right?"

Tim flipped away his beer can. "You savvy real good."

There was an uneasy silence: Who was going to start it? Darry solved the problem. He stepped forward under the circle of light made by the street lamp. For a minute, everything looked unreal, like a scene out of a JD movie or something. Then Darry said, "I'll take on anyone."

He stood there, tall, broad-shouldered, his muscles taut under his T-shirt and his eyes glittering like ice. For a second it looked like there wasn't anyone brave enough to take him on. Then there was a slight stir in the faceless mob of Socs, and a husky blond guy stepped forward. He looked at Darry and said quietly, "Hello, Darrel."

Something flickered behind Darry's eyes and then they were ice again. "Hello, Paul."

I heard Soda give a kind of squeak and I realized that the blond was Paul Holden. He had been the best halfback on Darry's football team at high school and he and Darry used to buddy it around all the time. He must be a junior in college by now, I thought. He was looking at Darry with an expression I couldn't quite place, but disliked. Contempt? Pity? Hate? All three? Why? Because Darry was standing there representing all of us, and maybe Paul felt only contempt and pity and hate for greasers? Darry hadn't moved a muscle or changed expression, but you could see he hated Paul now. It wasn't only jealousy—Darry had a right to be jealous; he was ashamed to be on our side, ashamed to be seen with the Brumly boys, Shepard's gang, maybe even us. Nobody realized it but me and Soda. It didn't matter to anyone but me and Soda.

That's stupid, I thought swiftly, they've both come here to fight and they're both supposed to be smarter than that. What difference does the side make?

Then Paul said, "I'll take you," and something like a smile crossed Darry's face. I knew Darry had thought he could take Paul any time. But that was two or three years ago. What if Paul was better now? I swallowed. Neither one of my brothers had ever been beaten in a fight, but I wasn't exactly itching for someone to break the record.

They moved in a circle under the light, counterclockwise, eyeing each other, sizing each other up, maybe remembering old faults and wondering if they were still there. The rest of us waited with mounting tension. I was reminded of Jack London's books—you know, where the wolf pack waits in silence for one of two members to go down in a fight. But it was different here. The moment either one swung a punch, the rumble would be on.

The silence grew heavier, and I could hear the harsh heavy breathing of the boys around me. Still Darry and the Soc walked slowly in a circle. Even I could feel their hatred. They used to be buddies, I thought, they used to be friends, and now they hate each other because one has to work for a living and the other comes from the West Side. They shouldn't hate each other . . . I don't hate the Socs any more . . . they shouldn't hate . . .

"Hold up!" a familiar voice yelled. "Hold it!" Darry turned to see who it was, and Paul swung—a hard right to the jaw that would have felled anyone but Darry. The rumble was on. Dallas Winston ran to join us.

I couldn't find a Soc my size, so I took the next-best size and jumped on him. Dallas was right beside me, already on top of someone.

"I thought you were in the hospital," I yelled as the Soc knocked me to the ground and I rolled to avoid getting kicked.

"I was." Dally was having a hard time because his left arm was still in bad shape. "I ain't now."

"How?" I managed to ask as the Soc I was fighting leaped on me and we rolled near Dally.

"Talked the nurse into it with Two-Bit's switch. Don't you know a rumble ain't a rumble unless I'm in it?"

I couldn't answer because the Soc, who was heavier than I took him for, had me pinned and was slugging the sense out of me. I thought dizzily that he was going to knock some of my teeth loose or break my nose or something, and I knew I didn't have a chance. But Darry was keeping an eye out for me; he caught that guy by the shoulder and half lifted him up before knocking him three feet with a sledge-hammer blow. I decided it would be fair for me to help Dally since he could use only one arm.

They were slugging it out, but Dallas was getting the worst of it, so I jumped on his Soc's back, pulling his hair and pounding him. He reached back and caught me by the neck and threw me over his head to the ground. Tim Shepard, who was fighting two at once, accidentally stepped on me, knocking my breath out. I was up again as soon as I got my wind, and jumped right back on the Soc, trying my best to strangle him. While he was prying my fingers loose, Dally knocked him backward, so that all three of us rolled on the ground, gasping, cussing, and punching.

Somebody kicked me hard in the ribs and I yelped in spite of myself. Some Soc had knocked out one of our bunch and was kicking me as hard as he could. But I had both arms wrapped around the other Soc's neck and refused to let go. Dally was slugging him, and I hung on desperately, although that other Soc was kicking me and you'd better believe it hurt. Finally he kicked me in the head so hard it stunned me, and I lay limp, trying to clear my mind and keep from blacking out. I could hear the racket, but only dimly through the buzzing in my ears. Numerous bruises along my back and on my face were throbbing, but I felt detached from the pain, as if it wasn't really me feeling it.

"They're running!" I heard a voice yell joyfully. "Look at the dirty ——— run!"

It seemed to me that the voice belonged to Two-Bit, but I couldn't be sure. I tried to sit up, and saw that the Socs were getting into their cars and leaving. Tim Shepard was swearing blue and green because his nose was broken again, and the leader of the Brumly boys was working over one of his own men because he had broken the rules and used a piece of pipe in the fighting. Steve lay doubled up and groaning about ten feet from me. We found out later he had three broken ribs. Sodapop was beside him, talking in a low steady voice. I did a double take when I saw Two-Bit—blood was streaming down one side of his face and one hand was busted wide open; but he was grinning happily because the Socs were running.

"We won," Darry announced in a tired voice. He was going to have a black eye and there was a cut across his forehead. "We beat the Socs."

Dally stood beside me quietly for a minute, trying to grasp the fact that we had really beaten the Socs. Then, grabbing my shirt, he hauled me to my feet. "Come on!" He half dragged me down the street. "We're goin' to see Johnny."

I tried to run but stumbled, and Dally impatiently shoved me along. "Hurry! He was gettin' worse when I left. He wants to see you."

I don't know how Dallas could travel so fast and hard after being knocked around and having his sore arm hurt some more, but I tried to keep up with him. Track wasn't ever like the running I did that night. I was still dizzy and had only a dim realization of where I was going and why.

Dally had Buck Merril's T-bird parked in front of our house, and we hopped into it. I sat tight as Dally roared the car down the street. We were on Tenth when a siren came on behind us and I saw the reflection of the red light flashing in the windshield.

"Look sick," Dally commanded. "I'll say I'm taking you to the hospital, which'll be truth enough."

I leaned against the cold glass of the window and tried to look sick, which wasn't too hard, feeling the way I did right then.

The policeman looked disgusted. "All right, buddy, where's the fire?"

"The kid"—Dally jerked a thumb toward me—"he fell over on his motorcycle and I'm takin' him to the hospital."

I groaned, and it wasn't all fake-out. I guess I looked pretty bad, too, being cut and bruised like I was.

The fuzz changed his tone. "Is he real bad? Do you need an escort?"

"How would I know if he's bad or not? I ain't no doc. Yeah, we could use an escort." And as the policeman got back into his car I heard Dally hiss, "Sucker!"

With the siren ahead of us, we made record time getting to the hospital. All the way there Dally kept talking and talking about something, but I was too dizzy to make most of it out.

"I was crazy, you know that, kid? Crazy for wantin' Johnny to stay outa trouble, for not wantin' him to get hard. If he'd been like me he'd never have been in this mess. If he'd got smart like me he'd never have run into that church. That's what you get for helpin' people. Editorials in the paper and a lot of trouble. . . . You'd better wise up, Pony . . . you get tough like me and you don't get hurt. You look out for yourself and nothin' can touch you . . ."

He said a lot more stuff, but I didn't get it all. I had a stupid feeling that Dally was out of his mind, the way he kept raving on and on, because Dallas never talked like that, but I think now I would have understood if I hadn't been sick at the time.

The cop left us at the hospital as Dally pretended to help me out of the car. The minute the cop was gone, Dally let go of me so quick I almost fell. "Hurry!"

We ran through the lobby and crowded past people into the elevator. Several people yelled at us, I think because we were pretty racked-up looking, but Dally had nothing on his mind except Johnny, and I was too mixed up to know anything but that I had to follow Dally. When we finally got to Johnny's room, the doctor stopped us. "I'm sorry, boys, but he's dying."

"We gotta see him," Dally said, and flicked out Two-Bit's switchblade. His voice was shaking. "We're gonna see him and if you give me any static you'll end up on your own operatin' table."

The doctor didn't bat an eye. "You can see him, but it's because you're his friends, not because of that knife."

Dally looked at him for a second, then put the knife back in his pocket. We both went into Johnny's room, standing there for a second, getting our breath back in heavy gulps. It was awful quiet. It was scary quiet. I looked at Johnny. He was very still, and for a moment I thought in agony: He's dead already. We're too late.

Dally swallowed, wiping the sweat off his upper lip. "Johnnycake?" he said in a hoarse voice. "Johnny?"

Johnny stirred weakly, then opened his eyes. "Hey," he managed softly.

"We won," Dally panted. "We beat the Socs. We stomped them—chased them outa our territory."

Johnny didn't even try to grin at him. "Useless . . . fighting's no good. . . ." He was awful white.

Dally licked his lips nervously. "They're still writing editorials about you in the paper. For being a hero and all." He was talking too fast and too calmly. "Yeah, they're calling you a hero now and heroizin' all the greasers. We're all proud of you, buddy."

Johnny's eyes glowed. Dally was proud of him. That was all Johnny had ever wanted.

"Ponyboy."

I barely heard him. I came closer and leaned over to hear what he was going to say.

"Stay gold, Ponyboy. Stay gold . . ." The pillow seemed to sink a little, and Johnny died.

You read about people looking peacefully asleep when they're dead, but they don't. Johnny just looked dead. Like a candle with the flame gone. I tried to say something, but I couldn't make a sound.

Dally swallowed and reached over to push Johnny's hair back. "Never could keep that hair back . . . that's what you get for tryin' to help people, you little punk, that's what you get . . ."

Whirling suddenly, he slammed back against the wall. His face contracted in agony, and sweat streamed down his face.

"Damnit, Johnny . . ." he begged, slamming one fist against the wall, hammering it to make it obey his will. "Oh, damnit, Johnny, don't die, please don't die . . ."

He suddenly bolted through the door and down the hall.

Chapter 10

I WALKED DOWN THE HALL IN A DAZE. DALLY HAD TAKEN the car and I started the long walk home in a stupor. Johnny was dead. But he wasn't. That still body back in the hospital wasn't Johnny. Johnny was somewhere else— maybe asleep in the lot, or playing the pinball machine in the bowling alley, or sitting on the back steps of the church in Windrixville. I'd go home and walk by the lot, and Johnny would be sitting on the curb smoking a cigarette, and maybe we'd lie on our backs and watch the stars. He isn't dead, I said to myself. He isn't dead. And this time my dreaming worked. I convinced myself that he wasn't dead.

I must have wandered around for hours; sometimes even out into the street, getting honked at and cussed out. I might have stumbled around all night except for a man who asked me if I wanted a ride.

"Huh? Oh. Yeah, I guess so," I said. I got in. The man, who was in his mid-twenties, looked at me.

"Are you all right, kid? You look like you've been in a fight."

"I have been. A rumble. I'm okay." Johnny is *not* dead, I told myself, and I believed it.

"Hate to tell you this, kiddo," the guy said dryly, "but you're bleedin' all over my car seats."

I blinked. "I am?"

"Your head."

I reached up to scratch the side of my head where it'd been itching for a while, and when I looked at my hand it was smeared with blood.

"Gosh, mister, I'm sorry," I said, dumfounded.

"Don't worry about it. This wreck's been through worse. What's your address? I'm not about to dump a hurt kid out on the streets this time of night."

I told him. He drove me to my house, and I got out. "Thanks a lot."

He waved me on. "I'm just naturally a great guy." He vroomed the motor and peeled out.

What was left of our gang was in the living room. Steve was stretched out on the sofa, his shirt unbuttoned and his side bandaged. His eyes were closed, but when the door shut behind me he opened them, and I suddenly wondered if my own eyes looked as feverish and bewildered as his. Soda had a wide cut on his lip and a bruise across his cheek. There was a Band-aid over Darry's forehead and he had a black eye. One side of Two-Bit's face was taped up—I found out later he had four stitches in his cheek and seven in his hand where he had busted his knuckles open over a Soc's head. They were lounging around, reading the paper and smoking.

Where's the party? I thought dully. Weren't Soda and Steve planning a party after the rumble? They all looked up when I walked in. Darry leaped to his feet.

"Where have you been?"

Oh, let's don't start that again, I thought. He stopped suddenly.

"Ponyboy, what's the matter?"

I looked at all of them, a little frightened. "Johnny . . . he's dead." My voice sounded strange, even to me. But he's not dead, a voice in my head said. "We told him about beatin' the Socs and . . . I don't know, he just died." He told me to stay gold, I remembered. What was he talking about?

There was a stricken silence. I don't think any of us had realized how bad off Johnny really had been. Soda made a funny noise and looked like he was going to start crying. Two-Bit's eyes were closed and his teeth were clenched, and I suddenly remembered Dally. . . . Dally pounding on the wall . . .

"Dallas is gone," I said. "He ran out like the devil was after him. He's gonna blow up. He couldn't take it."

How can I take it? I wondered. Dally is tougher than I am. Why can I take it when Dally can't? And then I knew. Johnny was the only thing Dally loved. And now Johnny was gone.

"So he finally broke." Two-Bit spoke everyone's feelings. "So even Dally has a breaking point."

I started shaking. Darry said something in a low voice to Soda.

"Ponyboy," Soda said softly, like he was talking to an injured animal, "you look sick. Sit down."

I backed up, just like a frightened animal, shaking my head. "I'm okay." I felt sick. I felt as if any minute I was going to fall flat on my face, but I shook my head. "I don't want to sit down."

Darry took a step toward me, but I backed away. "Don't touch me," I said. My heart was pounding in slow thumps, throbbing at the side of my head, and I wondered if everyone else could hear it. Maybe that's why they're all looking at me, I thought, they can hear my heart beating . . .

The phone rang, and after a moment's hesitation, Darry turned from me to it. He said "Hello" and then listened. He hung up quickly.

"It was Dally. He phoned from a booth. He's just robbed a grocery store and the cops are after him. We gotta hide him. He'll be at the lot in a minute."

We all left the house at a dead run, even Steve, and I wondered vaguely why no one was doing somersaults off the steps this time. Things were sliding in and out of focus, and it seemed funny to me that I couldn't run in a straight line.

We reached the vacant lot just as Dally came in, running as hard as he could, from the opposite direction. The wail of a siren grew louder and then a police car pulled up across the street from the lot. Doors slammed as the policemen leaped out. Dally had reached the circle of light under the street lamp, and skidding to a halt, he turned and jerked a black object from his waistband. I remembered his voice: *I been carryin' a heater. It ain't loaded, but it sure does help a bluff.*

It was only yesterday that Dally had told Johnny and me that. But yesterday was years ago. A lifetime ago.

Dally raised the gun, and I thought: You blasted fool. They don't know you're only bluffing. And even as the policemen's guns spit fire into the night I knew that was what Dally wanted. He was jerked half around by the impact of the bullets, then slowly crumpled with a look of grim triumph on his face. He was dead before he hit the ground. But I knew that was what he wanted, even as the lot echoed with the cracks of the shots, even as I begged silently—Please, not him . . . not him and Johnny both— I knew he would be dead, because Dally Winston wanted to be dead and he always got what he wanted.

Nobody would write editorials praising Dally. Two friends of mine had died that night: one a hero, the other a hoodlum. But I remembered Dally pulling Johnny through the window of the burning church; Dally giving us his gun, although it could mean jail for him; Dally risking his life for us, trying to keep Johnny out of trouble. And now he was a dead juvenile delinquent and there wouldn't be any editorials in his favor. Dally didn't die a hero. He died violent and young and desperate, just like we all knew he'd die someday. Just like Tim Shepard and Curly Shepard and the Brumly boys and the other guys we knew would die someday. But Johnny was right. He died gallant.

Steve stumbled forward with a sob, but Soda caught him by the shoulders.

"Easy, buddy, easy," I heard him say softly, "there's nothing we can do now."

Nothing we can do . . . not for Dally or Johnny or Tim Shepard or any of us . . . My stomach gave a violent start and turned into a hunk of ice. The world was spinning around me, and blobs of faces and visions of things past were dancing in the red mist that covered the lot. It swirled into a mass of colors and I felt myself swaying on my feet. Someone cried, "Glory, look at the kid!"

And the ground rushed up to meet me very suddenly.

When I woke up it was light. It was awfully quiet. Too quiet. I mean, our house just isn't naturally quiet. The radio's usually going full blast and the TV is turned up loud and people are wrestling and knocking over lamps and tripping over the coffee table and yelling at each other. Something was wrong, but I couldn't quite figure it out. Something had happened . . . I couldn't remember what. I blinked at Soda bewilderedly. He was sitting on the edge of the bed watching me.

"Soda . . ."—my voice sounded weak and hoarse—"is somebody sick?"

"Yeah." His voice was oddly gentle. "Go back to sleep now."

An idea was slowly dawning on me. "Am I sick?"

He stroked my hair. "Yeah, you're sick. Now be quiet."

I had one more question. I was still kind of mixed up. "Is Darry sorry I'm sick?" I had a funny feeling that Darry was sad because I was sick. Everything seemed vague and hazy.

Soda gave me a funny look. He was quiet for a moment. "Yeah, he's sorry you're sick. Now please shut up, will ya, honey? Go back to sleep."

I closed my eyes. I was awful tired.

When I woke up next, it was daylight and I was hot under all the blankets on me. I was thirsty and hungry, but my stomach was so uneasy I knew I wouldn't be able to hold anything down. Darry had pulled the armchair into the bedroom and was asleep in it. He should be at work, I thought. Why is he asleep in the armchair?

"Hey, Darry," I said softly, shaking his knee. "Hey, Darry, wake up."

He opened his eyes. "Ponyboy, you okay?"

"Yeah," I said, "I think so."

Something had happened . . . but I still couldn't remember it, although I was thinking a lot clearer than I was the last time I'd waked up.

He sighed in relief and pushed my hair back. "Gosh, kid, you had us scared to death."

"What was the matter with me?"

He shook his head. "I told you you were in no condition for a rumble. Exhaustion, shock, minor concussion—and Two-Bit came blubberin' over here with some tale about how you were running a fever before the rumble and how it was all his fault you were sick. He was pretty torn up that night," Darry said. He was quiet for a minute. "We all were."

And then I remembered. Dallas and Johnny were dead. Don't think of them, I thought. (Don't remember how Johnny was your buddy, don't remember that he didn't want to die. Don't think of Dally breaking up in the hospital, crumpling under the street light. Try to think that Johnny is better off now, try to remember that Dally would have ended up like that sooner or later. Best of all, don't think. Blank your mind. Don't remember. Don't remember.)

"Where'd I get a concussion?" I said. My head itched, but I couldn't scratch it for the bandage. "How long have I been asleep?"

"You got a concussion from getting kicked in the head —Soda saw it. He landed all over that Soc. I've never seen him so mad. I think he could have whipped anyone, in the state he was in. Today's Tuesday, and you've been asleep and delirious since Saturday night. Don't you remember?"

"No," I said slowly. "Darry, I'm not ever going to be able to make up the school I've missed. And I've still got to go to court and talk to the police about Bob's getting killed. And now . . . with Dally . . ."—I took a deep breath —"Darry, do you think they'll split us up? Put me in a home or something?"

He was silent. "I don't know, baby. I just don't know."

I stared at the ceiling. What would it be like, I wondered, staring at a different ceiling? What would it be like in a different bed, in a different room? There was a hard painful lump in my throat that I couldn't swallow.

"Don't you even remember being in the hospital?" Darry asked. He was trying to change the subject.

I shook my head. "I don't remember."

"You kept asking for me and Soda. Sometimes for Mom and Dad, too. But mostly for Soda."

Something in his tone of voice made me look at him.

Mostly for Soda. Did I ask for Darry at all, or was he just saying that?

"Darry . . ." I didn't know quite what I wanted to say. But I had a sick feeling that maybe I hadn't called for him while I was delirious, maybe I had only wanted Sodapop to be with me. What all had I said while I was sick? I couldn't remember. I didn't want to remember.

"Johnny left you his copy of *Gone with the Wind*. Told the nurse he wanted you to have it."

I looked at the paperback lying on the table. I didn't want to finish it. I'd never get past the part where the Southern gentlemen go riding into sure death because they are gallant. Southern gentlemen with big black eyes in blue jeans and T-shirts, Southern gentlemen crumpling under street lights. Don't remember. Don't try to decide which one died gallant. Don't remember.

"Where's Soda?" I asked, and then I could have kicked myself. Why can't you talk to Darry, you idiot? I said to myself. Why do you feel uncomfortable talking to Darry?

"Asleep, I hope. I thought he was going to go to sleep shaving this morning and cut his throat. I had to push him to bed, but he was out like a light in a second."

Darry's hopes that Soda was asleep were immediately ruined, because he came running in, clad only in a pair of blue jeans.

"Hey, Ponyboy!" he yelped, and leaped for me, but Darry caught him.

"No rough stuff, little buddy."

So Soda had to content himself with bouncing up and down on the bed and pounding on my shoulder.

"Gosh, but you were sick. You feel okay now?"

"I'm okay. Just a little hungry."

"I should think you would be," Darry said. "You wouldn't eat anything most of the time you were sick. How'd you like some mushroom soup?"

I suddenly realized just how empty I was. "Man, I'd like that just fine."

"I'll go make some. Sodapop, take it easy with him, okay?"

Soda looked back at him indignantly. "You'd think I was going to challenge him to a track meet or something right off the bat."

"Oh, no," I groaned. "Track meet. I guess this just about puts me out of every race. I won't be back in condition for the meets. And the coach was counting on me."

"Golly, there's always next year," Soda said. Soda never has grasped the importance Darry and I put on athletics. Like he never has understood why we went all-out for studying. "Don't sweat it about some track meet."

"Soda," I said suddenly. "What all did I say while I was delirious?"

"Oh, you thought you were in Windrixville most of the time. Then you kept saying that Johnny didn't mean to kill that Soc. Hey, I didn't know you didn't like baloney."

I went cold. "I don't like it. I never liked it."

Soda just looked at me. "You used to eat it. That's why you wouldn't eat anything while you were sick. You kept saying you didn't like baloney, no matter what it was we were trying to get you to eat."

"I don't like it," I repeated. "Soda, did I ask for Darry while I was sick?"

"Yeah, sure," he said, looking at me strangely. "You

asked for him and me both. Sometimes Mom and Dad. And for Johnny."

"Oh. I thought maybe I didn't ask for Darry. It was bugging me."

Soda grinned. "Well, you did, so don't worry. We stayed with you so much that the doctor told us we were going to end up in the hospital ourselves if we didn't get some sleep. But we didn't get any anyway."

I took a good look at him. He looked completely worn out; there were circles under his eyes and he had a tense, tired look to him. Yet his dark eyes were still laughing and carefree and reckless.

"You look beat," I said frankly. "I bet you ain't had three hours sleep since Saturday night."

He grinned but didn't deny it. "Scoot over." He crawled over me and flopped down and before Darry came back in with the soup we were both asleep.

Chapter 11

I HAD TO STAY IN BED A WHOLE WEEK AFTER THAT. THAT bugged me; I'm not the kind that can lie around looking at the ceiling all the time. I read most of the time, and drew pictures. One day I started flipping through one of Soda's old yearbooks and came across a picture that seemed vaguely familiar. Not even when I read the name Robert Sheldon did it hit me who it was. And then I finally realized it was Bob. I took a real good long look at it.

The picture didn't look a whole lot like the Bob I remembered, but nobody ever looks like his picture in a yearbook anyway. He had been a sophomore that year— that would make him about eighteen when he died. Yeah, he was good-looking even then, with a grin that reminded me of Soda's, a kind of reckless grin. He had been a handsome black-haired boy with dark eyes—maybe brown, like Soda's, maybe dark-blue, like the Shepard boys'. Maybe he'd had black eyes. Like Johnny. I had never given Bob much thought—I hadn't had time to think. But that day I wondered about him. What was he like?

I knew he liked to pick fights, had the usual Soc belief that living on the West Side made you Mr. Super-Tuff, looked good in dark wine-colored sweaters, and was proud of his rings. But what about the Bob Sheldon that Cherry Valance knew? She was a smart girl; she didn't like him just because he was good-looking. Sweet and friendly, stands out from the crowd—that's what she had said. A real person, the best buddy a guy ever had, kept trying to make somebody stop him—Randy had told me that. Did he have a kid brother who idolized him? Maybe a big brother who kept bugging him not to be so wild? His parents let him run wild—because they loved him too much or too little? Did they hate us now? I hoped they hated us, that they weren't full of that pity-the-victims-of-environment junk the social workers kept handing Curly Shepard every time he got sent off to reform school. I'd rather have anybody's hate than their pity. But, then, maybe they understood, like Cherry Valance. I looked at Bob's picture and I could begin to see the person we had killed. A reckless, hot-tempered boy, cocky and scared stiff at the same time.

"Ponyboy."

"Yeah?" I didn't look up. I thought it was the doctor. He'd been coming over to see me almost every day, although he didn't do much except talk to me.

"There's a guy here to see you. Says he knows you."
Something in Darry's voice made me look up, and his eyes
were hard. "His name's Randy."

"Yeah, I know him," I said.

"You want to see him?"

"Yeah." I shrugged. "Sure, why not?"

A few guys from school had dropped by to see me; I have
quite a few friends at school even if I am younger than
most of them and don't talk much. But that's what they
are—school friends, not buddies. I had been glad to see
them, but it bothered me because we live in kind of a
lousy neighborhood and our house isn't real great. It's
run-down looking and everything, and the inside's kind of
poor-looking, too, even though for a bunch of boys we do
a pretty good job of house-cleaning. Most of my friends at
school come from good homes, not filthy-rich like the
Socs, but middle-class, anyway. It was a funny thing—it
bugged me about my friends seeing our house. But I
couldn't have cared less about what Randy thought.

"Hi, Ponyboy." Randy looked uncomfortable standing
in the doorway.

"Hi, Randy," I said. "Have a seat if you can find one."
Books were lying all over everything. He pushed a couple
off a chair and sat down.

"How you feeling? Cherry told me your name was on
the school bulletin."

"I'm okay. You can't really miss my name on any kind
of bulletin."

He still looked uncomfortable, although he tried to grin.

"Wanna smoke?" I offered him a weed, but he shook

his head. "No, thanks. Uh, Ponyboy, one reason I came here was to see if you were okay, but you—we—got to go see the judge tomorrow."

"Yeah," I said, lighting a cigarette. "I know. Hey, holler if you see one of my brothers coming. I'll catch it for smoking in bed."

"My dad says for me to tell the truth and nobody can get hurt. He's kind of upset about all this. I mean, my dad's a good guy and everything, better than most, and I kind of let him down, being mixed up in all this."

I just looked at him. That was the dumbest remark I ever heard anyone make. He thought *he* was mixed up in this? He didn't kill anyone, he didn't get his head busted in a rumble, it wasn't his buddy that was shot down under a street light. Besides, what did he have to lose? His old man was rich, he could pay whatever fine there was for being drunk and picking a fight.

"I wouldn't mind getting fined," Randy said, "but I feel lousy about the old man. And it's the first time I've felt anything in a long time."

The only thing I'd felt in a long time was being scared. Scared stiff. I'd put off thinking about the judge and the hearing for as long as I could. Soda and Darry didn't like to talk about it either, so we were all silently counting off the days while I was sick, counting the days that we had left together. But with Randy sticking solidly to the subject it was impossible to think about anything else. My cigarette started trembling.

"I guess your folks feel kind of awful about it, too."

"My parents are dead. I live here with just Darry and Soda, my brothers." I took a long drag on my cigarette.

"That's what's worrying me. If the judge decides Darry isn't a good guardian or something, I'm liable to get stuck in a home somewhere. That's the rotten part of this deal. Darry is a good guardian; he makes me study and knows where I am and who I'm with all the time. I mean, we don't get along so great sometimes, but he keeps me out of trouble, or did. My father didn't yell at me as much as he does."

"I didn't know that." Randy looked worried, he really did. A Soc, even, worried because some kid greaser was on his way to a foster home or something. That was really funny. I don't mean funny. You know what I mean.

"Listen to me, Pony. You didn't do anything. It was your friend Johnny that had the knife . . ."

"I had it." I stopped him. He was looking at me strangely. "I had the knife. I killed Bob."

Randy shook his head. "I saw it. You were almost drowned. It was the black-headed guy that had the switchblade. Bob scared him into doing it. I saw it."

I was bewildered. "I killed him. I had a switchblade and I was scared they were going to beat me up."

"No, kid, it was your friend, the one who died in the hospital . . ."

"Johnny is not dead." My voice was shaking. "Johnny is not dead."

"Hey, Randy." Darry stuck his head in the door. "I think you'd better go now."

"Sure," Randy said. He was still looking at me kind of funny. "See you around, Pony."

"Don't ever say anything to him about Johnny," I heard Darry say in a low voice as they went out. "He's still pretty racked up mentally and emotionally. The doc said he'd get over it if we gave him time."

I swallowed hard and blinked. He was just like all the rest of the Socs. Cold-blooded mean. Johnny didn't have anything to do with Bob's getting killed.

"Ponyboy Curtis, put out that cigarette!"

"Okay, okay." I put it out. "I ain't going to go to sleep smoking, Darry. If you make me stay in bed there ain't anywhere else I can smoke."

"You're not going to die if you don't get a smoke. But if that bed catches on fire you will. You couldn't make it to the door through that mess."

"Well, golly, I can't pick it up and Soda doesn't, so I guess that leaves you."

He was giving me one of those looks. "All right, all right," I said, "that don't leave you. Maybe Soda'll straighten it up a little."

"Maybe you can be a little neater, huh, little buddy?"

He'd never called me that before. Soda was the only one he ever called "little buddy."

"Sure," I said, "I'll be more careful."

Chapter 12

THE HEARING WASN'T ANYTHING LIKE I THOUGHT IT WOULD be. Besides Darry and Soda and me, nobody was there except Randy and his parents and Cherry Valance and her parents and a couple of the other guys that had jumped Johnny and me that night. I don't know what I expected the whole thing to be like—I guess I've been watching too many Perry Mason shows. Oh, yeah, the doctor was there and he had a long talk with the judge before the hearing. I didn't know what he had to do with it then, but I do now.

First Randy was questioned. He looked a little nervous, and I wished they'd let him have a cigarette. I wished they'd let me have a cigarette; I was more than a little shaky myself. Darry had told me to keep my mouth shut no matter what Randy and everybody said, that I'd get my turn. All the Socs told the same story and stuck mainly to the truth, except they said Johnny had killed Bob; but I figured I could straighten that point out when I got my turn. Cherry told them what had happened before and after Johnny and I had been jumped—I think I saw a couple of tears slide down her cheeks, but I'm not sure. Her voice was sure steady even if she was crying. The judge questioned everyone carefully, but nothing real emotional or exciting happened like it does on TV. He asked Darry and Soda a little bit about Dally, I think to check our background and find out what kind of guys we hung out with. Was he a real good buddy of ours? Darry said, "Yes, sir," looking straight at the judge, not flinching; but Soda looked at me like he was sentencing me to the electric chair before he gave the same answer. I was real proud of both of them. Dally had been one of our gang and we wouldn't desert him. I thought the judge would never get around to questioning me. Man, I was scared almost stiff by the time he did. And you know what? They didn't ask me a thing about Bob's getting killed. All the judge did was ask me if I liked living with Darry, if I liked school, what kind of grades I made, and stuff like that. I couldn't figure it out then, but later I found out what the doctor had been talking to the judge about. I guess I looked as scared as I really was, because the judge grinned at me and told me to quit chewing my fingernails. That's a habit I have. Then he said I was acquitted and the whole case was closed. Just like that. Didn't even give me a chance to talk much. But that didn't bother me a lot. I didn't feel like talking anyway.

I wish I could say that everything went back to normal, but it didn't. Especially me. I started running into things, like the door, and kept tripping over the coffee table and losing things. I always have been kind of absent-minded, but man, then, I was lucky if I got home from school with the right notebook and with both shoes on. I walked all the way home once in my stocking feet and didn't even notice it until Steve made some bright remark about it. I guess I'd left my shoes in the locker room at school, but I never did find them. And another thing, I quit eating. I used to eat like a horse, but all of a sudden I wasn't hungry. Everything tasted like baloney. I was lousing up my school-work, too. I didn't do too badly in math, because Darry checked over my homework in that and usually caught all my mistakes and made me do it again, but in English I really washed out. I used to make A's in English, mostly because my teacher made us do compositions all the time. I mean, I know I don't talk good English (have you ever seen a hood that did?), but I can write it good when I try. At least, I could before. Now I was lucky to get a *D* on a composition.

It bothered my English teacher, the way I was goofing up, I mean. He's a real good guy, who makes us think, and you can tell he's interested in you as a person, too. One day he told me to stay in after the rest of the class left.

"Ponyboy, I'd like to talk to you about your grades."

Man, I wished I could beat it out of there. I knew I was flunking out in that class, but golly, I couldn't help it.

"There's not much to talk about, judging from your scores. Pony, I'll give it to you straight. You're failing this class right now, but taking into consideration the circumstances, if you come up with a good semester theme, I'll pass you with a C grade."

"Taking into consideration the circumstances"—brother, was that ever a way to tell me he knew I was goofing up because I'd been in a lot of trouble. At least that was a roundabout way of putting it. The first week of school after the hearing had been awful. People I knew wouldn't talk to me, and people I didn't know would come right up and ask about the whole mess. Sometimes even teachers. And my history teacher—*she* acted as if she was scared of me, even though I'd never caused any trouble in her class. You can bet that made me feel real tuff.

"Yessir," I said, "I'll try. What's the theme supposed to be on?"

"Anything you think is important enough to write about. And it isn't a reference theme; I want your own ideas and your own experiences."

My first trip to the zoo. Oh, boy, oh, boy. "Yessir," I said, and got out of there as fast as I could.

At lunch hour I met Two-Bit and Steve out in the back parking lot and we drove over to a little neighborhood grocery store to buy cigarettes and Cokes and candy bars. The store was the grease hang-out and that was about all we ever had for lunch. The Socs were causing a lot of trouble in the school cafeteria—throwing silverware and stuff—and everybody tried to blame it on us greasers. We all got a big laugh out of that. Greasers rarely even eat in the cafeteria.

I was sitting on the fender of Steve's car, smoking and drinking a Pepsi while he and Two-Bit were inside talking to some girls, when a car drove up and three Socs got out.

I just sat there and looked at them and took another swallow of the Pepsi. I wasn't scared. It was the oddest feeling in the world. I didn't feel *anything*—scared, mad, or anything. Just zero.

"You're the guy that killed Bob Sheldon," one of them said. "And he was a friend of ours. We don't like nobody killing our friends, especially greasers."

Big deal. I busted the end off my bottle and held on to the neck and tossed away my cigarette. "You get back into your car or you'll get split."

They looked kind of surprised, and one of them backed up.

"I mean it." I hopped off the car. "I've had about all I can take from you guys." I started toward them, holding the bottle the way Tim Shepard holds a switch—out and away from myself, in a loose but firm hold. I guess they knew I meant business, because they got into their car and drove off.

"You really would have used that bottle, wouldn't you?" Two-Bit had been watching from the store doorway. "Steve and me were backing you, but I guess we didn't need to. You'd have really cut them up, huh?"

"I guess so," I said with a sigh. I didn't see what Two-Bit was sweating about—anyone else could have done the same thing and Two-Bit wouldn't have thought about it twice.

"Ponyboy, listen, don't get tough. You're not like the rest of us and don't try to be . . ."

What was the matter with Two-Bit? I knew as well as he did that if you got tough you didn't get hurt. Get smart and nothing can touch you . . .

"What in the world are you doing?" Two-Bit's voice broke into my thoughts.

I looked up at him. "Picking up the glass."

He stared at me for a second, then grinned. "You little sonofagun," he said in a relieved voice. I didn't know what he was talking about, so I just went on picking up the glass from the bottle end and put it in a trash can. I didn't want anyone to get a flat tire.

I tried to write that theme when I got home. I really did, mostly because Darry told me to or else. I thought about writing about Dad, but I couldn't. It's going to be a long time before I can even think about my parents. A long time. I tried writing about Soda's horse, Mickey Mouse, but I couldn't get it right; it always came out sounding corny. So I started writing names across the paper. Darrel Shaynne Curtis, Jr. Soda Patrick Curtis. Ponyboy Michael Curtis. Then I drew horses all over it. That was going to get a good grade like all git-out.

"Hey, did the mail come in yet?" Soda slammed the door and yelled for the mail, just the way he does every day when he comes home from work. I was in the bedroom, but I knew he would throw his jacket toward the sofa and miss it, take off his shoes, and go into the kitchen for a glass of chocolate milk, because that's what he does every day of his life. He always runs around in his stocking feet—he doesn't like shoes.

Then he did a funny thing. He came in and flopped down on the bed and started smoking a cigarette. He hardly ever smokes, except when something is really bugging him or when he wants to look tough. And he doesn't have to impress us; we know he's tough. So I figured something was bothering him. "How was work?"

"Okay."

"Something wrong?"

He shook his head. I shrugged and went back to drawing horses.

Soda cooked dinner that night, and everything came out right. That was unusual, because he's always trying something different. One time we had green pancakes. Green. I can tell you one thing: if you've got a brother like Soda-pop, you're never bored.

All through supper Soda was quiet, and he didn't eat much. That was really unusual. Most of the time you can't shut him up or fill him up. Darry didn't seem to notice, so I didn't say anything.

Then after supper me and Darry got into a fuss, about the fourth one we'd had that week. This one started because I hadn't done anything on that theme, and I wanted to go for a ride. It used to be that I'd just stand there and let Darry yell at me, but lately I'd been yelling right back.

"What's the sweat about my schoolwork?" I finally shouted. "I'll have to get a job as soon as I get out of school anyway. Look at Soda. He's doing okay, and he dropped out. You can just lay off!"

"You're not going to drop out. Listen, with your brains and grades you could get a scholarship, and we could put you through college. But schoolwork's not the point. You're living in a vacuum, Pony, and you're going to have to cut it out. Johnny and Dallas were our buddies, too, but you don't just stop living because you lose someone. I thought you knew that by now. You don't quit! And anytime you don't like the way I'm running things you can get out."

I went tight and cold. We never talked about Dallas or Johnny. "You'd like that, wouldn't you? You'd like me just to get out. Well, it's not that easy, is it, Soda?" But when I looked at Soda I stopped. His face was white, and when he looked at me his eyes were wide with a pained expression. I suddenly remembered Curly Shepard's face when he slipped off a telephone pole and broke his arm.

"Don't . . . Oh, you guys, why can't you . . ." He jumped up suddenly and bolted out the door. Darry and I were struck dumb. Darry picked up the envelope that Soda had dropped.

"It's the letter he wrote Sandy," Darry said without expression. "Returned unopened."

So that was what had been bugging Soda all afternoon. And I hadn't even bothered to find out. And while I was thinking about it, I realized that I never had paid much attention to Soda's problems. Darry and I just took it for granted that he didn't have any.

"When Sandy went to Florida . . . it wasn't Soda, Ponyboy. He told me he loved her, but I guess she didn't love him like he thought she did, because it wasn't him."

"You don't have to draw me a picture," I said.

"He wanted to marry her anyway, but she just left." Darry was looking at me with a puzzled expression. "Why didn't he tell you? I didn't think he'd tell Steve or Two-Bit, but I thought he told you everything."

"Maybe he tried," I said. How many times had Soda started to tell me something, only to find I was daydreaming or stuck in a book? He would always listen to me, no matter what he was doing.

"He cried every night that week you were gone," Darry said slowly. "Both you and Sandy in the same week." He put the envelope down. "Come on, let's go after him."

We chased him clear to the park. We were gaining on him, but he had a block's head start.

"Circle around and cut him off," Darry ordered. Even out of condition I was the best runner. "I'll stay right behind him."

I headed through the trees and cut him off halfway across the park. He veered off to the right, but I caught him in a flying tackle before he'd gone more than a couple of steps. It knocked the wind out of both of us. We lay there gasping for a minute or two, and then Soda sat up and brushed the grass off his shirt.

"You should have gone out for football instead of track."

"Where did you think you were going?" I lay flat on my back and looked at him. Darry came up and dropped down beside us.

Soda shrugged. "I don't know. It's just . . . I can't stand to hear y'all fight. Sometimes . . . I just have to get out or . . . it's like I'm the middleman in a tug o' war and I'm being split in half. You dig?"

Darry gave me a startled look. Neither of us had realized what it was doing to Soda to hear us fight. I was sick and cold with shame. What he said was the truth. Darry and I did play tug of war with him, with never a thought to how much it was hurting him.

Soda was fiddling with some dead grass. "I mean, I

can't take sides. It'd be a lot easier if I could, but I see both sides. Darry yells too much and tries too hard and takes everything too serious, and Ponyboy, you don't think enough, you don't realize all Darry's giving up just to give you a chance he missed out on. He could have stuck you in a home somewhere and worked his way through college. Ponyboy, I'm telling you the truth. I dropped out because I'm dumb. I really did try in school, but you saw my grades. Look, I'm happy working in a gas station with cars. You'd never be happy doing something like that. And Darry, you ought to try to understand him more, and quit bugging him about every little mistake he makes. He feels things differently than you do." He gave us a pleading look. "Golly, you two, it's bad enough having to listen to it, but when you start trying to get me to take sides . . ." Tears welled up in his eyes. "We're all we've got left. We ought to be able to stick together against everything. If we don't have each other, we don't have anything. If you don't have anything, you end up like Dallas . . . and I don't mean dead, either. I mean like he was before. And that's worse than dead. Please"—he wiped his eyes on his arm—"don't fight anymore."

Darry looked real worried. I suddenly realized that Darry was only twenty, that he wasn't so much older that he couldn't feel scared or hurt and as lost as the rest of us. I saw that I had expected Darry to do all the understanding without even trying to understand him. And he *had* given up a lot for Soda and me.

"Sure, little buddy," Darry said softly. "We're not going to fight anymore."

"Hey, Ponyboy"—Soda gave me a tearful grin—"don't

you start crying, too. One bawl-baby in the family's enough."

"I'm not crying," I said. Maybe I was. I don't remember. Soda gave me a playful punch on the shoulder.

"No more fights. Okay, Ponyboy?" Darry said.

"Okay," I said. And I meant it. Darry and I would probably still have misunderstandings—we were too different not to—but no more fights. We couldn't do anything to hurt Soda. Sodapop would always be the middleman, but that didn't mean he had to keep getting pulled apart. Instead of Darry and me pulling him apart, he'd be pulling us together.

"Well," Soda said, "I'm cold. How about going home?"

"Race you," I challenged, leaping up. It was a real nice night for a race. The air was clear and cold and so clean it almost sparkled. The moon wasn't out but the stars lit up everything. It was quiet except for the sound of our feet on the cement and the dry, scraping sound of leaves blowing across the street. It was a real nice night. I guess I was still out of shape, because we all three tied. No. I guess we all just wanted to stay together.

I still didn't want to do my homework that night, though. I hunted around for a book to read, but I'd read everything in the house about fifty million times, even Darry's copy of *The Carpetbaggers*, though he'd told me I wasn't old enough to read it. I thought so too after I finished it. Finally I picked up *Gone with the Wind* and looked at it for a long time. I knew Johnny was dead. I had known it all the time, even while I was sick and pretending he wasn't. It was Johnny, not me, who had killed Bob—I knew that too. I had just thought that maybe if

I played like Johnny wasn't dead it wouldn't hurt so much. The way Two-Bit, after the police had taken Dally's body away, had griped because he had lost his switchblade when they searched Dallas.

"Is that all that's bothering you, that switchblade?" a red-eyed Steve had snapped at him.

"No," Two-Bit had said with a quivering sigh, "but that's what I'm wishing was all that's bothering me."

But it still hurt anyway. You know a guy a long time, and I mean really know him, you don't get used to the idea that he's dead just overnight. Johnny was something more than a buddy to all of us. I guess he had listened to more beefs and more problems from more people than any of us. A guy that'll really listen to you, listen and care about what you're saying, is something rare. And I couldn't forget him telling me that he hadn't done enough, hadn't been out of our neighborhood all his life— and then it was too late. I took a deep breath and opened the book. A slip of paper fell out on the floor and I picked it up.

Ponyboy, I asked the nurse to give you this book so you could finish it. It was Johnny's handwriting. I went on reading, almost hearing Johnny's quiet voice. *The doctor came in a while ago but I knew anyway. I keep getting tireder and tireder. Listen, I don't mind dying now. It's worth it. It's worth saving those kids. Their lives are worth more than mine, they have more to live for. Some of their parents came by to thank me and I know it was worth it. Tell Dally it's worth it. I'm just going to miss you guys. I've been thinking about it, and that poem, that guy that wrote it, he meant you're gold when you're a kid, like green.*

When you're a kid everything's new, dawn. It's just when you get used to everything that it's day. Like the way you dig sunsets, Pony. That's gold. Keep that way, it's a good way to be. I want you to tell Dally to look at one. He'll probably think you're crazy, but ask for me. I don't think he's ever really seen a sunset. And don't be so bugged over being a greaser. You still have a lot of time to make yourself be what you want. There's still lots of good in the world. Tell Dally. I don't think he knows. Your buddy, Johnny.

Tell Dally. It was too late to tell Dally. Would he have listened? I doubted it. Suddenly it wasn't only a personal thing to me. I could picture hundreds and hundreds of boys living on the wrong sides of cities, boys with black eyes who jumped at their own shadows. Hundreds of boys who maybe watched sunsets and looked at stars and ached for something better. I could see boys going down under street lights because they were mean and tough and hated the world, and it was too late to tell them that there was still good in it, and they wouldn't believe you if you did. It was too vast a problem to be just a personal thing. There should be some help, someone should tell them before it was too late. Someone should tell their side of the story, and maybe people would understand then and wouldn't be so quick to judge a boy by the amount of hair oil he wore. It was important to me. I picked up the phone book and called my English teacher.

"Mr. Syme, this is Ponyboy. That theme—how long can it be?"

"Why, uh, not less than five pages." He sounded a little surprised. I'd forgotten that it was late at night.

"Can it be longer?"

"Certainly, Ponyboy, as long as you want it."

"Thanks," I said and hung up.

I sat down and picked up my pen and thought for a minute. Remembering. Remembering a handsome, dark boy with a reckless grin and a hot temper. A tough, towheaded boy with a cigarette in his mouth and a bitter grin on his hard face. Remembering—and this time it didn't hurt—a quiet, defeated-looking sixteen-year-old whose hair needed cutting badly and who had black eyes with a frightened expression to them. One week had taken all three of them. And I decided I could tell people, beginning with my English teacher. I wondered for a long time how to start that theme, how to start writing about something that was important to me. And I finally began like this: When I stepped out into the bright sunlight from the darkness of the movie house, I had only two things on my mind: Paul Newman and a ride home . . .

that was then,
this is now

VIKING

A Division of Penguin Books USA Inc.
375 Hudson Street, New York, New York 10014
Penguin Books Ltd, 27 Wrights Lane, London W8 5TZ England
Penguin Books Australia Ltd, Ringwood, Victoria, Australia
Penguin Books Canada Ltd, 10 Alcorn Avenue, Toronto, Ontario, Canada M4V 3B2
Penguin Books (N.Z.) Ltd, 182-190 Wairau Road, Auckland 10, New Zealand

Penguin Books Ltd, Registered Offices: Harmondsworth, Middlesex, England

First published in 1971 by Viking Penguin Inc.
Published simultaneously in Canada
Copyright © S. E. Hinton, 1971
All rights reserved
ISBN 0-670-69798-2
Library of Congress catalog card number: 70-150116

Printed in the United States of America by R. R. Donnelley & Sons Company
Set in Baskerville

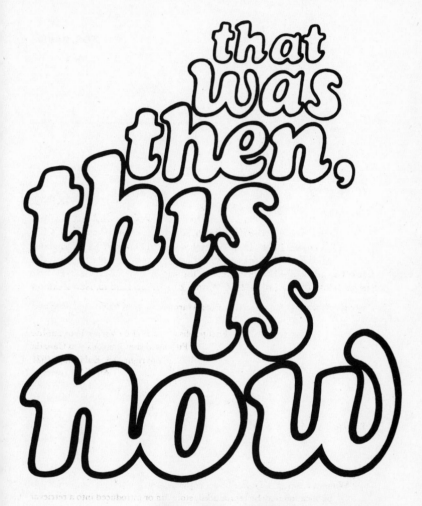

that was then, this is now

S. E. Hinton

THE VIKING PRESS   NEW YORK

FOR DAVID

1

Mark and me went down to the bar/pool hall about two or three blocks from where we lived with the sole intention of making some money. We'd done that before. I was a really good pool player, especially for being just sixteen years old, and, what's more, I look like a baby-faced kid who wouldn't know one ball from another. This, and the way Mark set me up, helped me hustle a lot of pool games. The bad deal is, it's against the law to be in this pool hall if you're under age, because of the adjoining bar. The good deal is, the bartender and owner was a good friend of mine, being the older brother of this chick I used to like. When this chick and me broke up, I still stayed friends with her brother, which is unusual in cases like that. Charlie, the bartender, was just twenty-two, but he had a tough reputation and kept order real good. We lived in kind of a rough part of town and some pretty wild things went on in Charlie's Bar.

I looked around for a plainclothes cop when we

went in—I can always tell a cop—but didn't find one, so I went up to the bar and hopped on a barstool.

"Give me a beer," I said, and Charlie, who was cleaning glasses just like every bartender you ever see, gave me a dirty look instead. "O.K.," I said brightly, "a Coke."

"Your credit ain't so hot, Bryon," Charlie said. "You got cash?"

"A dime—for cryin' out loud! Can't you let me charge a dime Coke?"

"Cokes are fifteen cents, and you already got three dollars worth of Cokes charged here, and if you don't pay up this month I'll have to beat it out of you." He said this real friendly-like, but he meant it. We were friends, but Charlie was a businessman too.

"I'll pay up," I assured him. "Don't worry."

Charlie gave me a lopsided grin. "I ain't worried, kid. You're the one who should be worried."

I was, to tell the truth. Charlie was a big, tough guy so a three-dollar beating up was something to worry about.

"Hey, Mark," Charlie called, "there ain't nobody here to hustle."

Mark, who had been scouting out the two guys playing pool, came up and sat down next to me. "Yeah, that's the truth."

"It's just as well," Charlie said. "You guys are going to get in real bad trouble one of these days. Some guy's going to get hacked off when he finds out what you're doin', and you're gonna get a pool stick rammed down your throats."

"No we ain't," Mark said. "Give me a Coke, Charlie."

"We don't have any credit," I said glumly.

Mark stared at Charlie disbelievingly. "You got to be kiddin'. Man, when did we ever not pay our bill?"

"Last month."

"You said you'd add it on to this month's. That's what you said. So I don't see why you can't add twenty cents to that."

"Thirty cents," corrected Charlie. "And, like I just told Bryon, if I don't get that money pretty soon, I'm going to take it out of a couple of hides."

"I'll get you the money tomorrow if you give us the Cokes right now."

"O.K." Charlie gave in to Mark. Almost everybody does. It was a gift he had, a gift for getting away with things. He could talk anyone into anything. "But if I don't get the money by tomorrow, I'll come looking for you."

I got chilled. I had heard Charlie say that to another guy once. I also saw the guy after Charlie found him. But if Mark said he'd have three dollars by tomorrow, he'd have it.

"Speaking of looking for you," Charlie continued, "the true flower child was in here asking for you."

"M&M?" Mark asked. "What did he want?"

"How would I know? Man, that is a weird kid. Nice guy, but weird."

"Yeah," Mark said. "I guess it would be hard to be a hippie in a hood's part of town."

"Speak for yourself, man," Charlie said. "This part of town don't make nobody a hood."

"You're right," Mark said. "But I really sounded profound there for a minute, huh?"

Charlie just gave him a funny look and got us the Cokes. It was later in the evening now, and some more customers came in, so Charlie quit talking to us. It got pretty busy.

"Where are you gonna get three dollars?" I asked Mark.

He finished off his Coke. "I don't know."

That bugged the heck out of me. Mark was always pulling stunts like that. I ought to know; Mark had lived at my house ever since I was ten and he was nine and his parents shot each other in a drunken argument and my old lady felt sorry for him and took him home to live with us. My mother wanted a hundred kids and could have only one, so until she got hold of Mark she had to be content feeding every stray cat that came along. There was no telling how many kids she might have picked up along the line if she could have afforded more than two—me and Mark.

I had been friends with Mark long before he came

to live with us. He had lived down the street and it seemed to me that we had always been together. We had never had a fight. We had never even had an argument. In looks, we were complete opposites: I'm a big guy, dark hair and eyes—the kind who looks like a Saint Bernard puppy, which I don't mind as most chicks cannot resist a Saint Bernard puppy. Mark was small and compact, with strange golden eyes and hair to match and a grin like a friendly lion. He was much stronger than he looked—he could tie me in arm wrestling. He was my best friend and we were like brothers.

"Let's go look for M&M," Mark said abruptly and we left. It was dark outside and seemed a little chilly. This was probably because school had just started, and it always seems like fall when school starts, even if it's hot. Charlie's Bar was on a real crummy street with a lot of other bars whose bartenders kicked us out when we strolled in, a movie house, a drugstore, and a second-hand clothes store that always had a sign in the window saying "We Buy Almost Anything"—and from the looks of their clothes, they did. When my old lady went into the hospital, we got so low on money that I bought some clothes there. It's pretty lousy, buying used clothes.

We found M&M in the drugstore reading *Newsweek,* which shows what a weird kid he was since there were plenty of skin mags and things to read. A little kid like him shouldn't be reading that junk, I know, but he should at least want to.

"Hey, Charlie said you was lookin' for us," Mark greeted him.

M&M looked up at him. "Yeah. How you guys doin'?"

M&M was the most serious guy I knew. He always had this wide-eyed, intent, trusting look on his face, but sometimes he smiled, and when he did it was really great. He was an awful nice kid even if he was a little strange. He had big gray eyes—the kind you see on war-orphan posters—and charcoal-colored hair down past his ears and down to his eyebrows. He probably would have grown a beard except thirteen was too young for it. He always wore an old Army jacket that was too big for him and went barefoot even after it started getting cold. Then his father got fed up with it and M&M got a pair of moccasins. He had a metal peace symbol hanging around his neck on a piece of rawhide string, and he got his nickname from his addiction to M&M's, the kind of chocolate candy that melts in your mouth and not in your hand. For years I'd never seen M&M without a bag of that candy. I don't know how he ate those things all day long, day after day. If I did that, my face would break out like nothing you've ever seen.

"You want an M&M?" He held out a bag toward us. I shook my head, but Mark took one, just to be polite, since he didn't like sweet stuff. "You wanted to see us for something?" Mark reminded him.

"Yeah, I did, but I forgot what for." He was like that. Real absent-minded. "My sister's home," he added as an afterthought.

"No kiddin'?" asked Mark tactfully, thumbing through a *Playboy*. "Which one?"

M&M had a million brothers and sisters, most of them younger. They all looked alike and it was really funny to see him out somewhere with four or five little carbon copies—with dark hair and big serious eyes— hanging all over him. If I had to be a baby-sitter day and night, I'd lose my temper and kill one of those brats, but then, M&M never lost his temper.

"My older sister, Cathy. You know."

"Yeah, I remember," I said, only I didn't remember too well. "Where's she been?"

"She went to a private school last year and this summer. She's been staying with my aunt. She had to come home, though, because she ran out of money. She paid for it all with her own bread."

"Must be smart," I said. I couldn't remember what she looked like; I had never paid any attention to her. "She as smart as you?"

"No," M&M said, still reading. He wasn't bragging, he was telling the truth. He was a very honest kid.

"Let's go over to the bowling alley," Mark suggested. The drugstore wasn't exactly jumping with action. It was a school night and nobody was hanging around. "You come too, M&M."

It was a long walk to the bowling alley, and I wished for the hundredth time I had a car. I had to walk everywhere I went. As if he'd read my mind, which he was in the habit of doing, Mark said, "I could hot-wire us a car."

"That's a bad thing to do," M&M said. "Taking something that doesn't belong to you."

"It ain't stealin'," Mark said. "It's borrowin'."

"Yeah, well, you're on probation now for 'borrowing,' so I don't think it's such a great idea," I said.

Mark could hot-wire anything, and ever since he was twelve years old he had hot-wired cars and driven them. He had never had an accident, but he finally got caught at it, so now once a week he had to go downtown on his school lunch hour to see his probation officer and tell him how he was never going to steal cars any more. I had been worried at first, afraid they were going to take Mark and put him in a boys' home since he wasn't really my brother and didn't have a family. I was worried about Mark being locked up. I didn't need to. Mark always came through everything untouched, unworried, unaffected.

"O.K." Mark shrugged. "Don't get shook, Bryon."

"Bryon," M&M said suddenly, "were you named after the lord?"

"What?" I said, stunned. For a minute I thought he meant God.

"Lord Bryon, were you named after him?"

The poor kid had *Byron* and *Bryon* mixed up. I decided to string him along. "Yeah, I was."

"Was there a Lord Bryon?" Mark said. "Hey, that's cool." He paused. "I guess it's cool. What'd this guy do, anyway?"

"Can't tell you in front of the kid," I answered.

M&M shook his head. "He wrote poetry. He wrote long, old poems. You ought to write poetry, just to keep up the tradition of the Bryons."

"You ought to keep your mouth shut," I replied, "before I keep up the tradition of punching wise guys in the mouth."

M&M looked up at me, and I realized from his hurt, puzzled look that he hadn't been trying to be smart. So I punched him on the shoulder and said, "O.K., I'll write poetry. How's this?"—and I recited a dirty limerick I'd heard somewhere. It made him laugh and turn red at the same time. Mark thought I had made it up, and said, "Hey, that was pretty good. Can you just pop them off like that?"

I only shrugged and said, "Sometimes," because then I'd take credit whether or not it was really due me. I was like that. I'd also lie if I really thought I could get away with it, especially to girls. Like telling them I loved them and junk, when I didn't. I had a rep as a lady-killer—a hustler. I kept up the old Lord Byron tradition in one way. Sometimes I'd get to feeling bad thinking about how rotten I treated some of these chicks, but most of the time it didn't even bother me.

"M&M, old buddy," Mark was saying, putting his arm across M&M's shoulders, "I was wondering if you might be able to loan your best friend some money."

"You ain't my best friend," M&M said with that disarming honesty, "but how much do you want?"

"Three bucks."

"I got fifty cents." M&M reached into his jeans pocket and pulled out a couple of quarters. "Here."

"Forget it," I said. Me and Mark looked at each other and shook our heads. M&M was unbelievable.

"It's O.K. I'll get fifty cents again next week, for baby-sitting."

"Is that all you get paid for watching all those kids? Fifty cents?" I couldn't get over it. Fifty cents a week?

"I think it's enough. I don't mind taking care of the kids. Who's going to do it if I don't. Both my parents work, so they can't do it. Anyway, I like my family. When I get married I'm going to have at least nine or ten kids."

"There goes the population explosion," Mark said.

"Well, now that your sister's home she can do a lot of the baby-sitting," I said, trying to be helpful. M&M could tell we thought he was crazy.

"Cathy's got a job after school; she can't help. I don't know what I have to do to convince you that I don't mind it."

"O.K., O.K., I'm convinced." I was also tired of the

subject and I had got to worrying about how we were going to get three dollars before tomorrow. Charlie didn't get his rough rep or his bar by being nice to people, especially ones who couldn't pay their bills.

By the time we got to the bowling alley it was ten o'clock. There weren't many people there. Mark and I watched a few games while M&M stared into a package of M&M's. I finally got bugged about it and asked him what in the Sam Hill was he doing.

"Take a look." He handed me the package, which was open at the top. "Put it right up to your eye."

I did, and all I saw was a bunch of candy.

"It's beautiful, ain't it?" asked M&M. "I mean, look at all the different colors."

"Yeah," I agreed, thinking, If I didn't know this kid better I'd say he was high.

"Let me look," said Mark, so I handed him the package. "Hey, this is groovy. Look at all the colors." He gave the candy back to M&M, looked at me, and shrugged.

M&M got up. "I gotta go home now. I'll see you guys later."

"We just got here," Mark objected.

"Yeah, well, I just came along for the walk, and now I gotta go home."

I watched him leave. "The kid's weird," I said. "That's all there is to it."

Mark lit up a cigarette, our last one, so we had to

pass it back and forth. "I know, but I still get a kick out of him. Come on, let's go catch up with him. There ain't nothin' to do around here."

Outside I spotted M&M at the corner. There were three guys trailing him. When you see something like that around here you know right away somebody is about to get jumped. In this case, it was M&M.

"Come on," Mark said, and we cut through an alley so as to come up behind those guys.

Three against three. The odds would have been even except that M&M was one of those nonviolent types who practiced what he preached, and me and Mark weren't carrying weapons. We slowed down to a walk when we came to the end of the alley. I could hear the voices of the three guys who were following M&M, and I recognized one of them.

"Hey, flower child, turn around." They were taunting him, but M&M just kept right on moving.

"It's Shepard," Mark whispered to me. We were waiting at the end of the alley for them to come by. They didn't. They must have had M&M up against the wall. We could hear them.

"Hey, hippie, don't you answer when you're spoken to? That ain't nice."

"Curly, why don't you leave me alone?" M&M sounded very patient. I moved over to the other side of the alley just in time to see Curly pull out a switchblade and reach over and cut through the rawhide string on M&M's peace medal. It fell to the ground.

M&M reached down to pick it up, and Curly brought his knee up sharply and hit M&M in the face.

Me and Mark looked at each other, and Mark flashed me a grin. We both liked fights. We ran out and jumped on them, and the one we didn't get took off, which was a wise thing for him to do. Since we had surprised them, it wasn't too hard to get them pinned. I had Curly Shepard in a stranglehold with one arm twisted behind his back, while Mark had the other guy pinned on the ground.

"How'd you like a broken arm, Shepard?" I said through gritted teeth, careful not to loosen my grip. His switchblade had fallen on the sidewalk, but I didn't know what all he might be carrying. He liked to play rough.

"O.K., you proved your point. Let us go, Douglas." Curly said a few more things that I'm not going to repeat. He must have figured out who it was twisting his arm when he saw Mark. Me and Mark were always together. Curly had a special grudge against me anyway. I used to go with his sister; she says she broke up with me, which was the truth, but I was spreading it around that I broke up with her and was giving all kinds of cool reasons. Curly was a little dumb—he belonged to a gang led by his brother Tim and known as the Shepard Gang. Really original. Tim was all right—at least he had a few brains—but I considered Curly a dumb hood. "Look, we didn't hurt him."

That was a lie, because M&M was sitting there

against the wall and already his cheek was swelling up and turning purple. He was trying to tie the ends of the rawhide string together and his hands were shaking.

"Let them go," said M&M. "I'm O.K."

I gave Curly's arm an extra twist for good measure and then gave him a shove that almost sent him sprawling. Mark let the other guy up, but when he was almost to his feet, Mark gave him a good swift kick. They left, cussing us out, partly in English and partly in sign language.

Mark was helping M&M up. "Come on, kid," he said easily. "Let's get you home."

The whole side of M&M's face was bruised, but he gave us one of his rare, wistful grins. "Thanks, you guys."

Mark suddenly laughed. "Hey, look what I got." He waved three one-dollar bills at me.

"Where did you get that?" I asked, although I knew good and well where he got it. Mark was very quick; nobody had to teach him how to hot-wire a car—or to pick a pocket.

"It was a donation," Mark said seriously, "for the Cause."

This was an old joke, but M&M fell for it. "What cause?"

" 'Cause we owe it to Charlie," Mark said, and M&M almost laughed, but instead winced with pain. I was really feeling good. I could quit worrying about Charlie's beating us up.

Mark suddenly poked me. "You still in the mood for a little action?"

"Sure," I said. Mark motioned toward the next intersection. There was a black guy standing there, waiting for the light to change. "We could jump him," Mark said, but suddenly M&M spoke up.

"You make me sick! You just rescued me from some guys who were going to beat me up because I'm different from them, and now you're going to beat up someone because he's different from you. You think I'm weird—well, you're the weird ones."

Both Mark and I had stopped walking and were staring at M&M. He was really shook up. He was crying. I couldn't have been more stunned if he had begun to dissolve. You don't see guys crying around here, not unless they have a lot better reason than M&M had. He suddenly took off, running, not looking back. I started to take a few steps after him, but Mark caught me by the arm. "Leave him alone," Mark said. "He's just all uptight from getting jumped."

"Yeah," I said. That made sense. That had happened to me before, and I could remember how scared it could get you. Besides, M&M was only a kid, just turned thirteen.

Mark picked something up off the ground. It was M&M's peace medal. It must have dropped off when

M&M started running. He hadn't tied the ends of the string together very well.

"Remind me to tell him I have this," Mark said, stuffing the medal and the string in his pocket. "Let's stop by and give this three bucks to Charlie before I buy some cigarettes with it."

"O.K.," I said. I didn't feel quite as good as I had before. I was thinking about what M&M had said about beating up people because they were different. There was a lot of truth to that. The rich kids in town used to drive around over in our part of the city and look for people to beat up. Then a year or so ago a couple of kids got killed in that mess and the fad slowly died out. But there were still gang fights around here and social-club rumbles, and things like Shepard's jumping M&M happened every day. I didn't mind it much, unless I was the one getting mugged. I liked fights.

"Come on," Mark called, "maybe there's somebody to hustle in Charlie's." I grinned and ran to catch up with him. Mark was my best buddy and I loved him like a brother.

2

The next afternoon after school Mark and me went downtown to the hospital to see my mother. She had just had a big operation, one that cost a lot of money. We had sold our car, an old Chevy—our TV, a little black-and-white job—and anything else we could find to sell, but we were still short of money. I had been trying for weeks to find a job. Mark scrounged around and came up with some money—I didn't ask him where he got it, and he didn't tell me, so I figured he stole it somewhere. Mark was really bad about stealing things. He stole things and sold them, or stole them and kept them, or stole things and gave them away. It didn't bother me. He was too smart to get caught. He had been stealing things since he was six years old. I wasn't above taking a pack of cigarettes from a drug-store, but that was about it. I was the hustler and Mark was the thief. We were a great pair. One thing about it, though. Mark couldn't see anything wrong with stealing stuff. I could. It didn't much matter to me whether or not Mark was a thief, but I still felt that stealing was wrong—at least it's against the law. I think Mark was only dimly aware of that fact. Stealing was a game to him, something to do for fun and profit, and he was careful not to get caught because that was one of the rules.

So that was how we lived, stealing stuff and selling stuff, trying to save money and eat at the same time. I never thought about it then, but I can see now that it was a pretty rough time for us.

Anyway, Mark and I hitched a ride almost all the way to the hospital. The guy who gave us a ride was a hippie with long hair and a beard and a Volkswagen bus. Those buses are very big with hippies, I don't know why. The guy said his name was Randy and that he went to college in town, majoring in English. I figure he was a pretty brave guy. Mark and I looked like tough guys—the kind who go around jumping hippies, which we had done once before. We had gone over to the city park where the hippies hang out, just to beat up somebody. I wouldn't do it again though. I hadn't realized those guys refuse to fight back, and what happened to the one we got hold of, it made me sick. Mark felt the same way. So after that we left them alone.

Randy was telling us about this really cool house where a bunch of his friends lived, an old house they all rented and everybody who wanted to could live there and groove in peace and good will. I didn't much believe him—there had to be a few sponges in a setup like that—and living with a bunch of people would get on my nerves, especially if they were hairy and dirty. But I was polite and said, "Sounds cool," even though it didn't particularly appeal to me. Mark was interested, though, and asked Randy all kinds of questions about where this place was and who all lived there and if he knew about any other places like that. Mark was interested in lots of things—he knew all about the Old West and was nutty about Warner Brothers' cartoons—so it didn't bug me when he got all excited about hippie living.

When we got out of the bus Randy held up two fingers and said, "Peace," and Mark held up M&M's peace medal, which he was wearing around his neck as a joke, and made a wisecrack. Then we looked at each other and cracked up laughing. But we weren't being hateful; it was just funny.

Mom was glad to see us, but she hadn't been lacking company. We had the kind of neighborhood where everyone knew everybody else's business, and all the ladies came up to see her, at least two a day. They also brought me and Mark junk like pies and potato salad. I got the pies and Mark took whatever else there was, since he couldn't stand sweet stuff. Cokes and an occasional M&M, just to be polite to M&M, was as much sweet stuff as he'd take. As a result, I was putting on weight—I wasn't in much danger of getting fat since it seemed like I was growing an inch taller a week—and Mark was staying as slight and slender as ever. You'd never guess Mark was as strong as he was by looking at him, but I knew from our wrestling matches that he was as tough as a piece of leather.

As usual, the last thing on Mom's mind was herself. We had no more than got there and got hugged when she started telling us about this poor kid across the hall who never had anybody visiting him.

"How do you know that?" I asked. "There's so many people comin' and goin' around here. How do you know about some kid across the hall?"

"The nurse told me. Poor kid, he's not any older than you and Mark—"

It figured—I mean her finding out about it. If there was a lame dog within three miles, she'd find it. It didn't bug me much though. Thanks to her, I had a brother.

"Bryon, promise me you'll go over and see him."

I frowned. "Look, I don't know the guy. I'm not going to just walk in and say, 'Hi there. Want a visitor? My mother tells me you don't have any.' "

"Bryon," Mom said, "just go talk to him. He won't talk much to the nurses. He's been hurt pretty badly, poor thing."

"I'll go see him," Mark said. "Bryon'll come with me." I gave him a dirty look but he continued, "Who knows, maybe one of us'll end up in the hospital sometime with nobody to come and see us."

That was just the kind of junk my mother eats up, and Mark knew it. When we left I stopped him in the hall. "What's the idea of telling her you were going to go see that kid?"

Mark shrugged. "I am going to. Why not?"

This was typical of Mark as it wasn't typical of anyone else. "Well, *I'm* not going. I'm going down to the snack bar here and get a hamburger. Ain't you hungry?"

Mark shook his head. "Naw. I'll meet you down there later."

I took the elevator to the basement, where the snack bar was. I sat on a stool at the counter—after sitting at the bar at Charlie's I had got used to it—reading the menu over and over, thinking about all the food I'd get if I could. I loved to eat. I could put away more food than anyone I knew. I was five-ten at sixteen and still growing, but I went through my lanky period at fourteen and I had a good build, of which I was proud. I should have gone out for football, I guess, but it didn't much appeal to me. I liked neighborhood football games, but all that practice for the real thing seemed like a bore to me. Besides, I knew I couldn't put up with a coach telling me how to play. I never have been able to accept authority. I don't know why. I figure it was because of this cop—these two cops—who beat me up once when I was thirteen years old. I had gone to the movies with these other guys—I forget where Mark was—and we drank a fifth of cherry vodka in Coke and got drunk. That stuff tasted terrible, but I was a dumb kid and I drank it just to show I was as super-tuff as the rest of them. When the movie was over and I was staggering around alone on the streets in the dark, these two cops picked me up, drove me out to a hill on the other side of town, slapped me around, and left me there. I never forgot it. It didn't stop me from drinking, but it sure ruined any respect I ever had for cops. Yeah, sure there are good cops somewhere. I just never met any. Ever since then I've made it a point to mouth off to cops. That's probably why I never met any good ones.

So I was sitting there, reading the menu, when I heard a voice say, "Can I take your order?" and I looked up at this really cute chick. She gave me a big smile and said, "Hi, Bryon! What are you doing here?" I was racking my brain trying to think where I knew her from; she did seem kind of familiar, so to stall for time I said, "I'm here to see my old lady. She's just getting over an operation. I didn't know you worked here."

"I just started this week. But you knew I just got back, didn't you?"

"Oh, yeah," I said, about to go crazy trying to remember who she was. She had this groovy long dark hair with a sheen to it like charcoal—long hair with bangs just drives me crazy. There aren't too many chicks who can wear their hair like that and still look good. And she had these big, beautiful gray eyes, dark gray with black eyelashes and the eyelashes were really long, but they weren't fake. I am a long-practiced studier of girls, and I can tell about things like that.

"Gosh, you've grown," she said. "You must be a foot taller than when I saw you last."

"Yeah, well, it's been a long time," I said. If I had grown a foot it must have been. "How you been doing?"

"Oh, pretty good. I was lucky to get this job. Listen, give me your order. I'm not supposed to stand around talking to the customers."

"Sure. I'll have a hamburger and a Pepsi."

She took my order and left, and I was about to lose my mind. She couldn't have been someone I had dated —I date a lot of girls, but I was sure I could remember them if I saw them again. Anyway, she seemed friendly, and, after you break up with someone, she's not usually friendly. She seemed so familiar I could have sworn I'd seen her recently. Whoever she was, I wanted to see her again. I had already noted that she wasn't wearing a boy's ring around her neck, or any other sign that she was somebody's personal property —I'm in the habit of looking for things like that. I have gotten into some tight spots with boyfriends I didn't even know existed.

"Here's your hamburger."

I looked up at her and she gave me this really great

smile, a smile that lit up her face. I knew I'd seen that smile recently, and then it struck me who it was, and I was so surprised that I said it out loud: "Cathy!"

"Yeah," she said, almost as surprised as I was, "who'd you think it was?"

"The last time I saw you you had short hair and braces," I said, forgetting that a lady-killer should never remind a girl of her gawky age when she was skinny and ugly, or fat and ugly, or short-haired with a mouth full of metal.

"Yeah, that's the truth. Bryon, you mean you didn't recognize me?"

"No, I didn't." I couldn't see why that should shock her so much. Even back in the days of braces and short hair we weren't exactly best friends. I had never paid any attention to her. "I just recognized you because you look so much like M&M when you smile."

"I am going to take that as a compliment," she said, giving me my check. "M&M is a beautiful child and he has a beautiful smile to match his mind."

"He's a good kid," I agreed. She turned to go, and I said, "Wait!" without thinking, so when she turned, I stuttered a little. "I mean—I haven't seen you in a while— I'd like to talk to you sometime—" I really wasn't living up to my self-image. I never stutter.

"All right," she said, "we'll talk sometime."

I wanted to ask when, but didn't. You should never be too eager with chicks. It gives them ideas.

I waited around for Mark, but he didn't show up so I took the elevator back to Mom's floor. I went and looked in the room across from Mom's where that kid was supposed to be. I saw him all right, but no sign of Mark. That kid had been hurt bad. He had bandages around his head and across one eye, both arms in slings, and stitches in his lower lip.

"Hey, are you Bryon?" He looked at me out of his good eye. "Mark said to wait for him here; he'll be right back. He went across the street to the drugstore to buy me some comics."

I could tell from the way he talked that he came from a neighborhood like mine. This was likely—it was a charity hospital. "Come on in," he said. "Pull up a chair."

I did. I didn't know what to say to him.

"You're Mark's brother? You don't look much alike."

For a minute I really felt good about Mark's telling this guy we were brothers. Of course, we didn't look alike—Mark with his gold hair and strange gold eyes and slight, tense body, and me, big and husky with dark brown hair and eyes—so I said, "No, I guess we don't."

"I got a brother—older—we don't look much alike either."

I looked around for a No Smoking sign. "Can I smoke in here?"

"Sure, as long as you don't get caught. Would you mind giving me a few puffs?"

"O.K.," I said. I lit up a cigarette and put it between his lips. When I took it back he said, "Thanks. I haven't had a cigarette in a week. My name's Mike Chambers."

"Mine's Bryon Douglas. Man, you look awful. What happened?" I asked. I was beginning to be glad I had come in after all. It must have been rough, being kept in a hospital that gave you the creeps, with nobody to talk to.

"I got beat up," he said with a wry smile.

I couldn't believe it. I thought he'd been in a car wreck or something. "What does the other guy look like?" I said finally.

"It's a long story," Mike said. "You got time for a long story?"

"Sure," I said. I really do like listening to stuff that's happened to other people. I guess that's why I like to read.

"Well, if it seems like I'm never going to shut up, just tell me. You and Mark are the first people I've talked to in a long time. There ain't much to say to these nurses." I could see that. What can you say to nurses?

"Well," Mike began, "I always had this soft spot for chicks. I was always making like Sir Galahad, opening doors for them and complimenting even the homely ones, and I beat out a lot of guys better looking than me and they never could figure out why. But it wasn't just a line with me. I guess I'm a sucker—I've been taken a few times, like 'loaning' money to chicks who came on with a sob story—but I'll always believe the best about a girl until I'm proved wrong, which is my own hang up.

"That explains the way I acted that night the gang and me was hanging around the drugstore and this black chick came in to buy some cigarettes. Me, I just see a nice-looking chick with really beautiful eyes, all black and inky-soft. I guess I'm a little funny that way, because Negroes just don't get me all upset. I mean, I can see a black guy and a white chick together, and it sure don't bother me, while most white guys can't stand to see that. Like the gang—the minute she walks in, they get all tensed up because black anyone, chick or otherwise, just don't happen to come around much where I live. I guess she worked downtown and got off late and just stopped in on her way to the bus stop. I think she told me that later. I don't remember too good now.

"So she gets her cigarettes and starts for the door, when a couple of guys block her way. Now the gang I hang with is a pretty good bunch of guys—a lot of heart and only a couple of wise apples in the group— but see, nothin' much had been happenin' and they were bored so they start picking on the chick, calling her Black Beauty and some other choice things. They were really getting rude, and I was feeling sorry for the girl. She kept her eyes down and just said, 'Let me by, please,' real soft-like. The guys started pushing her around, not enough to hurt her but enough to scare her plenty. She just gripped her purse with both hands and tensed all over like she was trying to keep from running, which was pretty smart. Running is just an invitation to be chased, and if she got caught it wouldn't be in a lighted drugstore. The old guy who runs the drugstore had disappeared. He was scared silly of the gang. I don't know why. We never done anything to him.

"When one of the guys grabbed hold of her and really got crude, I got fed up. I went over and said, 'Let her go,' like I meant it. They all looked at me for a while, like they were trying to make up their minds whether or not to jump me. We don't usually go around beating each other up, but it has happened. They finally decided not to. My big brother, he's got a pretty big rep as a tough guy in our neighborhood. He's in jail now, that's why he don't come to see me. It was his rep and not mine that stopped them, because I ain't never been known as a tough guy.

"So they turned her loose and went back to reading comics, and I followed the girl outside. She was looking up and down the street kind of desperate-like, and I knew she'd missed her bus. I said, 'Hey, uh, girl, if you've missed your bus I can give you a ride home.'

"She just kept her eyes down. Finally she said something—but, brother, I'm not going to repeat it. I saw then and there she thought I had evil intentions. I don't blame her. Hell, if I'd had to take what she just did, I'd be sore and suspicious too.

"I said, 'Look, I don't want a pick-up or anything . . .' She gave me a funny look so I added quick, 'Not that you're not real cute or anything— I mean, you'll have to stay here another hour to catch the next bus and I'll be leaving and I don't know what those other guys might do.'

"She saw the logic in that, because it was getting dark. Not too many cops come around that area; it's kind of a deserted street. You know how cops are; there's a million over on the Ribbon, making sure the nice kids don't kill each other or run each other down, while we can cut each other's throats and they don't give a damn.

"Finally she said she'd let me drive her home. I had my old Ford parked in the drugstore parking lot. It was really my brother's car but he said I could drive it any time he got busted, which is often. He's a pretty good guy, but if you've got a rep for fighting, somebody's always trying to take you on. The last time that happened, my brother busted a bottle over the guy's head and got charged with assault with a dangerous weapon. He never used weapons before, but he had finally got fed up with the whole routine. It wasn't his first offense, so they sat on him kind of hard.

"Anyway, we get into my Ford, and I can see the poor kid is still scared—she sits hugging the door on her side like she's going to jump out any second. I got a couple of good looks at her; she was real slender, looked like she'd sort of sway in the wind, and her hair was down to her shoulders and it must have been straightened. She had on a yellow dress and yellow shoes and she had her straw purse sitting on her lap. She held onto it with one hand and the door handle with the other. She really was cute.

"I started talking to her about just everything. Would her old lady chew her out because she was late? My old lady did. Man, they never liked anything you did, did they? But still, sometimes you couldn't get along without them. Did she go to school? I did but, boy, it was really a hell of a place to spend all day. I wanted to drop out but the old lady said she'd kill me if I did.

"I kept talking because that's what I do with animals when they're hurt and scared, and pretty soon they get over being scared. I've got a hang up with animals, too.

"I could tell she was beginning to calm down a little, at least she let go of the door handle. I even got her to smile once, I forget what I'd been saying. And then I said, 'I'm sorry about what happened to you back there,' and suddenly she started to cry.

"Man, that got me so shook. Nothing gets me shook

like chicks crying." Mike stopped here, and I gave him another drag on my cigarette.

"That's funny," I said. "Chicks crying bore me. Go on, Mike, finish your story."

"Well, I didn't know what to say to her. I finally said, 'Hey, don't cry,' which never does any good. She kept on sobbing and now and then I'd catch a word or two. I got the idea that she was fed up with getting walked all over by white people. I could see that. I get fed up with getting walked over by the fuzz, teachers, my old man, and the upper-class kids at school. So I could see that. Bryon, do you know that my old man keeps my mother from coming to see me? Said I was a dumb kid for ever gettin' into this hospital. So anyway, this chick, she tells me about her problems, and she uses some pretty bad language but nothing I ain't heard before from white chicks. I finally pulled the car over to the curb and reached into my pocket. She sat up straight and got all uptight.

" 'What we stoppin' for?' she says, and I said, 'I thought I had a handkerchief, but I guess I don't.' I pulled back out on the street. She looked at me for a minute— I kept staring straight ahead but I could tell she was watching me—and she said, 'Thank you.'

"I drove her home. She lived way out on the north side where most of the blacks live; you know where. It is a pretty lousy neighborhood, about as bad as mine. As I pulled up in front of her house, I could see a bunch of kids hanging around on her porch and in her yard.

" 'Well, here you are,' I said, a little nervous. For somebody who'd been practicing in her mind how to get the door open, she was pretty slow about getting out. That's how it seemed to me, anyway. I think she was tired out from crying so much.

"Then there was all these black kids around my car. Some big guy opened the girl's door and pulled her out and said, 'What's the matter, Connie? What happened?' You could tell she'd been crying.

"Then they opened my door and dragged me out. It seemed like there was a hundred black faces staring at me. I guess it was really just about a dozen, but it seemed like a hundred. I just stood there, backed up against the car. Talk about scared—man, was I scared. To top it off, the chick had started crying again so she couldn't talk."

Mike paused here for a minute. He was staring off in the distance, and when he started talking again, it was slowly, like he was living the whole thing over again.

"The big guy came around to my side of the car. 'You hurt her, white boy?'

" 'No,' I said, and it didn't sound very loud so I cleared my throat and said, 'No, I didn't,' so loud that it sounded like I was shouting. It was real quiet; you could hear somebody's TV from down the street and a dog barking a block away and Connie's soft sobbing. I could even hear my heart pounding in my ears. Then the big guy said, really quiet-like, 'What if we don't believe you?' And I got so scared I was about to cry and said, 'Ask her, huh, just ask her!' The guy called across the car, 'Connie, what you want me to do with this white cat?'

"And real soft—her voice was so soft, just like her eyes—she said, 'Kill the white bastard.'

"And sure enough, they almost did."

There was a long silence. I think Mike had forgotten I was listening to him. Then he took a long breath. "That's how I got here. I must be a dumb kid like the old man says though, because I still don't hate Negroes, least of all Connie. I mean, I can almost see why she did it. Almost."

I shook my head. "That's a rotten thing to happen to anybody."

"It sure is." Mark's voice came from behind me. He had been standing in the doorway, I don't know how long. "Come on, Bryon," he said. "Here's your comics." He tossed a couple of monster comics on the bed.

As we got into the elevator Mark said, "I'm inclined to agree with his old man. That is one stupid guy."

"You mean it?" I said. I had been thinking about Mike's story, and I could see his point about not hating the people who beat him up.

"Yeah, I mean it. Man, if anybody ever hurt me like that I'd hate them for the rest of my life."

I didn't think much about that statement then. But later I would—I still do. I think about it and think about it until I think I'm going crazy.

I had been hunting all over town for a job. I really needed one, but they're not easy to come by if you're sixteen years old with no experience, no contacts. I finally hit upon a great idea: I would ask Charlie for a job. After all, we were friends. He thought I was a smart kid, and having been one himself, he appreciated them. Besides, I figured I would really dig working in a bar.

Charlie's answer was short and to the point: No.

I was sitting at the bar, smoking a cigarette and trying to fight down my anger and disappointment. I had been hitchhiking all over town for a week trying to get a job. "Well, why not?" I asked, as soon as I thought I could talk without blowing my stack.

"For one thing, you know how often the plain-clothes cops stop in. Do you think they'd let a minor work here? You're lucky you can just come in and sit down. Besides, Bryon, it gets rough in here late at night—Yeah, yeah, you're a rough kid, they all think that, but you'd better just take my word for it that you'd be better off someplace else."

"Like where? There ain't no jobs in this town. I been all over. Don't think this crummy joint ain't last on my list." I was mad.

Charlie didn't get upset though, he just grinned. "Bryon, you're an honest kid in most ways, but you lie like a dog. Take Mark—I wouldn't trust him around anything that wasn't nailed down, but I'd believe anything he said. I'd trust you with my wife, if I had one. I trust your actions, but I double-check most of your statements. You just think about it, and I think you'll come up with the reason why you haven't got a job before now. You just think about it."

I was too mad to think about it right then, but I promised myself I would later. I listened to everything Charlie said, because he was really smart. He had been a high school dropout, but he could subtract and add in his head quicker than a machine, and he had also read almost everything I had, which was quite a bit of reading. Besides, he'd had it even rougher than me when he was a kid, and now he had his own business and was respected by the cops and the rough guys equally.

"O.K.," I said. "If you trust me so much why don't you let me borrow your car Saturday night?" This was a shot in the dark. I really never expected Charlie to let me borrow his car. But I had been thinking about Cathy quite a bit. I had even called her a couple of times—from a pay phone since we couldn't pay phone bills any more—and there was a dance coming up on Saturday night that I wanted to go to. But I didn't have a car.

"O.K., Bryon, you can borrow my car Saturday. Just bring it back with as much gas in the tank as there was when you took it."

I almost fell off the barstool. "You mean it? Really?"

Charlie gave a short laugh. "Yeah, I mean it. But you get into a wreck, and I'll swear you stole it. And I don't care if you let Mark drive it either. Any kid who's been hot-wiring cars and driving them for as long as he has without an accident, I'll trust with my car."

I didn't know how to say thanks. I've always had trouble thanking people, I don't know why. But Charlie just gave me one of those twisted grins of his, like he knew what my problem was and couldn't care less.

"I'll come by and get it Saturday," I said finally. Charlie said O.K., and I could tell he meant, "Get outa here before I change my mind," so I got. I wanted to get to a phone and call Cathy. For all I knew she already had a date.

She didn't, thank God. But she did ask me where I was going to get a car.

"A friend's loaning me his," I said. "We may be double-dating with Mark. You remember Mark, don't you?"

"Who could forget him?" she said, and something

gave me a funny feeling, something about the way she said it. It gave me a funny feeling. "Is this a dressy dance or a dance dance or what?" she asked.

"Casual," I said. "Pants would be O.K. It's just at the school gym. Maybe we could go get a Coke afterward"—but I was thinking, Maybe we'll stop by the park afterward, which is just the way I think.

Mark was surprised when I told him who I had a date with.

"Cathy! M&M's sister? How old is she?"

"Fifteen or sixteen, I guess. You want to double-date? Charlie's loaning me his car." I said this casually, like Charlie loaned me his car every day of the week, but Mark wasn't fooled. He never was, by me. "No kiddin'? How'd you manage that?"

I just shrugged. The truth was, I still didn't know how I had managed that.

"Well," Mark said, "I can't double with you. I already told some guys I'd go stag with them. I thought you would, too. Shoot, you haven't taken out a girl since you broke up with Angela Shepard."

"Yeah, well, if you'd gone with Angela for a while you'd be sour on girls, too. Man, I hate that chick."

"Too bad she can look so good and be so rotten," Mark said sympathetically. He never once said "I told you so." He had tried to tell me a long time ago that Angela was no good, but I hadn't paid any attention. It always seemed like Mark knew the score before I did—but it didn't do me any good. I wouldn't listen to him. I had to find out things for myself.

"Who all you going with?" I asked. We were in the kitchen doing dishes. Mark didn't particularly care for washing dishes, but I just couldn't stand a bunch of dirty dishes piled up in the sink.

"Terry Jones, Williamson, and Curtis."

"Then I'm glad I'm not going with you. I can't stand that Curtis kid."

"Come on, Bryon," Mark said easily. "He's a real nice guy. What'd he ever do to you?"

"He thinks he's so good-looking. That whole family's conceited."

Mark was trying to hide a grin. He was laughing at me. "You know good and well he's not conceited. He can't help it if he's good-looking; to tell the truth, I don't think he knows he is. You're jealous, Bryon, because Angela dumped you to make a play for Curtis, and he was smart enough to leave her alone."

"You can think what you want," I said, but I was almost laughing myself. Mark knew me pretty well. Sometimes that could be irritating, but most of the time it was funny.

I thought Saturday would never come, but it finally did. I hadn't looked forward to a date in a long time. With Angela, after a while our dates either ended in a make-out session or a fight. Both got boring.

I was kind of bothered about what to wear. It was a casual dance, so about anything would be all right, but I was bugged anyway.

I was in the bathroom shaving when Mark popped in. He had been down to Charlie's to pick up the car for me.

"Hey, hey, hey!" He leaned in the doorway, grinning at me. "Take it all off."

"You're just jealous 'cause you only have to shave once every two weeks."

Mark refused to be bugged. "You think I *want* to scrape my face every day? Thanks, but no thanks."

I glanced at him just to check out what he was wearing. Mark never paid any attention to how he dressed —I wouldn't be surprised if someday he completely forgot he was supposed to have something on and walked out into the street naked—but somehow he was always dressed right for the occasion. He had on a gold sweat shirt and wheat-colored jeans and tennis shoes.

"What are you wearin'?" Mark asked. His voice sounded funny.

I shrugged. "I don't know yet."

Mark turned to leave. "I gotta go now. I'm supposed to meet Terry over at his house. I left the keys in Charlie's car." As he was leaving he called over his shoulder, "I found this shirt out in the street, and it's lying on the bed if you want to see it." I heard the door slam and the sound of his light running steps on the porch.

I finished washing off my face and went into our room. Mark and I shared a bedroom which was pretty small—we have a small house—and it seemed even smaller with our twin beds. One was against each wall and that left only a path about three-feet wide to the closet. I wanted to get a look at this shirt Mark had "found out in the street."

It was real funny—that shirt happened to be just my size and dark blue, which happens to be a good color for me. For a minute I wondered whether he had bought it or stolen it—they were the same thing to Mark—but I decided to forget about it. After all, it's the thought that counts. Mark's clothes were almost all things I had outgrown. I grinned as I buttoned up the shirt. If Mark really cared about clothes he would steal some, but he didn't. But he knew me well enough to know what I would be thinking about.

If you have two friends in your lifetime, you're lucky. If you have one *good* friend, you're more than lucky.

Charlie's car wasn't anything you'd stop and stare at, but it was decent-looking. I felt funny when I stopped in front of Cathy's house. I had always thought of it as M&M's house, and now I thought of it as Cathy's house. I had never paid any attention to M&M's parents and I was about to go crazy trying to remember if

I had ever said anything rude or had got smart with them, but I couldn't remember. If I had, I hoped they wouldn't remember.

Cathy's father opened the door. He said, "Hi, Bryon" friendly enough—I guess as friendly as any father ever greets the kid who's taking out his daughter —so I figured I was safe. M&M was lying on his stomach on the floor reading a book with a little sister sitting on his back pulling his hair. I stepped over him. When M&M was reading you could blow up the house around him and he'd never notice. I'm that way myself.

Cathy's mother came from the kitchen wiping her hands on her apron, and in the kitchen some more little kids were fighting over who was going to rinse and who was going to dry.

"Cathy will be ready in a minute," Mrs. Carlson said. "Please sit down, Bryon. We haven't seen you in a while."

"I've been out looking for a job," I said, sitting down on a rubber duck. "Mark and I run into M&M every now and then."

"How can you tell him and Cathy apart?" Mr. Carlson said dryly. "I can't any more."

"Now, Jim. . ." Mrs. Carlson began nervously. "We agreed not to say any more about M&M's hair."

Even his own family called him M&M. I tried to remember for a second what his real name was, but I couldn't think of it. In the silence Cathy screeched, "You give me that brush, you brat!" I stifled a laugh.

"How have you been doing in school, Bryon?" Mrs. Carlson asked. She was pretending she hadn't heard Cathy.

This was the usual routine questioning you go through when you have to talk to your date's parents, but I didn't mind. At Angela's house her mother and her stepfather were always fighting and screaming and throwing things, and sometimes her brothers Tim and Curly would get in on it, and I'd sort of duck flying objects until Angela came out of her room, cussing and throwing things along with the rest of them. So you can see why sitting in the Carlson's front room answering questions wasn't really bothering me.

"I'm doing pretty well in school," I answered. "Mostly A's and B's." I decided I wouldn't say anything about flunking chemistry. The teacher and I had a personality conflict—and when I want to cause a teacher trouble, you'd better believe I can do it.

"M&M is flunking math and gym," Mr. Carlson said in the same tone he had used when talking about M&M's hair. "How anyone can flunk gym is beyond me."

I could tell that M&M was listening to the conversation but was staring at his book, pretending he wasn't. I understood what he was doing. I have stared at a book pretending I couldn't hear what was going on around me, too. If people think you can't hear them, they talk as if you couldn't. You can hear some pretty neat stuff that way.

"It's not as if M&M was an invalid," Mr. Carlson was saying when Cathy came out of her room.

"I'm ready," she said. She had on a yellow pants outfit that looked real cute on her.

I got up. "O.K., let's go." On the way out she gave M&M a friendly kick.

When we were in the car she said, "I wish Daddy would leave M&M alone. He's so sensitive, it hurts him for Dad to tease him about his hair or bawl him out for his grades. It seems to me they should be glad about his other grades—his English teacher says M&M has the most brilliant mind she's come across in five years of teaching—and be glad he's never gotten into any kind of trouble, instead of picking at him because of his hair." She sighed. "I guess since M&M and I are the oldest, we're the closest. I guess you know about that though. I forgot you have a brother too."

"Yeah, I know about that," I said. Of course, I never heard Mom gripe about anything Mark did—he could get away with things I wouldn't dare try. I never resented Mark for this. I took it as a matter of fact that Mark was different from other people and was therefore treated differently.

Cathy sighed, "Well, I'm not going to worry about it now. I want to have a good time tonight." She gave me a quick, shy smile. She was sitting close enough for me to put my arm around her, which I did. I was intending to have a good time too.

We could hear the music even before we got there. The band was supposed to be a good one—it was loud enough, which with a dance is at least half the way to being good. I was really proud of having such a cute date, and I was hoping Angela would be there. I wanted to show her up. I'd gone with Angela for months, longer than I'd ever gone with anyone. I wanted to show her that I had no intentions of going back to her. She had been telling everybody that I would. This was after she had made her big play for this Curtis kid and he had acted like he didn't know she was alive. Then she decided she wanted me back. You can imagine how that grabbed me.

The dance was going pretty good when we got there. I liked to arrive a little late, when things were swinging. I saw a bunch of people I knew. Cathy knew a lot of people, too, but not very well. She hadn't dated before she left for school, and I don't think anyone remembered her. She had been a shy, plain kid. Everybody was staring at us, wondering who she was. I was really feeling great. I liked being the center of attention. Cathy winked at me. She dug it, too.

I really liked her. I liked her a lot.

"Hey, Bryon!" It was Mark. I could tell even before I spotted him across the room, waving at us.

"Come on," I said. "Let's go see Mark."

We weaved in and out of the crowd, sometimes stopping to talk. I wasn't too happy when I saw that Mark and Curtis were standing together. Having had one girl ditch me to try for him, I wasn't thrilled with the possibility that it might happen again.

"Hi, Cathy," Mark greeted her. He had been drinking, but I doubt that anyone but me could tell. "I haven't seen you in a long time."

"I haven't been here to see," Cathy answered sensibly.

"I don't think you know Ponyboy Curtis—this is Cathy Carlson."

"Hi," Curtis said. He didn't look too happy. I think he had heard I wasn't crazy about him. He was a little guy, about the same size as Mark only with a better build. I think he thought I was going to pick a fight with him. I didn't want to. I guess he couldn't help what Angela Shepard did, and besides, I'd heard he was a pretty good fighter even though he didn't have the rep of a tough guy.

I watched Cathy. She didn't seem interested in him. The first time Angela saw him her eyes lit up like a tiger's. So I relaxed. "Where'd you get the booze?" I asked Mark, when Cathy couldn't hear.

He grinned. "Out in the car—Terry's car. He's got six six-packs, and only the four of us to drink them. Go out and help yourself. Terry won't mind, he's already passed out in the front seat."

Terry had always been a drinker. I decided I'd go out later and have a couple of cans. Maybe I'd get a couple for Cathy. I hoped she wasn't a very heavy drinker—Angela had got pretty expensive with her constant boozing.

Cathy and I watched Mark and Curtis as they started toward a group of girls. "Mark is a good kid," I said.

"I'd forgotten how beautiful he is," Cathy said. "I know girls who would give their eye teeth for hair that color."

I stopped breathing for a second. Cathy was looking at Mark, and I suddenly felt like I'd swallowed a spoonful of red pepper. I felt cold and hot and sick and mad all at once. I only felt it for a second, only for a second and then it was gone—but sometimes now I wonder how it would be to feel like that all your life. You know what the crummiest feeling you can have is? To hate the person you love best in the world.

"Hi, Bryon." The voice was familiar and I turned around. It was Angela. I just looked at her. She was smiling with that sassy smirk, and I wondered why on earth I'd ever given a damn about her. She was beautiful, little and dark, and, even when suddenly all the girls had long straight hair, hers hung to the middle of her waist in ringlets and curls. It was blue-black and shiny. Maybe all that heavy mass wouldn't look good on just anyone, but Angela had the kind of face that would probably be strikingly beautiful even if she shaved her head. But since I knew her so well, I could ignore the way she looked. "Hi, Angel," I said carelessly. "You here with Curtis?"

I meant to rub it in; I think he was the first guy she ever went after and didn't get. Her face contorted for a second, and she called me a few names and flounced off. She wasn't famous for an even temper.

"Who was that?" Cathy asked. I wondered if she was jealous. I hoped so anyway. "This chick I used to go with," I answered. Cathy glanced indifferently after Angela. "Certainly uses nice language," she remarked. "A real lady."

It hit me that Cathy wasn't jealous of Angela at all —not for her beauty or for having gone with me. She was the first girl I'd dated who wasn't scared some other chick would show her up. I didn't know what to make of it.

In the end, I decided it showed that Cathy had more sense than most girls. I wasn't worried about her liking Mark any more. I can tell when a girl is interested in a guy—like the minute I saw Angela looking at Curtis, I knew—and I could tell Cathy liked Mark just as a friend, as the brother of the guy she was interested in. Cathy liked me. I could tell that already.

She was a good dancer. We danced almost every dance. We were having so much fun I forgot all about going out to Terry's car for some beer. They had a cop there at the dance—they always did—but he was ignoring the kids who were staggering around obviously drunk. He was there just to prevent people from killing each other.

Apparently he wasn't even doing that much, because, suddenly above the music, we heard a scream from the back parking lot. Immediately everyone started running out there to see what was happening. I didn't. I hate people who stand around at an accident and pry and push and peer. I won't even stop to watch a fight if I don't know either guy who's fighting.

"Let's don't go," I said.

Cathy nodded. "O.K."

Just then Curtis pushed his way through the crowd. He had been one of the fighters, because his face was bruised and his lip was cut. "Bryon!" he yelled when he saw me. "Bryon, come quick! Mark's hurt!"

I went cold. Mark was hurt. I shoved my way through the crowd— I'm a pretty good size and when I shove I get through. There was a circle of people on the parking lot. I shoved through them too. Mark was lying on the ground, unconscious. One side of his face was covered with blood. I knelt beside him.

"Mark?" I said, but he didn't move. He was out cold. I took the end of my shirttail and wiped some of the blood off his face. He was bleeding from a bad gash on the side of his head, but that was the only injury I could see.

Curtis knelt down on the other side of Mark. "Is he all right?"

I shook my head. "Did anyone call an ambulance?"

He nodded. "I think the cop radioed for one."

I remembered the cop. I looked around for him; he had some kid in handcuffs a few feet away and was informing him of his rights.

"Is that the guy who did this?" I asked, and the kid in handcuffs looked over at me. He had heard me.

"Yeah," Curtis said.

I looked straight at that kid and said, "Buddy boy, you are dead. You had just better make up your mind to that. When I get through with you, you are going to be dead." I meant it. I was mad. The kid just looked away, like he was indifferent. But he was shook, I could tell.

"He meant to get *me*," Curtis said. "If that makes any difference."

"If he'd gotten you, he'd be doing me a favor," I said. I didn't really mean it, but I was upset. Curtis gave me a wry grin, like he understood. For the first time I felt I could like the guy. "What happened?"

Curtis shook his head. "I don't know. Mark and me were out here sitting on the car, not doing a thing, when this guy shows up and starts in on me. I don't know why, I ain't never seen the guy before. Finally he takes a swing at me, so I have to swing back, and pretty soon we're going at it. Then this character picks up a beer bottle Mark had thrown over there in the

58

grass and comes at me with it. About that time Mark steps in between us and says, 'Hey, come on, man, fight fair.' The kid just looks at him and, for no reason, cracks him across the side of the head with it. Then the cop shows up. Right in the nick of time," he added sarcastically.

When I took another look at the kid in handcuffs, Angela was talking to him. I got the picture. She had got this guy to pick a fight with Curtis—she was mad at him for ignoring her. I changed my mind. It would be her I'd get even with, not that poor dope she had used.

"Do you know Angela Shepard?" I asked Curtis. He shook his head. "No. I know her brothers pretty well, but I've never been around her much."

He was telling the truth. Curtis really didn't know that Angela had been after him. He probably thought I had it in for him for no reason at all.

"What does Angela have to do with this?" he asked.

"I'll tell you later."

Mark moved a little and groaned.

"Mark," I said softly, "listen! Don't move, just lie still. We're going to get you to the hospital."

He opened his eyes. The pupils were so large that I could see only a faint ring of gold around them. I picked up one of his hands. It was ice-cold. He was staring straight ahead and didn't seem to hear or see me. I was worried. "What's wrong with him?"

"Shock," Curtis said. He took off his jacket and put

it over Mark. I didn't have one, or I would have too. Mark was still bleeding. I couldn't stop it. It seemed that the ambulance would never get there.

When it finally did, I rode in the back with Mark. At last he seemed to recognize me. "Bryon?" he said, then he sort of laughed and groaned at the same time. "Man, am I hurtin'."

"Keep quiet," I said. I was almost crying, something I hadn't done in years. I was pretty worried.

"Listen, Bryon," Mark went on in a weak voice, "when we get there, at the hospital, stay with me, O.K.?"

"I'm not taking this trip for the ride," I said.

He closed his eyes. "O.K., just stay with me."

At the hospital they put ten stitches in his head. The X ray didn't show a fracture or anything, so they said we could go home. I didn't know how in the world we were going to get home—I'd left Charlie's car at the dance, and come to think of it, I'd left Cathy there too. I was a little worried about that, but mostly I was worried about getting Mark home.

He was sitting up, but he was still groggy and the painkiller shots he'd been given made him sleepy and high. He was probably still feeling all that beer he'd drunk at the dance too. He was in bad shape.

I thought about calling a taxi, but as it was I didn't know how I was going to pay for the ambulance. I was rescued unexpectedly by Cathy and Curtis. Any other time I would have been hacked off by the two of them showing up together, but right then I was glad to see them.

"I brought your car," Curtis said. "I figured you wouldn't have a way to get home. Is Mark going home?"

"Yeah, they said for him to stay in bed for a couple of days and to come back in a couple of weeks or so to get the stitches out. Help me get him in the car."

"Hey, hey, hey, Ponyboy!" Mark greeted him. "What are you doin' here?" Curtis and I pulled him to his feet and we each slung an arm across our shoulders.

"Come on, buddy boy," I said. "Time to go home."

Mark tried to walk, but almost fell, and we half-dragged, half-carried him out to the car. We got him stretched out in the back seat and climbed in.

"Hey," I said suddenly, "how'd you start the car without any keys?"

Cathy turned to him too. "Yeah, how did you?"

He was getting red. "I hot-wired it," he said finally. "Mark showed me how to weeks ago."

I almost laughed. That was just like Mark. "Don't make that a habit," I said.

Curtis shook his head. "I never done it before." I finally understood that Mark was right about that Curtis kid—he wasn't stuck up, he was shy.

I dropped him off near his house. I hated to just take Cathy home, but there wasn't much else I could do. Mark was singing to himself in the back seat. He had a good voice, but he had picked a lulu of a song. Cathy pretended not to hear it.

I walked her to the door. "I'm really sorry about the way things turned out," I said.

She grinned. "So am I—but thank goodness Mark isn't hurt any worse than he is. I had a good time, I really did—especially driving to the hospital with Ponyboy."

I looked at her quickly. She was teasing me to make me mad.

"Not really," she continued. "He's not my type—too quiet."

"That's one thing I'm not," I said. I wanted to kiss her, but I never know, some girls will kiss on a first date, some won't. I decided to play it safe and not kiss her. Besides, the porch light was on and there were four or five little faces peering out from behind the front-room curtains.

"I'll call you," I said finally.

By the time I got Mark home the shots had worn off. Sweat was running down his face and I think tears were too. But he gave me his typical grin. "I ain't feelin' so good, Bryon" was the most he'd say. I helped him into the house and got him to bed.

"You going to be able to sleep?" I asked when I turned out the lights.

"I don't think so. Man, have I got a headache. You tired, Bryon?"

"Nope," I said. I was sitting on the bed, leaning back against the wall, smoking a cigarette. The light of the moon was coming in the window and I could see Mark clearly. He had one arm folded under his head and was staring up at the moon.

"Well, if you ain't goin' to sleep, and I ain't, why don't we talk for a while?"

"That's fine by me," I said.

"Y'know, when I first came around tonight, after that kid cracked me, I was scared stiff. I thought I was dyin', I was so scared. I really felt weird. But after I got to thinkin' you were there with me, I calmed down. Bryon, you're the only family I got, you know that? I mean, your mom's been great to me and everything, but I don't feel like she's really *my* old lady. But I feel like you're my brother. A real one."

Mark had never had a real family. I remember once when we were very young I had remarked that he didn't look much like his father. And he had said, "He ain't my real father. My real father was a cowboy, here for the rodeo. The old lady said he had gold hair and gold eyes just like mine and that he won all kinds of prizes at the rodeo."

At the time I just thought, Gee, that's great, his real father is a cowboy. When I got older I realized what that meant, that Mark was illegitimate. It had never

63

seemed to bother him. But then, nothing did. Maybe it had, and I just never knew it.

"I must still be high." Mark's voice broke the stillness. "I don't know why I'm blabbering on like this."

"I always think of you as my brother," I said. I saw Mark's face in the moonlight. He was smiling.

Mark wasn't feeling any better the next day. When I asked him if his head still hurt he said, "Yeah." That was typical of Mark, who never admitted to being in real pain. I called the doctor from a pay phone, and all he said was that Mark would be in pain for a couple of days and that I should keep him quiet and give him aspirin. He was a big help.

I took back Charlie's car and told him what had happened. He didn't seem too interested, but he was having his own troubles. He'd got his draft notice.

I got home as soon as I could. I hated to leave Mark there all by himself. I didn't know which was bothering him most—the pain in his head or having to stay in bed. He probably would have tried to get up in spite of the doctor's orders, but he couldn't even sit up without getting dizzy. We didn't have the TV any more and Mark couldn't read too well. He couldn't even seem to get interested in poker.

"Why don't you read me a book?" he suggested,

after I had racked my brains trying to think of something to do.

"Read you a book?"

"Yeah. Don't you remember when we were little? You used to read me books all the time."

Mark was too lazy or too uninterested to read himself; he had never bothered to learn how to read very well in the first place. This probably accounted for his poor grades at school, because he was every bit as smart as I was.

I had read cowboy books to him when we were little —we were both going to be cowboys—books like *Lone Cowboy* by Will James. We'd climb the tree in the back yard and I'd read aloud, and then we'd play cowboys. "Do you remember? . . ." Mark said.

Somehow we spent the whole afternoon talking about when we were little kids. We had played a kid's version of gang fighting called "Civil War," and then later we had got in on the real thing. We fought with chains and we fought barefisted and we fought Socs and we fought other grease gangs. It was a normal childhood. I used to be able to get all uptight about a fight, look forward to it. Nowadays it was getting a little boring.

Mark had a great memory—better than mine, which is pretty good—and he brought up little goofy things we had done when we were young that I'd forgotten about. Like the time we climbed over the back fence at a drive-in movie and got caught. The drive-in manager put us in the back of a pickup truck to take us to the police station, but we jumped out while he was doing thirty miles an hour. Somehow neither of us was killed. We always wondered what that guy thought when he got to the police station and there was nobody in his truck.

We'd get up on the roof of a two-story shopping center and shoot water pistols at the people passing below, then have a good time running from the cop Mark had so thoughtfully drenched. We always had a car in those days, thanks to Mark's hot-wiring abilities. We'd take something that looked fast and go to the expressway and drag. It was sheer luck that when Mark was finally caught doing this, he was alone. I could have been booked too.

And mixed up between these episodes were poker games, sometimes drunken ones lasting all night, and pool games—I was a pool hustler at a very early age. And dates and parties and beer blasts on the dry riverbed. We were always with a bunch of guys. Sometimes it was the same bunch for a year or two, then people would drift away—usually if anyone got a steady girl it cut down on a lot of goofing around with the guys —and different people would drift in. But Mark was always the hub of this circle of people, and I was always with Mark.

"We've had some good times, huh, Bryon?" Mark

broke the silence. I guess we both had been reminiscing.

"Yeah," I said. I was sitting in my favorite position on the bed, leaning against the wall with my knees up, resting an elbow on my knee, and dangling a cigarette.

"Do you ever get the feeling that the whole thing is changin'? Like somethin' is coming to an end because somethin' else is beginning?"

"Yeah, I know exactly what you mean. Like now I couldn't care less about Angela, and I can remember when she seemed like the most important thing on earth."

"That's it!" Mark said excitedly, forgetting about his head and starting to sit up. He remembered suddenly, because he yelped and lay back down with a rueful grin. "Like we got into those gang fights—it was so important, it was the whole world if we won or lost—and the buddies we had then. We were like brothers, not just you and me, but all of us together. We woulda died for each other then. And now everybody's kinda slipped away, and then we woulda died for each other. Really, man, remember? It was great, we were like a bunch of people makin' up one big person, like we totaled up to somethin' when we were together."

"Now we total up to something by ourselves just as easy," I said. I understood exactly what he was talking about. Mark had the habit of thinking the way I did; the difference was that he said it and I usually didn't.

"Yeah, but still, don't you kinda miss that one-for-all, all-for-one routine? It's kinda sad, really, when you get to where you don't need a gang—I mean, like you did before."

"It's kind of a good thing too," I said, "when you know your own personality so you don't need the one the gang makes for you."

"Yeah," Mark sighed, "but there's a difference. I wonder what the difference is?"

"The difference is," I said evenly, "that was then, and this is now."

Mark flashed me that lion-like grin. "Bryon, you are brilliant."

We didn't say much the rest of the afternoon. We were thinking.

Mark missed one day of school. He still wasn't feeling real great by Monday, but I decided I could go anyway. He wasn't sick enough for me to stay home with him.

The fight had made Mark something of a hero, and the whole story was going around school in various versions, all different. Some of them were pretty funny. Everyone was mad at Angela, sympathized with Curtis, who had been in a lot of trouble before and was a kind of folk-hero, and made a big deal out of Mark's stepping in to keep the fight fair. When people asked me what happened, I told them, but I could see that they were going to believe what they wanted to believe and hearing the truth wasn't going to change their minds. People are generally like that.

I was in a funny mood Monday. That talk I had had with Mark really got to me. I felt like I was standing apart from all the rest of the kids and just watching. It was like I could see through them—see what they were thinking and why they did things—and it was really weird.

I went to a big high school. It graduated about seven hundred kids, and the senior class was the smallest class, so you can see how big it really was. Its district included a real crummy part of town—ours—and a pretty ritzy part of town. This can make for problems. It used to anyway, with the Socs beating up the greasers, but in these days, with all that love, peace, and groove stuff, the fights had slacked off. Besides, it was hard now to tell a Soc from a greaser. Now the greasers wore their hair down on their foreheads instead of combed back—this went for Mark and me too —and the Socs were trying to look poor. They wore old jeans and shirts with the shirttails out, just like the greasers always had because they couldn't afford anything else. I'll tell you one thing though: what with fringed leather vests and Levi's with classy-store labels in them, those kids were spending as much money to look poor as they used to to look rich. It was crazy.

There was another crazy thing I noticed for the first

time that Monday. I'm a smart kid, so I was put in classes with other smart kids. Most of these guys were what we used to call Socs. They were always friendly toward me, and I'd gone to quite a few parties at their houses and dated some of their chicks. All this time I had thought, Well, they like me. I'm big, friendly, wise-guy Bryon, so they like me. Now I saw it clearly. They didn't like me. The truth is they were probably scared of me. But I was a "poor white," and they were "liberals," so I got invited to the parties so everyone could see what hip, hip people they were. I had always wondered why at those parties people were always trying to get me to talk about politics and junk I'd never heard of. I don't keep up on those things. When I read, I like stuff like Hemingway—newspapers bore me. I lead with my left, and that's about as much as I know about Left, Right, and so on. I have a vague notion that the Left is Hippie and the Right is Hick, but I really don't know much else.

Now I knew. That Monday I could see through people and I knew what was going on. I figured if I'd been a black I'd have been twice as popular, but integration in our school wasn't really swinging yet, and there weren't very many Negroes there. These guys would probably have offered me their sisters' hands in marriage if I'd been black. I knew some Negroes, some really cool fighters out in Brumley. I'd have to remember to take a couple along to the next party with me.

Then they could talk about the Black Revolution and the Panthers—which they knew as much about as I did Right and Left.

I walked around the whole day laughing to myself. It was just that day—the next day I wondered what had hit me to make me act like that; and when I saw these Soc guys, they were just guys, friends of mine, and of course they asked me to their homes because we were friends—we were in the same English class and we got along. They were sincerely trying to change the world for the better, that was why they talked politics. They wore those clothes because that was their bag. That's what I thought the next day.

But not Monday. That Monday I knew.

Mark got better and went back to school. He went to school for lack of something better to do, because he sure didn't dig it the way I did. We didn't usually see each other much at school; we were never in the same classes. We walked to school together and usually got a ride home together with someone, but lots of times we didn't see each other until we got home.

So when Mark didn't show up for a while one afternoon the following week, I wasn't worried. He could have been any number of places. I didn't happen to guess the right one. He was at the police station.

I didn't know about it until Terry Jones came by. Terry was short, round, and a real nut.

"Bryon!" he yelled as he came running through the front door. "Hey, Bryon, did you hear what happened to Mark?"

I was making a peanut-butter-and-honey sandwich. I didn't get shook because something is always happening to Mark.

"What? And calm down, for Pete's sake. I ain't deaf."

"O.K.," Terry said carelessly. He sat down in a chair and looked around. "Having dinner?"

"Cut it, man. What happened to Mark?"

"Not much. He just got caught driving the principal's car."

I gagged. "What?" I said when I could talk. "He got caught doing what?"

"The principal had to leave school early today for some reason. He gets to his parking place, and no car. And then guess who shows up with it? Your friend and mine, Mark."

"You gotta be kiddin'," I begged. "Man, Terry, tell me you're kiddin'. Mark's on probation now for car stealing."

"That's the reason he was driving it," Terry said. "Can I have a sandwich?"

"Here," I shoved the peanut butter, honey, and bread at him. "Fix it yourself. Only first, if you don't want your head busted, tell me what's going on."

"I happened to be standing around when the aforementioned incident occurred." It figured. Terry was usually standing around. "And I hear Mark explain to the principal while the cops are bein' called that he has to go down to see his probation officer once a week and tell him how he ain't gonna steal no more cars. The deal is, he don't have no way to get downtown— there ain't no buses at that time, he don't have a car, and there ain't enough time to walk since he's on his lunch hour. So he borrows the principal's car, drives down to see the probation officer, and drives back. He's been doing this since school started, and if the principal didn't have to leave early today, he'd be doin' it yet."

"I don't believe it," I said slowly. "He's gonna be in jail for the rest of his life."

"I doubt it," Terry said, starting in on his second sandwich. "The principal was laughing by the time Mark got through talking to him."

I breathed a sigh of relief. Mark would come through. Even this. As if to prove this to me, Mark came strolling in. "Guess where I been? Got anything else to eat?"

"Let me see," I said. "Ah, yes. I see it in a vision— you were at the police station explaining how you had to borrow the principal's car because you had to see your probation officer."

"Terry told you, huh? Well, it's all straightened out now. The probation officer drives down to pick me up from now on. It was just one of those failures to communicate."

Mark sat down across the table from me, eating an apple. He was trying to look ashamed of himself, but it just wasn't coming off. I was trying to look disgusted with him, but that wasn't working either.

"I'm sorry," he said finally.

"No you ain't," I said. We were quiet for a while. Terry got up and left—he must have thought me and Mark were going to have a fight.

"Listen, man," Mark began, but I cut him off.

"Shut up, O.K.? As long as they ain't doin' nothin' to you, it's O.K. I guess you can get away with anything."

Mark leaned back in his chair. The sun came through the small kitchen window and glinted on his eyes, turning them a bright yellow. "I guess so," Mark said. He smiled, like an innocent lion.

5

The first time Mom knew anything about Mark being hurt was when we visited her in the hospital and she saw the stitches in his head. They were real noticeable against his gold hair. She just said, "How did that happen?" And Mark answered, "Fight," and the subject was dropped. That was a good thing about Mom— she'd cry over a dog with a piece of glass in his paw but remained unhysterical when we came home clobbered. About fights, she'd say, "Don't fight at school, you'll get expelled." About drinking, "I'd rather you didn't," so around her we didn't. She didn't know about some of the rest of the stuff we did—the pool games, the poker, the gang fights, the dry river-bed parties—but in that respect she wasn't any different from any other mother. Parents never know what all their kids do. Not in the old days, not now, not tomorrow. It's a law.

We stopped in to see that kid Mike, the one who'd been beaten up so bad. He looked worse than he had before; he said his old man had been in and chewed him out. The doctor had promised him that his father wouldn't be allowed to come to see him any more, but he was still shook.

He looked like a nervous wreck as well as a physical one. "I wish I was dead—or somebody else," he said. You just don't say things like that. I didn't stay long; things like that depress me. Mark stayed on to see if he could cheer up Mike. I wanted to go to the snack bar and see Cathy anyway.

She looked as cute as ever. She said, "Hi, Bryon," not too eager but friendly enough. I had called her a few times in the last couple of weeks and walked to her house to see her, but we hadn't been out. I didn't have a car and Charlie was still so mad about getting his draft notice that I didn't have the nerve to ask him for his car again. As a matter of fact, he was in such a rotten mood that I stayed away from his place altogether. We were friends, and I didn't think he'd ever take his temper out on me, but with big guys, it's safer to be careful.

"I'm on my break now," Cathy said, looking at the clock. This was an invitation for me to buy her a soda, so I said obligingly, "Want a Coke?"

"I knew you'd say that," Cathy said. She came around to my side of the counter and sat down next to me. I never could get over her honesty. Girls are usually careful not to let you know what they're thinking. Cathy hadn't dated before, maybe that was why she was so open. She didn't tell me that about not dating, of course. I found out from M&M. I found out a lot of things from M&M. I have never known anyone so unsuspicious as that little kid. He'd trust Jack the Ripper. He was a believer.

I kept comparing Cathy to Angela, I guess because out of all the girls I've dated—I started at thirteen—they were the two I liked best. I don't know if "like" is the right word for how I felt about Angela. I had been wrapped up in her, I had to see her every day, I had to talk to her ten times a day on the phone; but now, looking back on it, I don't remember ever liking her. Cathy was smart, but Angela knew more. That was strange. They both had guts—I can't stand chicken girls—but in different ways. Cathy wasn't afraid to say what she thought; Angela wasn't afraid to do what she wanted. Angela wasn't afraid of any boy on earth; Cathy wasn't afraid of any other girl. They were both gutsy in different ways.

My main problem with Cathy was that she liked me —and I wanted her to be crazy about me. I'm like that. I have a very bad ego hang up.

"Guess who called me?" Cathy said. "Ponyboy Curtis. He wanted to go out Friday night."

"No kiddin'," I said, while thinking, I'll murder that guy. "What'd you tell him?"

"I said I was busy. Am I?"

I was stunned again but didn't show it. "You are. I'll pick you up at seven." I had no idea what I was going to pick her up in, or where we'd go after I did pick her up, but I figured I could work that out later.

"We're goin' hustlin'," I told Mark as we walked home, trying to hitch a ride. This time no friendly hippie showed up to give us a lift.

"O.K."

"Tonight—for money."

"You'll need some money to get started with," Mark said, lighting a cigarette.

"I'll get it."

We ran into M&M at the drugstore, and as usual he was chomping on that crazy candy. At least he wasn't staring into the bag like it contained the eighth wonder of the world.

"I need some money," I said, deciding not to beat around the bush. "You got any?"

He looked at me with those serious, war-orphan eyes. "I got five dollars," he said. "I raked some lawns to get it."

I used to think he and Cathy looked an awful lot alike, but not any more. Sure, they both had those big charcoal eyes and matching hair, but Cathy laughed more, her expression usually twinkled with humor. M&M rarely smiled, and he always looked puzzled, serious, and trusting.

"That's a good deal. Can you loan it to me? Just for tonight. I'll pay you back tomorrow."

He pulled out his billfold and took all the money

out of it. "Be sure not to forget to give it back tomorrow. I need it. O.K.?"

"Kid, have I ever given you a dirty deal?" I said, winking at Mark.

"No," M&M said, and went back to his magazine. I never could figure that kid out. I liked him though, partly because he was Cathy's brother, partly because he was a good kid, and partly because he had lived to a nice old age in our neighborhood—for a sucker.

Mark had given him back his peace symbol. It hung around his neck on the rawhide string, and M&M kept twisting it absent-mindedly. I wondered if his father still gave him a bad time because of his hair.

We decided to hit Charlie's place first. Charlie grinned and waved at us when we came in, so I figured he was over his bad mood about being drafted.

"Guess what?" he said, just like a kid. It was the first time I'd ever seen him act like a kid. "They're not goin' to take me."

"How come?" Mark asked, plopping down at the bar. "Bad knee from playing football?"

Charlie shook his head. "Naw, because of my police record."

"You got a record?" I said. "I didn't know that. What'dya do?"

"When I was twelve years old I cut a guy's throat. You in here to play pool?"

I still don't know if Charlie was telling the truth or

just kidding us, sort of telling us that it was none of our business what his police record was for. Either was possible.

"Yeah, we're here to play pool. Any possibilities?"

Charlie nodded toward the poolroom. "There's a couple of guys in there. I watched them a little; you can take them."

"Good enough," I said, sliding off the stool.

"Hey, wait a minute," Charlie said. We turned. "Would it do any good to tell you to be careful?"

"Nope," said Mark bluntly.

Charlie kind of laughed and sighed at the same time. "I didn't think so."

We played pool until twelve o'clock that night. The two guys we played against were tough characters, out-of-towners from Texas. At first we played partners, me and Mark losing by a couple of balls. Then Mark started his routine about wanting to go home—"Come on, Bryon, you lost all the money you can spare"— while I played the eager kid—"I know I can win the next game." Then we played singles. I played the better of the two, a weather-beaten guy in his twenties who looked like an ex-con; for all I know he was. I don't know where else he could have picked up his lingo, because he used the worst language I've ever heard, and I've heard plenty.

I was careful not to win at first, and then, when I did start winning, I only made it by a few balls so it'd look like an accident. But once I started winning I didn't quit. By midnight I had twenty-five dollars and fifty cents.

"You're a darn good pool player," Dirty Dave said —he'd told us that was his name—or words to that effect. His friend, who had been standing around drinking beer for the last three hours, mumbled something about being "too good for his own good," but Dirty Dave shut him up.

"Closing time," Charlie said. He didn't have any other customers but us by that time; he had been watching the game for the last hour and a half.

"We're leavin'." Mark was sitting on the table of a booth and drinking a beer. I don't know where he got it, and from the surprised look Charlie gave him, Charlie didn't know where he got it either.

"See ya 'round, kids," the Texans said as they sauntered out. I was busy counting my money and Mark was stretching his legs.

"So the hustler strikes again," Charlie said. "How much did ya get?"

"Enough. Can I borrow your car again some time?"

"I guess so, just as long as you buy gas. Come on, beat it. I got some work to do. Next time you sneak a beer, Golden Boy, you're going to get stomped on."

"I didn't sneak nothing. I simply walked over and drew a beer. I can't help it if you didn't see it. I left a quarter on the cash register."

"You are good at bein' invisible, man, because anybody gets within ten feet of that cash register, I know it."

"You're gettin' blind in your old age," Mark said, apparently not caring if he got stomped on or not. I gave him a warning look, and he obediently shut up. I wasn't taking any chances—we left as soon as we could.

We didn't get far. Two dark shapes stepped out of the alley next to Charlie's and a voice drawled, "Step right into the alley, kiddies."

I froze, because the voice was Dirty Dave's. I thought about making a run for it, but the voice said, "I gotta gun," so I decided not to. I still didn't move. Mark suddenly said, "We don't want to see the alley, we seen it before," and he sounded like he was trying not to laugh.

"We're gonna give you a lesson on why not to hustle pool. Just step into the alley. Now."

I glanced at Mark over my shoulder. He shrugged, like he was saying "What else can we do?" So we walked past the Texans into the alley. I was beginning to shake. I was having visions of my thumbs being chopped off or my arms being broken—things like that happen to hustlers. When we reached the dead end of the alley, we turned and faced the Texans—the one guy was holding a gun on us while Dirty Dave was putting on some brass knuckles. I could just picture what my face was going to look like when he got through with me. I suddenly remembered Mark, who hadn't done anything but get me started. "Let Mark go," I said, and my voice was steady. I was surprised— I thought it would be shaking as bad as I was. "He didn't do nothin'."

Mark said quietly, "I'm not goin' anywhere," and Dave said, "You'd better believe it. You were settin' him up, and when I get through with hustler here, I'm goin' to give you a lesson too."

"Brass knuckles, guns, or whatever," Mark said in a voice I couldn't even recognize as Mark's, "you'll know you been in a fight if you tangle with me."

"I'm really scared, kid," he said. My eyes were used to the dim light by now; I could see past the Texans into the street. I was praying for a police car, something I never thought I'd ever do. Dave took a step toward me. I backed up against the alley wall. I was afraid that if I moved to grab up something to fight with, the other guy would shoot me.

Just at that moment somebody stepped into the other end of the alley and a voice said, "Drop the gun and freeze—I got a sawed-off shotgun here and I'd hate to scatter dirt all over this nice clean alley."

It was Charlie. I never thought I'd be so glad to see anyone.

"Bryon, Mark, come on out of there."

We couldn't resist smirking a little as we walked past the Texans. Even in the dark I could see the anger contorting their faces. It should have warned me, but it didn't.

"Thanks, Charlie," Mark said as we reached him. "You're a real pal."

"I hope you two learned something from this," Charlie began, but before we knew what was happening one of the Texans made a dive for the gun and fired at us. Charlie slammed both of us to the ground, but in an instant Mark freed himself, grabbed up the shotgun Charlie had dropped, and fired back at the Texans, who were scrambling over the alley wall. It all happened so quickly that I was trying to figure out what I was doing on the ground with my ears ringing from the blast before I realized what had taken place.

Mark was swearing and in the dim light he didn't even look like Mark. He looked perfectly capable of murder; his only regret was that he had missed. I didn't have any similar regrets; if he had missed, well, so had they. You can't feel too bad when you could have been dead but aren't.

"You can get off me now, Charlie," I said. Charlie didn't move. I rolled out from under him. "Hey, man, come on," I said. Then, in the white, sickly light from the street lights I saw that there was a neat, perfect hole above Charlie's left eye. He was dead.

I wouldn't talk about what had happened to anyone but Cathy and Mark. The next few weeks it seemed as if I was moving in slow motion while other people were speeded up. Mom came home from the hospital and I flunked chemistry and Angela got married to some creep friend of her brother's. I called Cathy every day. Mark was the one who explained everything to the police. The police were very impressed with Charlie's having saved our lives and all that. They were local cops who had known and liked him anyway. They told us we could have his car. I took it because I figured he would have given it to us if he had had the time.

I guess I was acting pretty strange during those weeks because one day Mark said, "Lookit, man, Charlie knew what kind of people came into his bar—why do you think he kept a shotgun handy? He knew those cowboys had a gun, he knew what kind of a chance he was taking."

"He told us to be careful," I said. I couldn't get it out of my mind, Charlie's warning us about hustling. "He didn't have to try to get us off the hook. Mark— can't you see? This ain't some story, some TV show, bang! you're dead, big deal. This is the real thing. Charlie is dead! He was all set for life, he wasn't gonna get drafted, he had his business, he was all set, and then we blew it for him."

"We didn't blow nothing, Bryon. Things happen, that's all there is to it."

"Not things like that," I said.

Mark didn't understand and Cathy did. I started spending more and more time with Cathy. Since I had the car, we went for a lot of drives and got a lot of Cokes together. We were always talking to each other about the way we felt—I tried telling her how I felt about Charlie, about how shook the whole thing had me. She told me about herself, about how she wanted to go to college more than anything, about how she worried about M&M, and about life in a big family, something I wasn't familiar with. She was so smart, yet she didn't know a lot of things. She was one of the few really innocent chicks I had ever run into. But I could talk to her about anything, talk to her better than I could anyone, even Mark.

After a few weeks we'd drive by the park and make out for a little while. It was different for me though, because I had quit thinking only about myself, quit pushing for all I could get.

Mark was acting strange these days, too. He would stare at me for long periods of time when he thought I wasn't watching, like he was trying to find the old Bryon in this stranger, like he was trying to figure out who I was. One night he even almost lost his temper with me when I told him I was going goofing around with Cathy instead of with him. It was as if he felt something slipping and was trying to hang on. I couldn't help him; I was trying to hang on myself.

He even acted like he was jealous of Cathy. In all the years I'd known him, in all the years I'd gone with different girls, he had never acted like that.

I was changing and he wasn't.

The Texans were finally caught and tried. I had to go
to the trial to testify. Mark did too. He watched me
closely at first—I guess he couldn't forget that by the
time the police had showed up at Charlie's I had been
hysterical. He didn't have to worry. I went through
the whole trial calm, collected, numb, and empty. I
felt like a tape recorder playing back something it had
impersonally recorded. The Texans were sentenced to
life after a trial that didn't last as long as I thought it
would, I guess because there wasn't any defense. I
didn't feel glad, or vengeful, or anything. I really
hadn't much cared whether or not they even caught
those guys. Charlie was dead, nothing was going to
change that.

I tried to figure out what made me so shook up
about it. I knew people died, although I still can't see
me doin' it. My father had died, so I knew that people
close to you died the same as strangers did. I guess I
just couldn't see standing there—alive, talking, thinking, breathing, being—one second, and dead the next.

It really bothered me. Death by violence isn't the same as dying any other way, accident or disease or old age. It just ain't the same.

That winter Mark and me were kind of celebrities because of our involvement in the trial. We were invited to Soc parties and we were stared at in the halls and even the teachers treated us differently. I just put up with it. Mark kind of enjoyed it. He felt bad about Charlie being dead though, enough to shut up people who tried to get him to talk about it.

Mark and me used to go down to the bar and just sit on the curb across the street and stare at the boarded-up windows. Just sit and stare and not say anything. It's funny how you don't think about people until after they're dead. Or gone.

Mom had to stay in bed for a month, so we were really getting hard up for money. I got to thinking about what Charlie had said when I asked him for a job. I decided I needed a haircut, clean clothes, and a really big change in attitude. I've told you that I don't like authority. This gives people the impression that I'm a smart-aleck kid. I'll admit I'm pretty mouthy. I got to thinking, Who's going to hire a mouthy kid who acts like he already knows it all?

"Even if you do know it all," Mark said one evening while we were sitting on the porch, "you don't have to let them know it."

"Very good idea." I grinned at him. We were getting along better lately—he had given up trying to keep us together the same as we used to be. I know now this must have been a struggle. Branching off from Mark couldn't affect me so much—I was all wrapped up in Cathy. He was on his own. I didn't know how he spent his time when I was with Cathy, and I didn't bother to find out.

"When you go so far as to get a haircut and iron a shirt, I know you're serious. We're really hard up, ain't we, Bryon?"

"Yep. Or hasn't the shortage of food bugged you at all?"

"I don't eat like some people. I'm goin' to start bringin' in some money. You wait and see, buddy, I ain't gonna sponge forever."

This was the first time in all the years that he had lived with us that Mark ever said anything about being dependent on us.

I looked at him quickly, and I wanted to say: "What do you mean, sponge? We love you and we want you here, and Mark, you're my brother and you've got a right to whatever I've got."

I didn't. I said, "Don't be a ding-a-ling." Now I wish I had told him how much he meant to us, to me and Mom, how he made us seem more like a family. But I never have been able to say things like that, to tell people I loved them, unless it was some nitwit chick I couldn't care less about. So I just gave him a punch on the shoulder. He grinned at me, but absently, like he was thinking of something else.

That night Cathy and I went for a drive. I wanted to tell her about my new approach to getting a job, but before I could she said suddenly, "I think M&M is smoking marijuana." She sounded worried.

I was puzzled. "So what?"

She gave me an incredulous look. "So what? Have you smoked it?"

"Yeah," I said. "You haven't?"

"No!"

"It ain't much. I'd rather have beer any day. I think a lot of these kids just dig it because it's in, it's against the law, and it's supposed to be cool. Me, I think it's O.K., but it sure ain't worth five years in a state prison."

"You won't smoke it any more?" It was a request, not an order, so I answered, "I said I wasn't nuts about it."

Cathy still seemed concerned. "Did you like it? Did it make you want to try stronger stuff?"

"Like acid? Nope, I can't say that it did. But maybe it affects some people like that. At least that's what I read in the magazines."

Cathy sat back with a sigh. "But it's different with you, Bryon. You're smart enough to enjoy yourself without artificial stimulants."

I didn't say anything to this, as I never turn down compliments. She continued, "But M&M, he's so trusting. If he's running around with people who give him grass, he'll take it. If someone handed him LSD and said, 'This is groovy,' he'd say O.K. and take it. I worry because, well, because before M&M always seemed so happy at home; he never seemed to need anything else. But lately he's gotten so much grief for his hair and some of his ideas. I wish Daddy would leave him alone. M&M isn't happy at home now, so he goes other places, I don't know where. I don't even know his friends any more."

"You love him a lot, don't you?" I said, vaguely jealous, feeling a mild form of whatever it was that Mark felt about Cathy.

"Sure, don't you?" Cathy said, amazed at the possibility that someone might not love simple, brilliant, trusting M&M.

"Yeah," I said, because at that moment I loved anything that Cathy loved, because I loved her. I did. I thought it was corny—love is always corny to anyone not experiencing it himself, and even now to me it was corny. But I couldn't help it. I thought about all the times I had said "I love you" to girls I didn't love—to some I didn't even like—and it had been so easy. And now I couldn't even look at her for fear she could tell somehow. It was really weird.

"I think you'd be a good influence on him," Cathy

was saying, and I realized I hadn't heard a thing she'd been saying. "I know what," she continued. "Let's pick up him and Mark and go get a Coke over on the Ribbon."

"O.K.," I said. The last thing I wanted just then was to be alone with her; I could easily say something really dumb.

We picked up Mark pretty quick—he was walking home from Terry Jones's house. We had to hunt and hunt for M&M, but we finally found him in the bowling alley.

The Ribbon was a two-mile stretch of hot dog and hamburger stands, drive-ins, and supermarkets over on the West Side, close to where the Socs lived. At night the parking lots were filled with kids sitting on their cars and waving, watching, and yelling at other kids driving by. You could drive up and down the street looking at people, or park your car and look at people. The cops sometimes came along and told everyone to get back into their cars, but the cops were mostly guys who had been patrolling the Ribbon for a long time. The kids had worn them down by being pleasantly smart-aleck and smilingly uncooperative, so unless the kids were openly smoking grass or fighting, the cops were content to sit on the cars with them and yell rude things to chicks driving by.

It was a great place to go to pick up chicks. If you followed a carload of them around for a while, they might pull over and exchange phone numbers with you. Everyone in town went there to see who was going with who and who had what car. If you found someone you wanted to drive around with, you parked your car and left it while you goofed around with maybe a dozen different people in one night. Just the driving up and down was a blast. There had been all kinds of editorials in the paper about it because a lot of pushers took advantage of the filled parking lots, and quite a bit of grass and money exchanged hands there, but mostly it was harmless. Fights down on the Ribbon had really died off in the last year. It had gotten pretty safe, except for drag racing, which caused a wreck or two a week.

"Boy, I hope I see someone I know," Cathy said. "Here I sit, surrounded by beautiful boys."

She gave me a teasing grin. Mark raised his eyebrows. "Well, if you feel that way about it . . ." He put his arm across her shoulders. We were sitting pretty close together because all four of us were in the front seat. Cathy was next to me, Mark on her other side, and M&M was hanging out the window, gravely watching people, waving if he was waved to, yelling back if he was yelled at, always slightly surprised at the crudity of the calls, as if he hadn't heard the same things a hundred thousand times before.

I put one arm across Cathy's shoulders too. She beamed. "It's so nice to feel wanted."

A couple of blondes in an orange Camaro came by on M&M's side of the car and made him an indecent proposition. I thought that kid was going to fall out the window, he was so shocked. The rest of us laughed.

The Ribbon was a two-lane street with an extra lane at the traffic lights for left turns. When we stopped at the light we were in the middle lane, with cars on both sides of us. The blond chicks in the orange Camaro were on our right, and they were still talking to M&M. I didn't catch much of the conversation, but Mark did and he was talking to them too, trying to see around M&M, who took up a lot of the window. On our left was a green outasite Corvette with a couple of guys in it, waiting for a left-turn signal. They looked like real snobs. You can tell just by looking that some guys are snobs. Especially ones with Corvettes. The one on the passenger side glanced over at us and—I still don't understand why—popped off with a really obscene remark. I sat stunned for a minute—the thought of Cathy's hearing such a thing just froze me. Then, so quick I didn't even realize what was happening, Mark reached past M&M, opened the door, pushed M&M out of the way, ran around to my side of the car, and punched the foul-mouthed guy in the nose, literally smashing his nose in. It was their turn to be stunned. Before they could move, Mark was back in the car. He jumped into the back seat and yelled, "Take off!" The light had turned green so I stepped hard on the accelerator. The Corvette was supposed to turn left, and all the cars behind it were honking, so they turned left. I thought maybe they'd come after us—they were older guys, maybe eighteen years old—but they didn't. We drove up and down the Ribbon without seeing them again.

"You're a fast worker," Cathy said. I wondered if she was mad at me because I hadn't been the one to punch that guy. She was my girl friend, I should have done it. I was halfway hacked off at Mark for showing me up.

"Well," Mark said in a mock serious voice, hanging over the front seat, "I get these impulses."

"Impulses to jump out of cars and hit people?" Cathy said dryly, and I realized she didn't think Mark was a hero for what he'd done. As a matter of fact, she didn't think too much of it.

"They hit us first," Mark said, sitting back in the seat. "A hit don't have to be physical. I couldn't hit them the way they hit us without hitting you, too."

I had always known that, in spite of his lousy grades, Mark was every bit as smart as I was. But it was still surprising whenever he proved it to me. Cathy was quiet. Then she turned around and looked at Mark for a long time. "I never know what to make of you, Mark."

"Why make anything of anybody? Why not just take people or leave them?" Mark was in a funny mood. I could tell; I had seen him in that mood before. He was never that way with me, but I'd seen him suddenly turn on people, like a teased lion who's had enough. I remembered the night Charlie was killed—Mark grabbing up the shotgun and firing away. I don't think I could have done that, even if I had known Charlie was dead at the time.

"I don't like being analyzed, baby," Mark said. "So don't."

I couldn't tell him to lay off, because he had a point. Cathy did like to turn everyone inside out and look at him. It didn't bother me, but I could see where it might bug some people.

"I'm sorry," Cathy said, even though she wasn't. I had to say something, so I said, "Let's get a hamburger."

We turned into a big drive-in called Jay's, which was always crowded. It was a set up with a stall for each car and a little deal that had a menu and a button on it. You pushed the button and a voice came out of the deal and said, "Order, please," and you told the speaker what you wanted—in this case it was three hamburgers, one steak sandwich, a cherry-pineapple Seven-up, and three Cokes—and about ten minutes later a chick appeared with the food. It was slightly spooky.

The place was crawling with kids. It was mainly a Soc hangout. There used to be a drive-in over on our side of town where the "hoods" went, but the Dingo was bombed and had burned down so we had started coming over here. Kids were driving through the parking area looking at the kids who were sitting in their cars. It was the same thing that was going on in the street, only on a smaller scale. They had a cop stationed at the drive-in to prevent trouble. He was on a first-name basis with a lot of the kids there; he was a friendly, good-natured cop who didn't mind getting splattered by a water pistol now and then. I didn't much care for him though, due to my feelings about cops in general. I began telling Cathy about the time the cops had beaten me up when I was thirteen.

"You shouldn't have been running around drunk in the middle of the night," she said.

"I never thought of it that way," I said.

"Who would?" came Mark's voice from the back seat. I realized right then that whatever chance Mark and Cathy had ever had of becoming friends was gone. I had already sensed in Cathy the same hostility toward Mark that he had for her. That put me in a really great position.

"Hey, there's Terry Jones. I'm going over to see him," Mark said suddenly. He gave the cop a quick glance—you weren't supposed to get out of your car at the drive-in. They came up with this rule about a year ago because all this switching from car to car was causing fights, and what was worse, cars were left empty in the stalls for hours at a time while the owners were running the Ribbon in someone else's car. This doesn't make money for the drive-ins.

"Mark doesn't like me much, does he?" Cathy said. M&M looked at her, astonished. For the first time I was sick of her honesty.

"You don't like him either," I said.

Not used to having her honesty turned back on her, Cathy was silent for a minute. "I guess we're fighting over you. Isn't that funny?"

"A real riot," I said dryly. I looked across the street, watching some little twelve- and thirteen-year-old teeny-boppers make fools of themselves—smoking, trying to act cool, pushing each other, screaming and swearing so loud I could hear them. I had a sudden recollection of Mark and me at twelve, smoking our heads off, clowning around, hoping someone—usually some little long-haired chick—would notice us and see how cool we were. All of a sudden it seemed like I was a hundred years old, or thirty at least. I wondered if, when I got to be twenty, I would think how stupid I was at sixteen. When I remembered us, it didn't seem possible that we had looked as silly as these teenybop-pers, but I guess we had. At least then we weren't wor-ried about looking silly. We were sure of ourselves, so sure we were the coolest things to hit town. Now I wasn't so sure.

That was strange too: in the past I thought in terms of "we," now I was thinking in terms of "me."

"There sure isn't anything to do in this town," Cathy said, breaking in on my thoughts of the good old days.

"We could go to a movie," I said, even though I didn't have the money to go to the movies. Or money to go bowling, or money to go out to dinner, or money to ride go-carts, or to go to the amusement park.

"No, I don't want to go to the movies. There's nothing to do in this town except drive up and down."

"That takes gas," M&M said, "and gas takes money," even though neither Cathy or me had mentioned money.

"Well, let's go drive up and down some more," I said, flipping a switch on the magic dealie that signals a car-hop to appear and pick up our tray.

I was thinking about what Cathy said. There was nothing to do except drive up and down the Ribbon, even though we lived in a fairly large city. It wasn't New York, but for our part of the country it was a good size. All the adults in town screamed about the kids driving up and down, but what did they expect us to do? Sit and twiddle our thumbs like they probably did when they were young? No, thanks.

We drove up and down the Ribbon again—it was getting hard to find a place to turn around. Usually the shopping center at the far end was good for a quick turn-around, but somehow the cops figured out that that was against some law that had been gathering dust for years, so they sat in the shopping-center lots giving out tickets. If a kid got a ticket he immediately went around collecting money from friends and strangers. Usually he got at least a nickel or a dime from each person. I have never known anybody who took advantage of this custom by collecting money when he didn't really have a ticket. This would have been like squealing on someone you saw cheating, or refusing to lend or give or sell your senior theme to some promising junior.

A block beyond the shopping center, under the bypass, the Ribbon ended as suddenly as it began at a movie theater two miles back. Abrupt and unexplainable. There was another shopping center beyond the bypass but for some reason it was not considered part of the Ribbon, so it wasn't full of cops. We turned around there to head back, which is against the unwritten rules of the Ribbon, but I didn't feel like messing around, sitting in the left-turn lane for half an hour waiting to turn.

"Drive by the hot-dog stand," M&M said, so I pulled in to drive through the parking lot, which was filled with kids sitting on their cars. We got tied up in a long line of cars driving through the hot-dog-stand lot. M&M suddenly got out of the car.

"Where are you going?" Cathy asked.

"I got some friends around here," M&M said. He should have. At least three quarters of the guys out there had hair to their shoulders.

"Well, when can we pick you up?"

"Not ever. I'm not going home," M&M said and walked off toward a group of kids sitting on a station wagon.

There were cars honking behind me so I had to drive on, even though Cathy was yelling, "Stop, we can't just let him walk off like this."

"I'll drive back through," I said, trying to hush her up, because I don't like hysterical chicks. She calmed down right away.

"That little mess. Wait till I get a hold of him."

She didn't though. When we came back through he was gone, and nobody seemed to know where. I parked the car and Cathy and me ran around asking different kids. We drove up and down the Ribbon until one o'clock in the morning looking for him. I found Mark sitting on Terry's car—Terry had gone somewhere with a couple of girls. We picked him up and drove home in silence.

Cathy was crying without making any noise, and, for the first time in my life, I wasn't annoyed with a girl for crying.

Instead, I felt really bad. It was the first time I'd ever felt bad for anyone except Mark.

I went with Cathy to break the news about M&M to her parents and to explain why we were so late. Her father was sitting up waiting for us, and when I saw his face I was glad that I had a real good excuse, even though I was quite a bit bigger than him. Her mother got up and came into the front room in her housecoat. She got real upset when we told her what had happened, but her father said, "He'll be home tomorrow —that kid's been going through this stage for months now."

"It's not just a stage!" Cathy cried. "You can't say, 'This is just a stage,' when it's important to people what they're feeling. Maybe he will outgrow it someday, but right *now* it's important. If he never comes home it'll be your fault—always picking on him about silly, goofy things like his hair and flunking gym!" She sat down and began to cry again. Her father just looked at her and said, "Honey, I know it's because you're worried that you're talking like this. M&M'll be home tomorrow. He's a sensible kid."

"Then why didn't you ever tell him so?" Cathy sobbed irrationally. "I don't think he's coming home tomorrow. He doesn't do things on the spur of the moment; he thinks things out. He's not going to come home!"

By now two or three younger kids had wandered in, dressed in their underwear or not dressed at all. They got enough out of the conversation to gather that M&M was gone and they began crying too. It was a big mess and I felt really uncomfortable. Mark was waiting out in the car, and, as it was two in morning and I had to go to school in a few hours, I wanted to leave; only I just didn't want to leave Cathy. I wished I could take her home with me. Her father said, "Bryon, thank you for your help. I think you'd better be going home, your mother is probably worried."

I could have told him that Mom never worried about Mark and me—she loved us but let us run our own lives—but I only said, "Yes, sir." I suddenly noticed that where he wasn't bald his hair was charcoal-colored too and that his eyes, though smaller with age, were the same as Cathy's and M&M's. I wondered if it was strange, seeing your eyes in someone else's face. I was tired and thinking funny.

"Everyone uptight?" asked Mark when I got back into the car.

"Yep," I said. "I don't blame them."

"They don't have nothin' to worry about," Mark

said. "Half the kids on the Ribbon are living in someone else's car or house or garage. Shoot, I remember last summer, you and me sometimes didn't come home for weeks—we were bumming around the lake or somebody's house. Remember when Williamson rented that apartment for a couple of months with two other guys? I bet half the kids in town stopped there overnight."

"Yeah, but M&M is just a kid."

"So are we. Nothing bad happens to you when you're a kid. Or haven't you realized that?"

"Youth is free from worry," I said sarcastically. "You've been listenin' to too many adults."

"I don't worry. I'm never scared of nothing, and I never will be," Mark said, "as long as I'm a kid."

"You can get away with anything," I said, because that phrase came through my head whenever I really thought about Mark.

"Yeah, I can." He was quiet. "You used to be able to."

I looked at him, and suddenly it was like seeing someone across a deep pit, someone you couldn't ever reach. It was like the car had widened into the Gulf of Mexico and I was seeing Mark through a telescope.

"What's happening?" I said, half out loud, but Mark was asleep.

M&M didn't come home the next day like his father

thought he would. Cathy and I ran up and down the Ribbon every night for a week, but it wasn't fun any more because we were looking out for M&M. We never did find him. We must have stopped sixty million little long-haired kids, thinking they were M&M, but none of them was. I began watching for him everywhere.

I got a job in a supermarket and I did a pretty good job of changing my attitude, outwardly at least. I couldn't help thinking smart-aleck things, but I could help saying them. Sacking groceries wasn't the most fun job in the world, but I was bringing in money. Mark was bringing in money, too, more than he ever had before. I couldn't imagine him stealing all of it, so I figured he must have gone in serious for poker. I never asked him where he got it, and Mom didn't either. Of course, she would never think Mark was getting it dishonestly. Besides, none of us was in any position to turn away extra money.

One night a couple of weeks after M&M disappeared, Mark and me went goofing around by ourselves again. It was almost as if we had never felt a gulf between us, never been separated by something we couldn't see. We drove up and down the Ribbon, trying to pick up chicks and get into drag races, even though our car wasn't all that fast. I was kind of half-hearted about picking up chicks, too, as I was more serious about Cathy than I let on, even to Cathy herself.

"Hey," Mark said suddenly. "Lookit who's over there in the parking lot."

It was Angela and a bunch of other chicks—her type, by the way they dressed and the way they were acting. You can always tell when a girl wants to be picked up.

"Let's pull in," Mark said. He was smiling.

"Sure," I said, feeling, with the old sense of thrill, that something was up, something was going to happen. We pulled into the parking lot, and immediately we were surrounded by girls.

"Outa the way," I said superiorly. "I want to see Angela."

"Bryon!" she yelled, and jumped for me the minute I got out of the car. "Bryon, I'm so glad to see you!"

She was pretty drunk. I let her hug me though, catching Mark's wink. "Where ya been keeping yourself, Angel?" I said. "How's married life?"

She let go with a string of swear words which told me pretty well what she thought of married life, her in-laws, and her husband.

"I never cared about him anyway. I thought I was having— I mean, I thought I was, but I wasn't—and that's the only reason I married him, the louse." She was half-crying now, between obscenities. "You're the only boy I ever cared about, Bryon."

"Sure," I said. I still hated the sight of her. She was as beautiful as ever, so striking that she could have been a movie star, but I remembered all the trouble she had caused, compared her to Cathy, and hated her. I let her hug me and bawl into my shirt front because Mark was winking at me.

"Angel, let's go for a ride," Mark said. "You and Bryon can talk over old times and maybe I can get some more booze for you."

"Sure," Angela said, always eager for free booze. I couldn't believe she was that glad to see me.

We drove around for a while, Angela telling us all of her problems—her husband didn't have a job, her brothers were both in jail, her old man was drunk all the time, and her father-in-law was always slapping her bottom. I had always taken her family for granted—they weren't so different from most of the families in our neighborhood. But now that I had seen Cathy's home—not rich, not much more than poor, but where everybody cared about each other and tried to act like decent people—the picture Angela was painting was making me sick. I could hardly stand for her to be hanging onto my arm.

At Mark's request I pulled into a parking lot across the street from a liquor store. Mark got out and disappeared. He was looking for somebody to buy the booze. You can't legally buy booze until you're twenty-one in this state, so we always have to get some old guy to buy it for us, usually somebody's big brother. If you can't come up with one of them, there was bound to be some rummy hanging around who was willing to buy it if you gave him a little extra to buy something for himself. I sat in the car and talked to Angela, who had completely given up to tears—it was the first time since I had known her that I had seen her cry. She was a tough little chick. Her eye makeup was running all over my shirt front, but that didn't bother me as much as the way it was running down her face in dark streaks. She almost looked like she was behind bars.

Mark hopped back into the car with some rum, and we got a carton of pop at a one-stop store and took off for the lake. It was too cold to go swimming, but the lake is always a good place to go. There are a mess of them—lakes, that is—around here.

"I get so sick," Angela was saying. "I feel like I can't take it any more, life is so lousy. I'm lousy, everything is lousy. I can't stand it at home, I can't stand it at school, I can't stand it anywhere. I always thought, hell, I can get what I want. Get what I want and everybody can go to hell. But it doesn't work that way, Bryon. I'm going to hell right along with them. I'm already there."

Tomorrow she would be tough again, hard-as-rock Angela Shepard. Tonight she was tired. And drunk.

She passed out on my shoulder. We were stopped on a little dirt road, one of the millions that run along the lake and through the woods surrounding it. Mark sighed, "I thought she was never gonna shut up. I sure hate to see gutsy chicks break. Destroys my faith in human nature."

"You're never gonna break, huh?"

"Nope," Mark said. He pulled a pair of scissors out of his pocket. "Picked these up at the one-stop." He reached over and began cutting off Angela's beautiful long blue-black hair. Close to her head.

"You ain't gonna cut it all off?" I said, stunned.

"Yeah, I am. Setting up Curtis like she did, gettin' me cracked like that. She coulda had me killed."

"That's right," I said, and suddenly all the hatred I had had for Angela, for her brother Curly, for everything she stood for, came back. I sat and watched Mark cut off all her hair. He tied it all up neatly when he had finished the job. It was a couple of feet long. Even with her hair gone and her makeup streaked all over her face, Angela was a beauty. She would always be. A lot of good it did her.

We drove home about three that morning. Mark and me finished what was left of the rum. We dumped Angela and her hair in her front yard. She never even woke up. I didn't think she'd remember getting into the car with us, but her girl friends would probably tell her that. She'd know who had cut off her hair.

She wouldn't do anything about it though, because one thing I knew about ol' Angel, she was proud. She'd say she had her hair cut at the beauty shop. She'd say, "I was sick of all that hot mess." She'd never let on.

I started crying on the way home from Angela's and Mark had to drive. Sometimes rum affects me like that.

I was still crying when we got home. We sat on the porch and I cried while Mark patted me on the back and said, "Hey, take it easy, man, everything's going to be all right."

I finally quit and sat sniffing and wiping my eyes on my shirt sleeve. It was a quiet night. "I was thinking . . ."

"Yeah?" Mark said, in the same easy, concerned voice. "What were you thinkin', Bryon?"

"About that kid Mike, the one in the hospital. We talked to him a couple of times, remember?"

"Yeah, I remember. He got beat up tryin' to do a black chick a favor."

"How come things always happen like that? Seems like you let your defenses down for one second and, man, you get it. Pow! Care about somebody, give a damn for another person, and you get blasted. How come it's like that?"

"You got me, Bryon. I never thought about it. I guess 'cause nothin' bad has ever happened to me."

I looked at him. Nothing bad had ever happened to him? His parents had killed each other in a drunken fight when he was nine years old and he saw it all. He had been arrested for auto theft. He had seen Charlie shot and killed. He had nearly been killed himself by some punk kid he had never seen before.

Nothing bad had ever happened to him? Then I knew what he meant. Those things hadn't left a mark on him, because he was Mark the lion—Mark, different from other people. Beautiful Mark, who didn't give a damn about anyone. Except me.

I suddenly knew why everyone liked Mark, why everyone wanted to be his friend. Who hasn't dreamed of having a pet lion to stand between you and the world? Golden, dangerous Mark.

"You are my best friend, Mark," I said, still a little drunk. "Just like a brother to me."

"I know, buddy," he said, patting me again. "Take it easy; don't start bawling again."

"I sure wish I knew where M&M was," I said, and tears were running down my face again in spite of myself. "I like that dumb little kid. I wish I knew what happened to him."

"He's O.K. Take my word for it."

"You know where he is!" I said. "He's been gone all these weeks and you know where he is!"

"Yeah, I do. If he wanted to come home, he'd come home. Don't worry."

"You gotta take me to where he is, Mark," I said, knowing I sounded like a drunken nitwit—but I couldn't help it, seeing how I was so drunk.

"Sure, Bryon, don't cry. I'll take you there tomorrow. But don't count on him comin' home."

"Cathy is awful worried about him. You know, Mark, I think I'm gonna marry Cathy."

"Come on, man," Mark said, trying to pull me to my feet. "Yeah, marry Cathy and be sure and name all the kids after me. Let's go in the house. Try an' be quiet, O.K.? You don't want the old lady to see you like this. I shoulda known better than to let you drink all that rum."

"Didn't you drink any?"

"Naw, I was drinkin' plain Coke."

"I drank all that rum by myself?" I couldn't believe it. I'm not much of a boozer.

" 'Cept for what Angela drank." Mark was helping me up the steps. I was weaving back and forth. If he hadn't been hanging onto me, I would have dropped flat on my face.

"Poor Angel—we shoulda left her alone, Mark. That was a mean thing to do, cut off her hair like that."

"Please, Bryon, for Pete's sake, don't cry any more." He half-dragged me into our room and pushed me onto my bed. I passed out. I could hear Mark moving around the room, feel him taking my shoes off and pulling the blanket up over me, but it was all as if he was real far away, or I was way down inside myself.

"What'd I ever do to deserve you, Mark? Pull a thorn outa your paw?"

"Bryon, buddy, you are as wiped out as I've ever seen you. I think you'd better shut up and go to sleep."

"When did we start runnin' around together, Mark? Remember?"

"We've always been friends. I can't remember when we weren't."

"How come your old man shot your mother? She shot him back, but it was too late because she was dying anyway." I really was drunk, because I had never mentioned that to Mark in all the years I had known him.

"It was me. I was under the porch—I could hear them real plain. And the old man was sayin', 'I don't care, I ain't never seen a kid with eyes that color. Nobody on my side of the family has eyes that color—not on yours either.' And the old lady says, 'That's right. Why should he look like anybody in your family? He ain't yours.' And then they start yelling and I hear this sound like a couple of firecrackers. And I think, well, I can go live with Bryon and his old lady."

"Did you really think that?" I opened my eyes, and the room was turning around slowly. It was making me sick. Something was making me sick.

"Yeah, I did. I didn't like livin' at home; I got sick of them yelling and fighting all the time. I got whipped a lot, too. I remember thinking, This'll save me the trouble of shooting them myself. I don't like anybody hurtin' me."

"I'm glad you came to live with us."

"Me too. Now you really better shut up, man."

"Why you tryin' to shut me up?" I said, making an effort to sit up. It made me even sicker, so I lay back down. "You got a cigarette?"

"Right in the old secret place." Mark pulled back his mattress and got a pack of cigarettes. He always kept an extra pack there. When we were little and didn't want Mom to know we smoked, we kept our cigarettes hidden. It wasn't till much later that we found out she had known about it all along.

I couldn't light my cigarette for some reason. Mark lit it for me and stuck it in my mouth. He sat back on his bed watching me, his elbows on the window sill. I could see the end of his cigarette glowing.

"Charlie, he tried to help somebody out and look what happened to him," I said. This was connected with what he'd said about Mike somehow, but Mark followed my train of thought, just like he always had.

"Charlie wasn't about to let a couple of his friends get beat up by some hicks. What happened then, well, that was just the way things turn out sometimes."

"Yeah, but listen, Mark, if somebody had said to him, 'Is savin' a couple of dumb kids from gettin' beat up worth your life?' he woulda said, 'Hell, no!' Charlie woulda said that, Mark."

"Sure he woulda said that. But you don't know what's comin'. Nobody does. He sure knew he was taking a chance. Bryon, he musta known those guys had guns. He knew they were rough guys. He took a chance, and he got a rotten break. That's it."

"It doesn't make any sense. Like you gettin' busted with that bottle. A little harder and you woulda been dead."

"But I ain't. This is the way it is, Bryon. Angela Shepard is a tough little chick who set out to get a shy guy who didn't know she was alive, so she sweet-talks some dummy into fighting for her, and I happen to be friends with Curtis, happen to be sittin' on the car with him when the dummy picks the fight with him, and I happen to be a little high. So I step in between Curtis and the punk. Now, if Angela wasn't tough, if she was a nice girl from the West Side—maybe she woulda left well enough alone and given up on Curtis. If Curtis was a playboy like you, he woulda picked her up when she wanted to be picked up. If that kid wasn't so dumb, he would have never taken on Curtis, who is no slouch of a fighter, man, I can tell you. If I had had a date that night, I woulda been somewhere else. But Bryon, that ain't the way things went. You can't walk through your whole life saying 'If.' You can't keep trying to figure out why things happen, man. That's what old people do. That's when you can't get away with things any more. You gotta just take things as they come, and quit trying to reason them out. Bryon, you never used to wonder about things. Man, I been gettin' worried about you. You start wonderin' why, and you get old. Lately, I felt like you were leavin' me, man. You used to have all the answers."

"I can't help it, Mark. I can't help thinking about things. Like Mike and Charlie and M&M and you— it's all mixed up and I can't help it."

"You can help *thinking* about it." He leaned over

his bed, reached across the short space that separated us, and yanked my cigarette out of my fingers.

"You're going to go to sleep and burn us alive," he said.

I remember I was going to say, "No I ain't," but I was asleep before I could get the words out.

I was real hung over the next morning. Besides that, I had to get up early and go to work. Mark woke me up. He was a human alarm clock and never needed more than five hour's sleep a night. Me, if I don't get at least nine hours, I feel dead. I felt dead that Saturday morning. I wished I was, anyway. I was feeling so bad that I actually stuck a loaf of bread in a grocery bag and dropped three cans of soup on top of it. Bread always goes on top. In a supermarket this is like the Ten Commandments all rolled into one. It was a wonder I didn't lose my job that Saturday.

I carried groceries for this one young housewife type, and when I put the bags in her car she handed me her phone number. I was feeling so bad I groaned, "Lady, you gotta be kidding."

Like I said, it was a wonder I didn't lose my job. It was two in the afternoon before the sound of the cash register quit blasting my ears, and it was quitting time before I finally felt I could eat something. This shows you how sick I was.

I had a date with Cathy that night, but she had to work late. I would pick her up at the hospital snack shop at ten. This was fine with me, as I wanted a chance to go look for M&M. Mark knew where he was.

When I got off work, I found Mark sitting in my car.

"I figured you'd want to hunt for M&M," he said. "How's your head?"

"Better. Man, don't ever let me guzzle like that again."

Mark shrugged. "You wanted to. You had to get good and drunk because I was cutting Angela's hair off and you couldn't take it."

I flipped a remark that I had said many times before, but not to him. Even from my side of the car I felt him tighten, getting ready to spring. The gulf was between us again. For some reason, I was hacked off because he didn't need to sleep nine hours, because he wasn't hung over.

"You sound like Cathy," I said.

"Heaven forbid."

"What have you got against her, anyway?"

"What's she got against me?"

"You're a bad influence." I don't know why I said that, because Cathy sure as hell never said anything like it.

Mark was quiet for a minute, then he said something really rotten. I had it coming for what I'd said to him, but he didn't have to drag Cathy into it. I gripped the steering wheel. "You want to get outa this car and have it out?"

"You don't want to swing on me, do you?" It was partly a statement and partly a request. I was quiet.

"I'm sorry," Mark said, and I kept driving. This was as close as we ever came to having a fight.

I followed the directions Mark gave me. We went into this old part of town which used to be a really classy place maybe thirty or forty years ago, with these huge old houses that were probably a big deal when they were built. They just looked gloomy now; most of them were divided into flats.

On Mark's say-so I pulled into a driveway in front of one of them. There was a sign hanging from the porch ceiling that said "Love" in red-and-green letters.

"He's here?" I asked, because I wasn't sure what was going on.

"Last time I was here he was." Mark got out of the car. You can tell when somebody is familiar with a place. Mark had been here many times before. "Come on."

I got out of the car, wondering what in the world Mark could have been doing here. Mark didn't knock, he just opened the front door and walked in. I followed him. The whole inside of the house was freaked out with posters. A girl with long, streaked, blond hair, wearing blue jeans and a paint-splattered shirt, was lying on a beat-up couch. She had the deadest, most colorless face I had ever seen.

"Hello, Cat," she said to Mark. She knew him; she didn't call everybody "Cat."

"Peace, baby," Mark said. I tried not to laugh. I dig hippies O.K.— I mean, they've got some great ideas, but sometimes it was funny.

"Freaked out?" Mark said politely, as if he were saying "How are you these days?"

" 'Way out, man." She was staring at the ceiling so intently that I glanced up there, just to make sure the answer to the universe wasn't written across it. If it was, I couldn't see it. Maybe she could.

Mark stepped over a stringless guitar and went upstairs. I stumbled after him, looking around. Somebody was in the kitchen singing. Each of the steps was painted a different color. It was a good effect, but they were awful dirty.

Mark stepped into a bedroom. There were about six or seven kids in it. One kid was lying on a bed watching his fingernails. The others were sitting cross-legged in a circle, talking about some book. I hadn't read it so I didn't get the conversation, but these kids were not dumb. They were all in blue jeans and old shirts and fringed vests. A couple of them were smoking grass.

"Hi, Cat," a guy with a beard and a flowered shirt said.

"I'm looking for M&M," Mark said. "You seen him?"

"Baby Freak? He ain't been around today. The kid's flying, man. He's going to crash."

"You didn't let him take anything, did you?" I said. This may have been against house rules, as nobody had said anything to me yet, but this place was getting on my nerves.

"There isn't any 'letting' here," this fat chick says. "We're free."

I looked her over with the practiced eye of a playboy and popped off with something really good. Then I raised two fingers and said "Peace." This seemed to earn their forgiveness, because they all went back to their literary discussion.

Now the kid on the bed was painting his fingernails with green water-color.

On the way out we passed the blond chick. She was reading a book and smoking grass.

"You seen Baby Freak?" Mark asked.

She shook her head. "Sorry. See you around, Cat." Even sitting up she looked dead.

When we got back into the car I said, "You dating her?"

"Sometimes. Like the lady said, they're free."

I thought about that a long time. I am the first to admit I've got hang ups. I don't think I'd ever consider myself really free.

But I'm not sure I'd consider them free, either.

"Just because it ain't your bag, don't knock it," Mark said, after we had driven in silence for a while.

"I didn't say anything."

"Grass, rum, both are a high."

"Yeah, well, listen, man, rum's going to maybe get me a weekend in the drunk tank. Grass could get me five years in the pen."

"That law ain't necessarily right."

"It's the way things are." I was puzzled. I had never known Mark to smoke pot. I wondered why he was defending it.

"I don't smoke it, so quit worrying," Mark said, reading my mind as usual. "I just don't like to see you judging people."

"What the hell is bugging you? I didn't say anything."

Mark was quiet. Then he said, "You remember when the Socs used to come through here looking for somebody to beat up?"

"Yeah."

"You remember when me and you beat up that hippie kid in the park?"

"Yeah," I said.

"I'm a tough punk, Bryon, but I ain't dumb."

We drove the rest of the way home in silence.

I picked Cathy up at the hospital. I didn't tell her

about going to the hippie house to look for M&M. I didn't see any sense in getting her all upset. After all, I hadn't found him.

We drove up and down the Ribbon, then stopped by the park on the way home. This was becoming standard procedure. I was getting more and more serious about Cathy, and this was really strange for me. I had always had a love-'em-and-leave-'em attitude. Even with Angela, I guess it was more a pride thing than a love thing. I still hadn't told Cathy I loved her though. It was like my never thanking Charlie for letting me use his car. It was something I just couldn't do when it meant anything.

"Hey, Cathy," I said, while we were on the way home. "If I got a ring, would you wear it?"

"Yeah," she said. That's how we started going steady.

After I dropped Cathy off at her house, I headed for Terry Jones's place. I was supposed to pick up Mark there, but when I got to the house, nobody was home. Terry's parents were out of town for the weekend, which normally meant it was party-and-poker time at the Joneses'. I figured everybody had gone out scouting for booze and broads, so I sat down on the front steps to wait.

It was a cool night, but not too cool. It was getting to be spring. It had been a real weird winter. Last fall Mark and me had thought just alike, as one person;

now we couldn't even talk. Charlie had been alive and griping about our Coke bill. I had been a hustler, both with pool and chicks. M&M had been reading *Newsweek* and getting his kicks baby-sitting. Now everything was different.

While I was sitting there, smoking and thinking, a car pulled up. I thought it was some guys coming to party and so forth, so I didn't pay any attention. The four guys were standing right in front of me before I came to and realized that two of them were Tim and Curly Shepard.

"I thought you guys were in the cooler," I said pleasantly, just like I didn't know they were here for the sole purpose of stomping out my guts.

"We're out now," Tim said. He scared me. He was what I would call a rough guy. Curly was mostly mouth, but Tim backed up anything he said. He really was a hood. I know most people call any kid from over here on the East Side a hood, but Tim really was.

"I guess so," I said, still smoking, not blowing my cool. If I kept them talking long enough, maybe Mark and Terry and God knows who else would show up.

"Seen Angela lately?" Tim said. Curly was keeping his mouth shut—even he was awed by his big brother. There was something about Tim Shepard—his scarred face, his fighter's slouch, the flickering of his black eyes —that really let you know he meant business.

"Yeah, as a matter of fact, I saw her over on the Ribbon last night, and she went for a drive with me." I decided I didn't need to drag Mark into this—it was plain they weren't worried about him.

"No kidding? Did you know Angel got her hair cut this morning? At least that's what people say. She told me something different."

I was sweating. I could feel it running down my back and wetting my palms, and my cigarette was shaking, so I ground it out on the porch. But I sounded calm as I said, "What's she telling you?"

"She says you got her drunk and cut her hair off. That the truth?"

"Yeah, that's the truth, and I'm sorry it happened." I decided to tell it straight for once, without all this hedging and playing the game. "It was a rotten thing to do and I'm sorry."

"You ain't half as sorry as you're going to be," Tim said, and the two guys I didn't know rushed me, pinned my arms, and held me while Tim and Curly took turns punching me.

I passed out finally, but not as soon as I had hoped I would.

When I came to, Mark was wiping my face off with a wet rag.

"Bryon, you O.K.? Don't move, man."

I bit back a groan because I could tell there were

other guys in the room. Normally I wouldn't have to knock myself out playing the tough guy for just Mark, but I did have a rep to keep.

"What happened? Who did this to you?"

"Shepards," I said finally, but it hurt to draw the breath to say it. Something was stabbing me in the sides. My whole face was throbbing and I couldn't open my eyes. They were swollen shut. There was a funny taste in my mouth—I guessed it was blood.

"You want to go to the hospital?" Mark asked. He sounded so worried that I felt sorry for him.

"No," I said. I didn't want to go anywhere. I felt that if I moved I'd fall apart. "Can I stay here?" I figured I was in Terry's house somewhere. I could tell I was lying on a bed.

"Sure, man, you stay here." I recognized Terry's voice. "Brother, you look like you been through a meat grinder."

"That's what it feels like too," I said, even though this witticism cost me more stabbing pains in my sides. A reputation is one hell of a thing to have; you got to kill yourself to keep it.

"I'll call the old lady," Mark said. "Then we'll go look up the Shepards."

"Mark!" I said. "I want to talk to you, personal-like."

"Sure, buddy. Clear out, you guys." And because he was Mark, they obeyed him.

"Listen, it hurts like hell to talk, so I'm only goin' to say it once, an' I don't want to argue."

"Sure." Mark's voice sounded puzzled. I wished I could see him; I knew he wasn't going to dig what I had to say. I could tell he was sitting on the edge of the bed, and I reached for where his hand should have been and caught it. "I don't want anybody to fight the Shepards."

"What?"

"I don't want to keep this up, this getting-even jazz. It's stupid and I'm sick of it and it keeps going in circles. I have had it—so if you're planning any get-even mugging, forget it." I was trying to keep my voice from trembling with pain, but not only did talking hurt my sides, it was killing my face.

"I got you, Bryon," Mark said after a silence. "You just take it easy." He left to call Mom, and I heard him yelling at the rest of the guys to keep the record player down. He stayed all night on the other side of the bed, guarding me.

Mark drove me to the hospital the next day and I got fifteen stitches in my face and had my ribs taped. As luck would have it I got the same doctor that had sewed up Mark a few months before when he had been busted with a bottle. He remembered Mark all right; most people did. He gave us a disgusted look and said, "Don't you punks ever do anything besides fight?"

Mark growled something real cute, but I couldn't get mad. I felt sick, ashamed of myself, even though I hadn't done anything. All I could think about was Mike's getting beat up for driving a black girl home. I kept remembering him saying he didn't hate the guys who did it. Well, I didn't hate the Shepards either. I tried to explain this to Mark as we drove home. I was so wrapped up in what I was trying to get across to him that I was startled when Mark suddenly burst out, "Whatdaya tryin' to do to me, Bryon?"

"What?" I said, confused. Mark had turned white and his voice was shaking as if he was about to cry. I couldn't believe that; I had never seen Mark cry except from physical pain.

"How do you think I feel, man? You won't let me get the Shepards for you, and here you go givin' me this song and dance about how you don't feel bad about gettin' beat up. You think I don't know they beat you up for something I did? And here you are, practically sayin' you had it comin', when it was me who cut Angela's hair, it was me who planned it, and me who did it—and it's you who gets beat up for it. Like that damn fool, Mike, he feels like he had it coming, feels guilty for something somebody else did. Man, that is sick! How do you think I felt, finding you lying there in the yard? I knew it was the Shepards. If they had killed you it woulda been my fault. That is eating me up, Bryon, and you won't even let me get even for you."

He was crying. I just went sick inside. "Mark, it ain't your fault. It's just that I'm sick of fighting. I'm sick of this circle of beating up people and getting beat up. It's stupid." I reached over and gave him an easy punch on the shoulder. "I ain't dead, man; there's nothing to worry about."

Mark took a deep breath, and, even though his voice was normal, he was gripping the steering wheel so hard that his knuckles were white. "I don't know what's the matter with me. I never worry about 'what if?' I never did until me and Terry came home and found you lyin' there smashed up. Then I think, 'what if?' and look what happens to me." He shrugged. "You don't want to get even with the Shepards, that's your business."

We just couldn't get through to each other. He didn't understand why I didn't dig fights any more; I didn't understand how he could accept everything that came along without question, without wanting to change it.

Mom nearly had a fit when she saw me. She was well by then, back at her job. I almost gave her a relapse. I had never been so messed up. A black eye she could take, stitches in my lip she could take, smashed ribs she could take, but not all at the same time. I was feeling so lousy that I didn't mind her fussing at me. I pretended that it was her who made me go to bed, but I was glad to be there.

"You want me to call Cathy?" Mark asked after I had been put to bed.

"Yeah—you mind?" He could get to a pay phone and I couldn't.

"Sure, I mind. Beating up the Shepards would be easier. But for you, buddy, I'll do it." He gave me his famous Mark grin. "I know she'll be glad to hear from me."

I tried to grin back at him, but it was difficult. It's pretty lousy to have the two people you care about most hate each other.

I must have dozed off after Mark left. I felt pretty bad—the painkiller shots had worn off and I was running a fever. I don't know how long I was asleep, but when I came to, Cathy was sitting next to the bed.

"Hi, Bryon," she said, and her voice and her face were so serious that for a dazed second I couldn't figure out if it was Cathy or M&M. I really felt dizzy and drunk and confused.

"How do you feel?" she asked, when I couldn't say anything; I just lay there and looked at her stupid-like.

"Oh, all right," I said, which made a lot of sense. "I'm glad you're here."

"Are you?" she said, and she was crying. There, I had both her and Mark crying within twenty-four hours. I must be really something.

"Cathy, I am really glad you are here," I said. "I love you."

"O.K.," she sobbed. "O.K." Then she reached over and held my hand. I took a quivering breath and looked at the ceiling. That hadn't been so hard after all. If I could do that, maybe there were a few other things I could take care of.

"Well," Cathy said finally, gulping back her tears, "your mother says you'll be all right in a couple of days." She sort of half-laughed. "You just look so awful, Bryon."

"You look great," I said. She didn't really, I guess, because you never do see a girl who looks good while she's crying except in the movies, but to me she looked good.

"I'll be fine in a day or two; then we can go find M&M. I got a lead on him," I said. My mind was clearing up.

"Really?" Like I hoped, this took her mind off me for a little while, and like I hoped, not much.

"Yeah. Mark says he's seen him at this hippie commune-house."

Cathy looked shocked. "One of those free-love places?"

"I don't think that's the right word for it." I couldn't help grinning. "Anyway, he's been staying there. I went over to look for him yesterday, I think"—I was still a little confused as to what day it was, or what time. "He wasn't there then, but maybe we can find him. Don't worry, the place wasn't that bad. He could have been in worse places."

"All right." She smiled at me like I knew everything on earth, like whatever I said went, and it really made me feel good. "We'll go look for him when you get better."

She reached over and gave me a quick, light kiss. Because of the stitches in my lip, this hurt. But not much.

I took a couple of days' sick leave from work—I didn't want to go to work looking like some prize fighter. But as soon as I was able I took the car and went for a drive by myself. I had been thinking about a lot of things. Cathy, Mark, M&M, and Charlie. I drove around for two hours before I finally made up my mind.

I drove out to the cemetery, the cheap cemetery where people who don't have money get buried. I hadn't gone to Charlie's funeral, but I knew where he was buried.

I finally found his grave. This was not easy since there wasn't much of a marker. There weren't any big headstones in the whole place. I went and stood in front of his barren grave. No flowers, no nothing. Just the place where what was left of Charlie lay. I said out loud, "Thanks for letting me use your car, Charlie. Thanks for saving my life."

This wasn't hard to do. I wished I'd done it when he could have heard me. I don't know, maybe it was a dumb thing to do, but I sure felt better.

I picked up Cathy two nights later and we went looking for M&M. Mark had gone out somewhere; he was spending more and more time away from home. Mom was worried about him, I could tell. By now she was also bugged about where he was getting the money he kept bringing home. I still figured he was doing some serious poker playing, but I didn't want to tell Mom that, as she didn't have too high an opinion of poker, or gambling in general. Me getting mixed up in that pool-hustling business hadn't done much to glorify gambling, either.

"I just love your mother," Cathy said as we left the house. She and Mom were getting along pretty good. This was fine with me, as I dug her parents O.K., too. Right now Cathy was hacked off at her old man; she blamed him for M&M's running away. But I liked the guy.

"Most people do," I said. "She knows everybody within twenty miles of here. The mailman brings her all the stray kittens he finds, and the neighborhood grocer gives her free cat food."

We were feeling real good driving to the hippie house. We laughed and kidded and horsed around all the way. I figured we had a pretty good chance of coming home with M&M this time.

There were two Volkswagen buses parked in the driveway of the old house; I knew they belonged to the hippies because of the flowers and slogans painted on them. One read "War Is Unhealthy for Children and Other Living Things." Really bright.

"This is where he is?" Cathy sighed. "I still can hardly believe that baby is living in a place like this."

I guess big sisters always think of little brothers as babies, no matter how old they are. "Maybe it was good for him," I said. "Maybe being on his own made him grow up a little." I only half-believed this; I had always had a good opinion of M&M's mind, but being smart ain't being mature, as I have often proved. "Anyway, we can't be sure he even wants to come home with us."

"If he doesn't, Daddy is going to call the cops and have them bring him home. He doesn't want to, but he keeps saying M&M has had his fling, and it's time he came home. This is my only chance to get him home without dragging the police into it."

"I didn't know that. Well, let's hope he comes with us. Maybe I could slug him and carry him home."

Cathy laughed. "No, let the cops do it if it comes to that. I'd rather have him hate the police than you."

We walked up to the house. There were kids on the porch, just watching the street. I stopped to talk with a Biblical-looking guy.

"I'm lookin' for Baby Freak. He around?"

"Yeah, he is." The guy was staring directly into my eyes. He had friendly, trusting eyes. "Are you a friend of his?"

"Yeah, a good friend. This is his sister."

Cathy gave him the big smile she won me with. The guy smiled back.

"He's upstairs, I think." Suddenly the guy looked worried. "He's been floating for a couple of days now."

"Oh, no kiddin'," I said, keeping my cool, and Cathy followed my example.

"Talk to his travel agent," the hippie said. "He's the cat with the red hair, inside."

"Travel agent? What's that?" Cathy whispered as we went in. I didn't want to tell her, didn't want her to feel the sudden cold waves of fear that I was feeling, so I said, "I don't know."

We found who we were looking for—a big, heavy guy with fire-colored hair, beard, and mustache.

"We're looking for Baby Freak," I said. I was beginning to see why M&M had acquired this other nickname: most of the kids there were at least seventeen or eighteen, with a lot of college-age kids. It was a real crowded place, but now I can't remember what everyone was doing. At least some of the kids were smoking grass; you could tell that by the smell. I was hoping the place didn't get raided while we were there. You can get busted just for being at a place where people are smoking pot.

"Yeah?" Red said. "Man, that kid is on a bad trip."

Cathy made a funny, yelping little sound.

"Some of these freaks have been dropping acid. Baby wanted to try it, so I sat with him. Bad trip, man, really bad. He's calmed down a little now, but all day today me and some of these other cats been holding him, keeping him from jumping out the window."

I felt like I was going to throw up. Cathy was as white as a sheet. "Can we see him?" she said, in a tiny, expressionless voice.

"Sure."

We followed him up the stairs. He led us to the

same room Mark and I had gone to the last time we were there. This time no one was there except the blond chick, who was curled up on the bed asleep, and someone huddled in the corner. To my surprise, Red walked over to the huddle. "Hey, man, there's people here to see you," he said softly.

"Are they spiders?" The person didn't raise his head, but the voice was M&M's.

"No, man." Red laughed gently. "They're squares."

M&M looked up, and I hardly recognized him. His hair was to his shoulders, he was a lot thinner, he was dirty, and the expression on his face was one I had never seen on him before—suspicion.

"M&M, baby, it's me—Cathy." Cathy kneeled down in front of him. He was staring at her, not seeing her.

"Square spiders?" he said, and his face was contorted in fear. "I don't want to see any spiders."

"It's me, Cathy," she said again. "Your sister. Don't you want to go home?"

"I went to my stomach," M&M said in a high, unnatural voice. He was talking too fast. "I went down into my stomach and all these spiders came out. I never knew there were spiders in my stomach. I was there ten years, and all that time these spiders kept chewing on me. They were big spiders."

Cathy choked back a sob. "Baby, what have you done to yourself?" she said in a whisper.

He seemed to see her. "Cathy? I screamed and

screamed and screamed, but nobody came to help me."
He was shaking. He didn't look right. He looked sick.
"I kept trying to get back, but the spiders held me
down. Held me down and chewed on me and the colors went in and out. I listened to the colors and they
were screaming too. Red and yellow screamed loudest.
The spiders were eating them too."

"He kept trying to jump out the window," Red said.
"All day. We took turns holding him down."

What did the guy want, a medal? He had given him
the stuff in the first place.

"Cathy," I said. "We ought to take him to the hospital."

She looked at me quickly. "Hospital?" Then she
nodded. "Let me call Daddy first." She looked at Red.
"Do you have a phone I can use?" She followed him
out of the room.

"There was this other color," M&M said to me seriously but half-afraid, as if he thought I'd turn into a
spider any minute. "I don't know its name; it told me
but I forgot. It said I was being paid back for all the
carrots I ate. I didn't know— I thought— I didn't
know about the carrots before. I don't think it was my
fault." He was crying, tears were pouring down his
face, but he hadn't changed his expression. He looked
so thin and scared, not a bit like the M&M I knew.
"Do you think I should be paid back for something I
didn't know about?"

"No," I said, clearing my throat. "I don't think it was your fault." I put my arm around him and held him. He was shaking real bad.

Cathy came back. "Daddy's going to meet us at the hospital. Can you carry him?"

"Yeah," I said. I picked him up easily; he couldn't have weighed more than ninety pounds.

"I'm so tired," M&M said. "I was gone so long, and I didn't have any sleep." I carried him down the stairs and out of that house. Nobody made any move to stop me. Nobody seemed to care.

Cathy drove us to the hospital. Halfway there M&M started suddenly and screamed, "Where am I?"

"It's O.K., kid, you're going to be O.K."

"Where am I?" he was screaming in terror. "Why don't I know where I am?"

I was just sick. I didn't know how Cathy was managing to drive the car. I never felt so bad before. I just held onto M&M. There wasn't any sense in trying to talk to him. I felt then that he was as much my little brother as Cathy's. That's how bad I felt.

Mr. Carlson was waiting for us at the hospital. We drove right up to the emergency entrance, and there he was. I got out and picked M&M up again, but I didn't have him for long. Mr. Carlson took him and carried him into the hospital, holding him very close, very tight.

M&M was telling him about the spiders.

We stayed there at the hospital until the doctor could talk to us. He couldn't tell us much—physically M&M would recover, but mentally . . .

"Will he always be like he is now?" Cathy said. She had really been brave—no crying, no hysterics. Only by the tense, tight way she was ripping the hem out of her shirt was she showing how bad she was shook.

The doctor replied, "I have no way of knowing. He might get better, or he may have lost his mind forever. Either way, I don't believe he'll ever be completely the same. LSD is a powerful drug, people react to it differently. If these kids would only . . ."

I tuned him out. I won't listen to sermons. Besides, I was hacked off at that doctor. He shouldn't be saying things like that. He should be saying that M&M would be fine, that tomorrow morning he would be the same again. Couldn't he see how what he was saying was tearing Mr. Carlson to pieces? Couldn't he see what it was doing to Cathy? What kind of a doctor was he, anyway?

"I want to drive you home," I said to Cathy.

She shook her head. "I don't want to go home. I want to stay here."

"Cathy, I want you to go home," Mr. Carlson said. "You can't do anything here and I want you to be with your mother when she hears about this. M&M will be asleep for a few hours. I'm going home in an hour or so. Wait until I get there before you tell your mother." His voice broke. "What are we going to tell her?"

"Come on," I said, putting my arm around Cathy, guiding her to the car.

"Wait a minute," Mr. Carlson said. "Bryon, I want to tell you how much I appreciate all you've done. I'm really proud of you, son."

That was the first time any man had ever called me "son" without making me mad. I didn't know what to say, so I just nodded to him and gave Cathy a squeeze.

In the car Cathy broke down and cried. I drove to the park and stopped. I held her while she cried. She was almost hysterical. I was crying too. I couldn't stand seeing her hurt like that. I just couldn't stand it. "Don't cry like this, baby," I said. My voice was shaking. "Cathy, don't. It won't do any good."

"Oh, my God," she sobbed. "What if he's lost his mind forever? He was such a sweet kid, the sweetest damn kid in the whole world."

This was the first time I had ever heard her swear. I tried to think about this fact, to focus on something

like that before I lost control and became hysterical
too. "He's going to be all right," I said. "He'll be just
like before."

"No he won't." Cathy was trying to stop crying now.
"He won't ever be the same." This set her off crying
again. My shirt front was soaked clear through. She
just hung onto me and cried while I patted her head.
Finally she sat up. "I love you so much, Bryon," she
said. "I don't know what I'd have done without you."

"I love you, too, baby," I said. This was getting easier to say. "And don't worry about what the doctor
said. He's one of those hippie-haters. M&M will be
O.K., I know it."

"I'd better go home now," Cathy said. "I have to be
there when Mamma hears. Oh, this is just going to kill
her."

I let her out at her house, but I didn't go in. I figured this was a family matter, and I wasn't a member
of the family yet.

I was surprised to see how late it was when I got
home. Mom was asleep. I went into my room and lay
down without bothering to turn off the light. Mark
wasn't home yet. I was tired. I felt empty and drained.
Nothing can wear you out like caring about people. I
was tired, yet I knew I wouldn't be able to sleep. I
closed my eyes, but I kept seeing pictures: all these
people were spinning around in my head—Mark and

Charlie and Mike and Angela, Cathy and M&M and Mr. Carlson, and Tim and Curly Shepard. Life had seemed so simple once, now it suddenly seemed so complicated. I could remember a time when my only worry had been paying Charlie the three bucks I owed him. Things used to be simple and now they weren't. I wanted a cigarette bad. I halfheartedly searched my pockets, but I knew I didn't have any. Then I remembered Mark's spare carton and rolled off the bed and reached under his mattress. I felt something strange and pulled it out. It was a long cylinder-like thing. I unscrewed one end and all these pills came rolling out.

I am not dumb by any means. I have never used drugs except for a couple of tries with grass, but I knew what they looked like. I looked at this bunch of pills—there were hundreds of them, and it was like a machine in my head went *click, click, click.* And it came up with an answer I didn't want.

Mark was selling this stuff. This was 'way too many pills for anybody to have if he was just taking them himself, and besides, I would have noticed something different about Mark if he had been taking them. You can't use drugs and not show it—I knew too many kids who were users not to know that. Mark was selling. Mark was a pusher. That was where he was getting his money. That was why he had known about the hippie house; that was why they had known him; that was why he had known where to look for M&M.

M&M. Cathy.

M&M was in the hospital, and maybe he was messed up for life—and Mark was selling the stuff that made him that way. Maybe this wasn't LSD, but it was a step in that direction, and God only knows what all Mark had been selling. I thought about that blond, dead-looking chick and about M&M screaming about spiders and about Cathy half-hysterical with grief. I thought about Mr. Carlson and the bitter doctor, and the whole mess was swirling around in my head, and it felt like it would burst wide open.

When I thought about the cause of all this misery, I became very cool. I very calmly called the cops. M&M had lost his mind and Cathy was hurting, and I did something about it. Then I sat down on a chair in the front room and waited. It seemed only a minute later when Mark came in.

"Hey, still up?" he said. Then he stopped. "What's the matter— Bryon, you look awful! What is it?"

I held out the cylinder.

"Oh," Mark said, after a pause. "You found them, huh? Well, don't worry, buddy, I don't take them. I have a good enough time like I am."

"Just how are you, anyway?" I said.

"What?" Mark said, confused.

"M&M is in the hospital—acid trip. They think he may have lost his mind."

"Man, that is awful. That poor kid." Then he

looked at me. "Bryon, don't look like that. I said I don't take them. Don't you believe me?"

"I believe you," I said dully.

"We needed the money, you know. I tried getting a job, but with my police record nobody'd hire me. Then I met this guy on the Ribbon—he set me up. I figure I don't have to take it to sell it, so what's the worry?"

"M&M—" I began, but I was too tired, too numb to talk.

"Is that what's buggin' you? Listen, I didn't sell M&M anything. He got it from somebody else. Lookit, Bryon, they're going to get it from somebody if they want it, so why can't I make some money? I never forced it on anybody. I never tried to talk somebody into using drugs so I could make a buck."

He could have talked all night and I wouldn't have changed my mind. This was wrong. For the first time in years I thought about the golden-eyed cowboy who had been Mark's father. Was Mark a throwback? To what? I wondered tiredly why I had never seen it before: Mark had absolutely no concept of what was right and what was wrong; he didn't obey any laws, because he couldn't see that there were any. Laws, right and wrong, they didn't matter to Mark, because they were just words.

"Bryon, what is it?" Mark cried suddenly. "Listen, if it bugs you that much I'll quit. I'll stop selling if you don't like it. Shoot, I never thought it would bother you. I sort of thought you knew about it."

Don't drag me into this, I thought. Don't try to make me out to be blind, just because you are. Aloud I said, "I called the cops," and I felt as if I was talking in my sleep. Mark went white.

"What?" he said softly, disbelievingly. "What did you say?" We could already hear the siren. "Bryon, you know what something like this would do to me with my record. Bryon, tell me you're lyin'." Mark was pleading desperately.

I thought maybe he would run for it, but he didn't. He just sat down in a chair opposite me. He was white and his eyes were black with a rim of gold around them. He looked the way he had when he had been clobbered with that bottle. "Bryon," he said quietly, like he was trying hard to understand, like he was totally confused, like he thought maybe I would answer in a foreign language, "why are you doing this to me, buddy? Bryon, just tell me."

I couldn't tell him. I didn't know.

The police arrived, and of course Mom woke up. She didn't know what was going on. She could only stand helpless in the kitchen doorway while the police questioned me, rounded up the drugs, and slapped handcuffs on Mark. They advised Mark of his right to remain silent, and he did. He just stood there, quivering, watching me while I told the cops the things that would put him behind bars for years.

Then a cop said, "Let's go, kid," and it seemed to dawn on Mark what was happening. He looked quickly from the cops to me and cried, "My God, Bryon, you're not gonna let them take me to jail?"

Didn't he know I had just put him there? The cop jerked Mark around and shoved him out the door. Suddenly it was deadly quiet—just the distant siren and Mom's quiet sobbing.

I went into the bathroom and threw up. I was sick.

The next morning I really thought that I had dreamed the whole thing. I thought I had had a nightmare, one I only vaguely remembered. It seemed a long time before it finally got through to me what had happened. Then I was tired and sick, and I wondered why people didn't die from being so mixed up.

Why had I turned on Mark? What had I done to him? I tried to remember how shook I had been about Cathy and M&M, tried to justify what I had done. But I didn't know now. If I had asked Mark to quit selling pills, he would have. I didn't have to do what I did. Last night it had seemed the only right thing to do. Now Mark was in jail. It would kill him. It would kill him.

It would kill him.

"Bryon, are you going to work?" It was Mom. I was sitting on the edge of the bed, holding my head in my hands. It felt like it was going to burst wide open.

"Mom," I said wearily, "what have I done? You don't hate me, do you?"

She came in and sat down on Mark's bed. "Bryon,

150

you are my only child and my son and I couldn't hate you. I love you."

"You loved Mark, too," I said, only beginning to realize how this mess was going to affect her. Mark, her stray lion, behind bars.

"Yes, I loved Mark and I still do. But you are my son and you come first. What Mark was doing was wrong. Maybe the juvenile authorities can help him."

"You know they can't." I was too worn out to play games—let's pretend everything will turn out all right, let's pretend it's all for the better.

"We'll just have to make him understand it was wrong and that what you did was for his own good."

I took a good long look at her. She was my mother and I loved her, but there wasn't any sense in carrying on the conversation. She was tired and hurting, too, but she had hope and I didn't and we couldn't talk.

"I gotta get ready to go to work," I said.

"Bryon, don't hate yourself," Mom said, but that was easier said than done.

I went through the day mechanically, numb, and hardly knowing what I was doing. I had a rep as a wise-cracker and a clown, so this got me a lot of ribbing, but I hardly heard it. I was glad to get home and lie on my bed, smoking one cigarette after another, not thinking—scared to think.

I heard someone at the door, but since Mom answered, I didn't pay any attention.

"Bryon, you have company," Mom finally called.

It was Cathy. It occurred to me with a shock that I hadn't thought about her all day long.

"Bryon, your mother told me what happened. I'm so sorry." She looked tired and nervous but I couldn't work up any sympathy for her.

"Are you?" I said "Why?"

"Bryon!" she said, tears jumping to her eyes. "You know I know how you feel!"

"Oh," I said. "No, I hadn't realized that."

She was quiet, bewildered. I knew I was hurting her, but I couldn't seem to stop myself. It was as if I was outside myself, watching while someone named Bryon Douglas hurt his girl friend. I couldn't stop him, and I wasn't much interested in the first place.

"How's your brother?" I said. Suddenly it was just some brother of hers in the hospital, not M&M, not my friend, not somebody I too cared about.

"He seems better—but I don't know, he's still mixed up."

That makes two of us, I thought sarcastically.

"I thought"—she swallowed, she was a proud person and it was hard for her to be humble—"I thought maybe you'd come up to the hospital today or call me or something. Then your mother told me what happened."

"Aren't you glad?" I said. "You never liked Mark— you thought he was beautiful, but you didn't like him. Aren't you glad he's out of the way?"

"Bryon, why are you doing this to me?" she said, and suddenly I could hear Mark, as plain as day, saying, *"Why are you doing this to me, buddy?"*

"I'm sorry," I said. "I can't talk today, Cathy. I'll call you tomorrow."

"O.K.," she said, still puzzled and hurt but no longer humble. "Call me tomorrow."

I wasn't going to call her tomorrow and she knew it.

I wondered impersonally why I didn't love her any more. But it didn't seem to matter.

Mark had a hearing, or a trial, or whatever—I never paid any attention to the formalities. I had to testify. I did. I hadn't seen Mark since they had come to get him. He looked relaxed and amused, tipping back in his chair, glancing over everyone in the courtroom with an easy, almost friendly expression. When I was questioned about my relationship with Mark and answered, "We were like brothers," Mark laughed out loud. When he was questioned, he admitted selling drugs and shrugged. I think it was his attitude that made the judge go hard on him, even though by then judges were beginning to crack down on pushers. Mark was only sixteen; he had always been able to talk his way out of anything. But this time he didn't try. When the judge sentenced him to five years in the state reformatory, he didn't even change expression. I felt like someone had knocked the breath out of me, and I heard Mom's little cry of protest, but Mark got to his feet and casually strolled out with the officers. He hadn't looked at me once.

The next months were a blur—I went to school and went to work and went home and studied. I ended up with straight A's that semester, something that surprised me more than anyone, because I couldn't remember a thing I had studied. I didn't date. Once, at the drugstore, I ran into M&M.

His hair was much shorter than it had been in years, and he was still thin.

"I haven't seen you around in a while," he said.

"Yeah, I been busy. How ya been?"

"O.K.," he said, but he looked half-scared, and his old expression of complete trust and intent interest was gone entirely. He looked like a little kid—I had forgotten he was just a little kid. "But, I don't know— It can come back, they told me. I could have a flashback, it could come back. And if I ever have any kids —something about chromosomes—they could be messed up. I don't think I'll ever have any." He was quiet for a minute. "I don't remember things too good any more; all my grades are shot."

I couldn't help feeling sorry for him. He had been such a bright, sweet kid. I remembered the time—it seemed years ago—when Mark and I had teased him about wanting a large family. Well, that was taken care of.

154

"You used to go with Cathy, didn't you?" he said. The poor kid, he was really confused. He was reading a monster comic.

"Yeah, for a while."

"She liked you better than anybody," he said. "I know it. She's dating some guy named Ponyboy Curtis now. She likes him O.K. too."

I couldn't feel any anger, any jealousy, any anything except a halfhearted hope that they would hit it off together. Any grudge I had ever held against Curtis was gone, so was any feeling I had ever had for Cathy. It seemed impossible that I could once feel so emotional about someone, and then suddenly feel nothing.

"I'll see you around," I said. But I hoped I wouldn't. M&M made me sad, and I hadn't felt anything for so long—it was slightly scary.

I spent that summer working full time and trying to get to see Mark at the reformatory. But every time I went they told me that Mark was causing trouble at the reformatory so he couldn't have visitors. I got promoted from sack boy to clerk. I didn't come to work hung over and I didn't give the manager any lip. I seemed to have become a mixture of things I had picked up from Charlie, Mark, Cathy, M&M, Mom, and even obscure people like Mike and the blond hippie-chick and the Shepards. I had learned something from everyone, and I didn't seem to be the same person I had been last year. But like a mixture, I was mixed up.

Angela came into the store once wearing short shorts and a tight blouse. It was funny, but she looked even better with short hair. I guess I'll never see a girl as good-looking as she is. She came through my counter, staring at me coolly, daring me to say something. Poor little chick. I didn't hate her any more than I loved Cathy. I felt sorry for her.

"How've you been, Angel?" I said, but not smart-like. I really wanted to know.

"Well enough. I hear you dumped little what's-her-name on Curtis. Well, they deserve each other."

I just shrugged and rang up her stuff. She was going to be bitter all her life, and all that beauty was wasted.

"You know, I'd thought for a long time you were really low, Bryon," she was saying, "but what you did to Mark really proved it."

"Angel, you look really good with short hair," I said, and I don't know whether or not it scared her, but she shut up.

One night when I was lying on the floor reading a book, Mom came in and sat down. "Bryon, you got even with Mark for Cathy, then you got even with Cathy for Mark. When are you going to stop getting even with yourself?"

I rolled over and got up and went for a drive. I couldn't talk to Mom, especially when she was telling the truth.

Finally, at the end of August, I got to see Mark. He couldn't leave the reformatory, so I had to go in. He had been in so much trouble that the authorities considered my visit a last-ditch effort to straighten him out. If it didn't work, they were going to send him to the state prison. They told me they hoped I could influence him.

They didn't say how.

I thought we'd have to talk through a wire dealie, like you see in prison movies, but instead we were left alone in a room which I remember as strangely empty.

"Hi ya, buddy," Mark greeted me. "Slumming?"

I couldn't speak. I had a real bad pain in my throat. Mark had changed. He had lost a lot of weight, but somehow it had stretched his skin over his bones and slanted his eyes. He hadn't lost his looks, but exchanged them. He looked dirty somehow, and hard, things I had never seen in him before. His strangely sinister innocence was gone, and in its place was a more sinister knowledge. He seemed to be pacing, like an impatient, dangerous, caged lion.

"How goes it?" I managed finally. "What's the action like in here?"

"If I told you how it was in here," he said, "you'd be sick." There was a silence. Then he continued, "I didn't have to see you. I wanted to, though. I had to make sure."

"Make sure of what?"

"Make sure I hated you."

I suddenly remembered that time, so long ago, when Cathy had looked at Mark and for a moment I had hated him. I wondered what it felt like to experience that feeling all your life—to hate the person you loved best.

"Mark . . ." I began miserably. "Mark, I didn't know what I was doing . . ."

"Can it, buddy." He glanced around. "Groovy place, ain't it? Seems like home now."

"I hear you've been causing trouble."

"Yeah. I don't seem to be able to get away with things any more."

I thought I would break down and cry then, but I didn't. "Listen," I said, "you straighten up and they'll let you out early on probation or parole or whatever it is, and you can come home. I'll get you a job at the store—"

"Like hell you will," Mark said, in the same, easy, pleasant voice he had used all along. "I ain't never goin' back there again. When I get outa here, you ain't never going to see me again."

"We were like brothers," I said, desperate. "You were my best friend—"

He laughed then, and his eyes were the golden, hard, flat eyes of a jungle animal. "Like a friend once said to me, 'That was then, and this is now.' "

I broke out in a sweat and was suddenly glad of the

walls and the guards and the bars. I think if he could have, Mark would have killed me.

I haven't tried to see Mark since then. I heard in a roundabout way that he was sent to the state prison. I've just been sort of waiting around for school to start, not much caring whether it does or not. I don't seem to care about anything any more. It's like I am worn out with caring about people. I don't even care about Mark. The guy who was my best friend doesn't exist any longer, and I don't want to think about the person who has taken his place. I go over everything that happened last year, trying to figure out what I could have done different, what I would do different if I had the chance, but I don't know. Mostly I wonder "what if?" What if I had found out about Mark some other time, when I wasn't half out of my mind with worry about Cathy? What if I hadn't met her in the first place, would I still have grown away from Mark? What if M&M had had a good trip instead of a bad one? What if someone else had turned Mark in—would there still be hope for him?

I am too mixed up to really care. And to think, I used to be sure of things. Me, once I had all the answers. I wish I was a kid again, when I had all the answers.